A Casterglass Christmas

A Casterglass Christmas

A Keeping Up with the Penryns Romance

Kate Hewitt

TULE
PUBLISHING

Dedication

Dedicated to Rachel and Sophie, my Cumbrian friends!
Love you!

Acknowledgements

With every book I write, I must thank the wonderful Tule editorial team, including my editor Sinclair, copyeditor Helena, and proofreader Marlene who all help to make my books the best they can be. Also thanks to the Tule team that helps to get my books out into the world, including Meghan, Jane, Maggie, Cyndi and Nikki. And special thanks to my readers, who have loved my Cumbrian-set books and asked for more! Lastly, thanks to all the friends I've made when I lived in Cumbria—you were like family when I lived there! Thank you for making it such a special place.

Chapter One

"MUM, THERE'S NO signal!"

Sixteen-year-old Poppy waved her phone in Althea's face as she turned onto the sweeping drive, its extensive gardens now shrouded in darkness—and sleeting, icy rain. Christmas in Cumbria. *Very* merry.

"Poppy, I'm trying to drive."

"There's no *signal*," her daughter shrieked again, as if Althea hadn't heard her the first thirty-two times she'd mentioned it since they'd turned off the M6 and entered the Land that Time Forgot.

"Poppy, please." Althea tried to keep her voice light even as she gritted her teeth. Part of her disaster recovery plan was, for some reason, to speak musically rather than maniacally, and also not to throw things. A low bar, perhaps, but at least it meant she was succeeding at something. "Besides, we're just about there. You can use the Wi-Fi once we're inside."

"Casterglass has crap Wi-Fi—you *know* that." Poppy flung her phone on top of her leather bag—Prada, only the best for her daughter, naturally—in the footwell and folded her arms mutinously, which was, Althea thought, a pointless gesture. She already knew her daughter didn't want to come to Casterglass for Christmas. She'd made that abundantly clear when she'd talked about the parties she'd miss, the revision she needed to do—as if—and the fact that Casterglass was not even in the middle of nowhere, but on its farthest edge. On the last point, Althea had to agree with her.

Over the last twenty years of her unfortunately regrettable marriage Althea had visited her family home only sporadically, even as she'd recalled it with affection, at least mostly. It hadn't helped that her soon-to-be-ex-husband Jasper had never wanted to come. He'd always liked the *idea* of her home being a castle and her father a baron, but not the somewhat less than sparkling reality.

"Where is it, Mum?" Twelve-year-old Tobias, morose and mostly silent in the back seat for the entire six hours' drive from London, now peered through the rain-streaked window for a glimpse of his ancestral home—Casterglass Castle, family seat of the Penryns since 1277.

"Around the corner, sweetheart." The Land Rover was heading up the drive at a crawl, the rain lashing the car in a way that felt like a personal attack. Everything was dark, rainswept, romantic in a *Wuthering Heights* sort of way, which was exactly *not* Althea's mood. As far as she was concerned, she'd sworn off romance forever, and definitely brooding heroes. Besides, she'd take a holiday on Turks and Caicos to Cumbria any day. However. Needs must.

"Here we are," she sang out, as musical as ever. All she needed was a piano accompaniment and a microphone. Poppy groaned, more of a huff really, as if six hours of complaining had finally taken the wind out of her determinedly bolshie sails, but Tobias, bless him, had pressed his nose to the window as Casterglass Castle loomed out of the darkness like something from a low-budget drama, the kind of thing you'd see at ten p.m. on BBC Two—an adaptation of one of the lesser known Jane Austen novels, or Anne Brontë, perhaps.

Althea had stuck more to Jilly Cooper and Marian Keyes, but she *thought* that's what it looked like. Home, in all of its musty, dank, crumbling glory, against a stormy night sky.

"Well, let's go say hello," she said, her melody faltering slightly as she opened the door of the car and a sheet of rain blew in, soaking her thoroughly. Typical Cumbrian weather, but it was still a shock every time.

"Why are there no lights on?" Poppy asked, an uncharacteristic waver of uncertainty in her voice, for the hulk of grey stone was looking particularly forbidding on this rainy night, its bleak Norman frontage like a blank face, the narrow arrow-slit windows resembling hostile, squinty eyes.

"There will be lights on in the back," Althea promised, a bit too gaily. Dread was pooling like sludge in the pit of her stomach. Somehow, she always managed to forget how coming home made her feel, until she was walking up to the door. A combination of affection and foreboding, having no idea what state the house would be in, or what sort of reception she might get, or how she could make any of it better.

"When were we last here?" she asked her children, who both gave her blank looks. Long enough that they didn't remember.

"Grandad's birthday," Poppy said sullenly, after a moment. She was clutching her phone to her chest like a security blanket. She'd been texting furiously for most of the car trip, no doubt reading and responding to all the messages about the parties she would now miss, because her mean old mother had decided to hightail it home when her philandering husband had finally philandered too far. "But you and Tobias came by yourselves after that," Poppy added.

"I think I was ten?" Tobias suggested hesitantly, swiping his dark eye-hiding fringe away from his face.

"Ah yes, I remember." It had been after one of Jasper's more obvious affairs; Althea had been too humiliated to weather it like the kind of storm they were currently in, and had gone and hid instead. Eventually, as usual, things had blown over, or at least everyone had pretended that they had.

On that occasion Poppy had point-blank refused to go with her, and Ben, now at university, had been on a school ski trip, so it had just been her and Tobias, rattling around Casterglass's many rooms with her parents. Tobias had, she recalled, bonded a bit with her younger sister Persephone, who had only been twenty at the time and had spent her whole life at Casterglass. Born when Althea had already escaped to university, her youngest sister remained a somewhat uneasy enigma to her.

Well, here they were, about to have a happy family reunion. Or not. Taking a deep breath, Althea tried the handle of the front door, a mammoth, rusted iron ring that looked like it should belong on the wall of a dungeon, complete with accompanying skeletal hand.

"It usually just takes a bit of twisting…" she told her waiting—and wet—children a bit breathlessly, only to have the rusted hunk of iron fall off right in her hand. With an exclamation of shock, she dropped it, narrowly and thankfully missing her foot. It clunked on the stone steps and then rolled off into the darkness. "Oh…well," she said a bit lamely, and received another huff from Poppy in return.

"Is there another door?" Tobias asked.

"Oh, there's loads of doors!" Althea's voice was going from musical to manic. She swiped her wet hair out of her face as she surveyed the terrain. The castle's normally manicured lawns—admittedly she tried to come to Cumbria in summer, when they were verdant and lush—looked decidedly less than well kept. The lawn was tufty and muddy and not something she wanted to slog through, but she had no choice because the door she knew would be open, to the kitchen, was around the side.

"Come on," she called to her brood like they were Cub Scouts on a camping trip. "We'll go round the side."

Althea tried to ignore the squelching under her black suede Ted Baker boots as she made her way around Casterglass's forbidding front to the Victorian addition in the back that was far friendlier, and where the rooms the family actually used were. A light shone out of the sitting room that boasted a stunning vista of the purple-fringed fells, and the sight of that little, ember-like glow amidst all the darkness heartened her.

She hadn't told her parents about leaving Jasper, or was it Jasper who had left her? A bit of both, she supposed, but frankly she wasn't even sure how much they would care, although perhaps that was being a bit too mean. Just because your parents were a bit scatty and eccentric didn't mean they were actually *indifferent*. Did it?

"Come on," she told her two children who were lagging behind, and she headed for the kitchen door. Its handle turned easily enough, and Althea breathed a sigh of relief as she stepped into the kitchen, the comforting rumbling of an Aga like a soundtrack to the room as well as her childhood. In the gloom lit only by the moonlight outside, filtering from behind the storm clouds, she saw everything exactly as it had always been: the battered red Aga along one wall, the rectangular table of scarred oak seating twelve taking up one end of a room the size of a basketball court, or at least half of one. Several Welsh dressers lined another wall, filled with dusty Willow Ware. On the other end of the kitchen there was a sofa and several squashy armchairs, every one of them piled with old newspapers and magazines.

"What is that *smell*?" Poppy exclaimed in disgust as she stepped into the kitchen behind Althea. "It's absolutely rank."

Althea took a sniff, and then wished she hadn't. The usual musty, dusty smell of home had definitely been dialled up a notch or five. And knowing her family, it could be originating from anything or anywhere.

"I'm not sure," she hedged as she put down her bag by the door. "Maybe some milk's gone off."

"Or a whole cow." Poppy shuddered as she looked around the room. "This looks like something from an episode of *Hoarders*."

Althea let out a slightly strangled laugh. The kitchen was the most comfortable and *normal* room in the entire castle. Wait until her daughter caught sight of the library with its many tottering stacks, or the ballroom with its army of mannequins from her mother's brief bout with dressmaking, or the armoury, which had eight centuries of rusty shields stacked like dustbin lids. And those were the more manageable parts of a castle that had eight hundred years of history, and even more junk.

"Let's see if we can find Granny and Grandad," she said in a faux-cheerful voice. She'd emailed to say she was coming, but with her parents that didn't mean anything. If they'd even checked their email, which they still considered new technology, they had most likely forgotten about her message by now.

Quietly she crept through the castle, her two children in tow, down a narrow corridor that led from the warren of rooms that made up the erstwhile servants' quarters, to the rooms that Althea had always considered most liveable—a sitting room, her father's study, and half a dozen bedrooms squashed above. This was the only part of the castle that had a *chance* of being somewhat warm, for a few hours at least after the heating had been cranked up to full blast. The rest of the castle was freezing even in the middle of summer—a Cumbrian summer, which wasn't saying much. If the thermometer registered twelve degrees in July the locals considered it 'red-hot'.

Why had she come back here again? Oh, right, because she'd had no other options. Good to remember.

"Here we are." Althea pushed open the door to the sitting room, a room decorated in varying shades of 1970s browns, with throws and pillows in several violent combinations of orange plaid. Her parents didn't do redecorating. The best part of the room was the deep window seat overlooking the stupendous view, which of course couldn't be seen at night during a rainstorm.

Now rain pelted the glass like bullets, and the howling wind made the panes flex in a way Althea remembered from her childhood but which made both her children take an instinctive step backwards, as if afraid the windows might explode on impact. Which, fair enough, they might. Althea recalled more than one winter storm growing up that had resulted in shattered glass. The room was disappointingly empty, despite the homely light Althea had seen from outside, and she turned back to the door, uncertain which part of the castle to try next.

"Where is everyone?" Poppy asked, and her daughter's usually aggressive attitude faltered for a moment, filling Althea with a sudden rush of maternal feeling. Poppy had been rather hard work these last few years, obsessed with social media and her group of pouty, twig-like friends, and completely dismissive of everything and anyone else. Althea suspected she was at fault for letting too much slide over the years, but that knowledge didn't make dealing with her daughter any easier.

"They'll be around somewhere," she said now, as brightly as she could.

"They knew we were coming, right?"

"Yes, of course." This, Althea knew, sounded somewhat unconvincing. What she really meant was—*I think they knew at one point, but they've most certainly forgotten.*

"Darling!" The plummily enthusiastic yet decidedly vague tones of her mother—so familiar from her childhood—had Althea turning to see her wafting down the hall wearing something in a garish shade of pink that was a cross between a muumuu and a toga.

"Mummy." Yes, she, a forty-one-year-old, soon-to-be-divorced woman of the world, called her mother Mummy.

Because she was pseudo-aristocratic, and that was what you did, even when you were old enough to be drawing a pension.

Her mother air-kissed both her cheeks without managing to make any actual contact before she stepped back, blinking owlishly at the three of them. She had two pairs of glasses perched on top of her head, another pair that she was actually wearing, and she sported a long necklace of what looked like bottle caps that reached down to her navel. "Was it today you were coming? It must have been. I'm sorry, I haven't done a thing about your rooms. I was finishing a chapter on Catullus…"

"We can do it, don't worry." Her mother's response was entirely expected. Having gained her PhD in Classics from Oxford in her twenties, she had spent the last thirty years writing books that could be used as doorstops but were in fact the primary texts of obscure postgraduate courses and could not be found on Amazon, never mind in an actual bookshop. She didn't make much money off them, but she certainly loved her work.

"Hi, Granny," Tobias offered uncertainly as Violet Penryn, Lady of Casterglass, turned to him with an abstracted smile.

"Oh, hmm, yes? So lovely to see you again, my dear." She patted Tobias awkwardly on the shoulder before she continued drifting down the hall. "Have you eaten? I'm sure we can rustle something up…"

Poppy threw Althea a dark look, no doubt thinking of the smell emanating from the kitchen, and she gave her a reassuring smile in return that had no basis in reality. The thought of her mother rustling up anything in the kitchen was terrifying in the extreme.

Her mother was, Althea knew, what in another time would have been called an original. Nowadays people would just call her weird, and that was if they were feeling generous.

The daughter of a (very) mildly famous archaeologist who had been widowed when Violet was a child and died before Althea was born, Violet had spent most of her childhood on a dig in Persia.

"Persia?" Althea had once asked uncertainly, during one of her mother's dreamy recollections of foraging for skulls and brushing off mosaics in some oasis-filled desert. "Didn't Persia stop being a country, like, a hundred years ago?"

"Oh no," her mother had replied with a vague smile, "it was definitely Persia."

Sometimes Althea wondered if her mother had made it all up, and had actually grown up in a council house in Birmingham. If so, kudos to her for carrying on the charade for so long, and so convincingly. Her mother's mask hadn't slipped once.

"Now let's see…" Violet mused as they followed her into the kitchen. "I'm sure there was some leftover ham somewhere. We had it for supper a few days ago…"

"We can sort it, Mummy," Althea said as they followed

her into the kitchen. Was some ancient, rancid ham the source of that utterly revolting smell? Judging by the look on Poppy's face, she certainly thought so.

"Oh no, no, let me do something…" Violet said, which was cue for her to stand in the middle of a room, looking lost.

Now that she was back in the kitchen, the horrid smell really was overpowering. Poppy was pointedly holding her nose and Tobias was breathing rather loudly through his mouth. "Mummy…" Althea ventured cautiously. "Has something, um, gone off? Because there's a sort of smell…"

"A smell?" Violet sniffed thoroughly, unfazed. "Oh no, darling, that's just my sourdough starter. I know it's a *bit* whiffy, but that seems to be the point of the thing, doesn't it? And you can keep them for *ages*. Olivia was telling me all about it. Grandmothers pass it down from generation to generation!" She laughed merrily. "Perhaps I'll bequeath it to you one day…"

If it was the source of the smell, then no thanks, Althea thought with a shudder. "Where is it?" she asked, and her mother pointed vaguely to the larder, a narrow, stone-floored room adjacent to the kitchen that was usually piled with broken blenders and the like. Althea ventured inside, nearly gagging at the reeking odour that seemed thick and viscous in the air, a cross between something dead and something that perhaps needed to be put out of its misery. There was a bowl on the slate shelf, an old-fashioned mixing bowl of cream enamel that had probably been used by the ninth baron of Casterglass's cook (her father was the twelfth). The smell seemed to be emanating from there.

Althea edged closer, covering her mouth and nose with her scarf, as she peered into the bowl and then took a hasty, horrified step backwards, trying not to regurgitate the soggy tuna baguette she'd bought at a roadside M&S several hours ago.

"Did you find it, darling?" her mother called.

"Er…yes." Althea came back into the kitchen. "Mummy, didn't you realise it needed to be *covered*?"

Violet gave her a look of mild, blank curiosity. "Covered?"

"The bowl. Otherwise…" Otherwise flies would get into it and the whole thing would become a liquefying, maggoty mess that would haunt her nightmares. Althea's stomach roiled. If she'd needed a reminder why she didn't come home very often, she'd had eight in the last five minutes.

"Well, no, darling, because it's got to *ripen*, doesn't it?" her mother said oh so reasonably. "Now where's your father? He'll be so pleased to see you."

And off she wandered, murmuring to herself, as Althea steeled herself to go back into the larder and fetch the wretched bowl.

"Is Granny…*okay*?" Poppy asked in a low voice once Althea had dumped the bowl outside and left it to soak in the rain. She rummaged in the cupboards under the sink for a cleaning product that was less than a decade old.

"Okay?" she repeated, sounding almost as distracted as her mother. "What do you mean?"

"She's just a bit…off, you know? A bit…weird."

Althea let out a hollow laugh as she rose from where she'd been kneeling on the floor with a crusted bottle of Flash. "That's just the way she is, Pops. The way she's always been." For a second Althea felt a pang of sorrow that her daughter didn't really *know* her mother, but then she considered what her mother was like and decided that was not an entirely bad thing. Her mother wasn't cruel or unkind or anything like that, but during Althea's childhood her vagueness had sometimes skated close to neglect.

"Don't worry," she told Poppy. "You'll get used to her." She frowned as she started shaking the bottle of Flash, hoping for a few ancient drops to trickle out. "When did you last see her? Was it Grandad's seventieth? I can't even remember."

"I don't know… They came to London a year ago, I think…but…" Poppy trailed off, but Althea knew the gist of what she'd been going to say. Her parents did, rather miraculously, manage to scrub up and act normally when they were in the outside world. In their natural habitat, they reverted to true and bizarre form, without even realising it.

"Like I said, you'll get used to them," Althea said, and she started to hunt around for some fairly clean tea towels.

"Is there anything to eat?" Tobias asked, sounding woebegone, and she gave him a quick, sympathetic smile. Their plastic-wrapped sandwiches felt like a long time ago. "I'm sure I can find some pasta or something."

"What about a takeaway?" Tobias asked hopefully, and Althea suppressed another hollow laugh. The nearest restaurant was fifteen miles away, and it was a grotty pub near Millom that had carpets that smelled like wee.

"No, sorry, love, there isn't. But I'm sure I can find something to make here, and tomorrow we'll do a big shop." There was, at least, a decent supermarket in Ulverston, which was only a little farther than Millom.

"Althea, my golden girl!" Her father's booming voice had Althea putting down the Flash and grubby tea towel as her father came bounding into the room, all ruddy cheeks and flyaway hair, tweedy charm personified, his arms outstretched for a bear hug that would make her bones rattle. Walter Penryn, the twelfth baron of Casterglass, affectionate, absent-minded, and unfortunately pretty much useless when it came to anything but orchids, but still eminently lovable.

"Hi, Daddy." Althea tried not to wince as her father squeezed the breath out of her before stepping back to give her a thorough once-over.

"You look a little pale. Have you eaten?"

"I'm just about to—"

"Your mother has made some lovely sourdough—"

"Thanks, I think we'll just have pasta." Althea had spied a packet of unopened spaghetti in the larder, far enough away from the offending sourdough starter to deem safe. "Where's Seph?" she asked as she rinsed out a pot several times before filling it from the tap, which screeched in protest as it had done for as long as she could remember.

"Seph?" her father repeated, as if he'd never heard the name before. "I have no idea."

"She does still live here, doesn't she?" Althea half-joked, squashing a guilty qualm that she didn't really know what her little sister was up to. Persephone was only twenty-two, after all, and considering the state of her parents, perhaps she should keep an eye out a bit more than she had been, although Persephone never seemed to appreciate her well-intentioned conversational gambits, usually greeting them with a somewhat sullen silence and dark look.

"Yes, yes, of course she lives here." Her father almost sounded affronted, before his face, so suddenly it seemed almost comical, fell. "For now."

The pot was almost overflowing and quickly Althea turned off the protesting tap. "What do you mean, Daddy? Is Seph thinking of moving out?" Her sister had spent her entire life at the castle, first being homeschooled and then doing an Open University course online. She worked for a local farmer and had never seemed remotely interested in exploring the wider world. Althea had invited her to visit several times, but Seph had refused, which admittedly had brought some relief. Althea didn't think her husband and sister would have got on all that well. "Daddy?" she prompted while her father regarded her in what she realised was a rather miserable silence.

In the ensuing second's pause she felt as if the already cracked tectonic plates of her world shifted yet again; it was as if all the disdained familiarity around her suddenly became irrevocably and unbearably dear. Her father's face was as sorrowful as a basset hound's as he said heavily, "Well, my darling, the truth is I'm afraid it looks like we're going to have to sell up."

Chapter Two

"SELL UP?"

Althea repeated the words dumbly as she lifted the lid of the Aga and basked in the blast of comforting heat for a few seconds before she plonked the pot on the stove. "What do you mean?"

"Well, you know how expensive running a place like this is." Her father sounded uncharacteristically feeble. "And we haven't got as much in the coffers as we'd like…"

"Well, I *know* that." Her whole childhood had been a study in Dickensian levels of poverty, shrouded in the popular mystique of the shabby genteel. She remembered hearing in a history lesson about the children of some erstwhile exiled French king who were left starving in the nursery of the palace, and while her classmates had shaken their heads in wonder (or more likely, stared out the window in boredom) she'd thought: *I know exactly how that feels.* All right, she may never have actually been *starving*, but it had been close. Her parents had never been diligent about things like shopping or cooking, and money had always been found down the back of the sofa or similar. Yet somehow all four of the Penryn children had survived, so Althea supposed she shouldn't complain too much.

She ripped open the packet of spaghetti and dumped it into the pot. "I mean, we've always sailed a bit close to the wind, haven't we?" she tossed over her shoulder with a smile, before she clocked her father's bereft expression. Wait, he wasn't *serious*? "Daddy…?"

"I'm sorry, sweet pea."

He hadn't called her sweet pea since she was about six. A sudden terror seized Althea, akin to what she'd felt when she'd lost three-year-old Poppy in Selfridges when she'd decided to get her make-up done for a date night with Jasper. She'd found Poppy after five horror-filled minutes, and the date night had been the usual disaster.

"What do you mean?" Althea asked, her voice sounding ridiculously squeaky. "I mean, why now? What's hap-pened…?"

"Well, the roof needs replacing." Her father tried for wry jocularity, but she could see he looked pained. And he really was serious.

"Wait…what…" Her head was spinning, and her children were *actually* starving. She needed to get them fed first, and then she might consider opening one of the precious bottles of Chateau Margaux '36 that the tenth Earl of Casterglass had laid down in the cellar.

"I'm sorry to break it to you like this, darling—"

"No, wait. Just wait." Althea took a deep breath and turned back to the spaghetti bubbling away on the stove. "We're going to talk about this properly."

Somehow she managed to make three plates of pasta, complete with sauce from a jar that was, amazingly, only a month past its expiry date. Poppy and Tobias both wolfed theirs down but despite her earlier hunger, Althea could barely manage a mouthful. *Sell* Casterglass? Amazingly such a possibility had never, ever crossed her mind. Casterglass seemed as immutable as…as rain in Cumbria, or Jasper being unfaithful. Neither fact was, Althea acknowledged, something she wanted to dwell on particularly, but *still*. Casterglass was as much a part of her as her soul, her skin, even if she hadn't always liked that fact. Even if sometimes she'd wished it otherwise.

After they'd eaten their pasta, or in her case, pushed it around on her plate, she headed upstairs to find the least damp bedrooms to lay claim to. Her mother had not put in another appearance and her sister had not shown up at all. Her father had tottered back to his study; he'd been working on a definitive guide to orchids for the last fifteen years, and didn't look to be finished anytime soon.

"I think these sheets are clean," she told Poppy bracingly as she shook out a fitted sheet that had been worn to a velvety if fragile softness. They'd claimed three bedrooms on the top floor, above her parents' and Seph's rooms, and Tobias had gone to investigate his. This part of the house was a jumble of steep stairs, narrow corridors and low ceilings, only to suddenly emerge into pleasantly spacious rooms.

Poppy skulked in the doorway, one slim leg wrapped around the other as she twirled a strand of hair around her finger and regarded her mother's preparations dubiously. Althea didn't think she'd ever seen her look so young and uncertain.

"How long are we staying here?" she asked as Althea smoothed the sheet over the bed. "I mean, I know for Christmas…"

"We'll see how it goes, I think." Althea had yet to explain to any of her children the entire state of affairs—no pun intended, of course—between her and Jasper. All they knew was there had been a massive row, their father had swanned off to Switzerland for the entire holiday, and Althea, humiliated and heartbroken, had run back home. She suppressed a sigh as the depressing reality of her situation hit her all over again. *Jasper's finally had enough of you. And that's actually a good thing.*

The trouble was, he'd hinted that she wasn't welcome back, and Althea didn't know if that was his indifference talking or his intransigent solicitor persona. In any case, she didn't even know if she *wanted* to go back, although she had no idea where else she would go.

Life felt overwhelming, impossible, which was why she'd come home. Wasn't that what you did, when things got too much? Too bad home was a freezing, falling-down castle, but there you were. She loved it anyway. Sort of.

"But what does *that* mean?" Poppy demanded, interrupting the downward spiral of her thoughts, her voice high and thin as she put both feet on the floor. "I have school, you know? I'm in the middle of *A levels*?" She spoke in that cutting, sarcastic tone sixteen-year-olds seemed to have got down to a tee. At least Poppy had, but then perhaps she'd learned it from her father.

"I know you are, Poppy," Althea answered as she reached for a pillowcase. "And I don't want to upset your education, naturally. It's just...things are complicated right now, as you know. When your father returns from Switzerland, we'll have to talk things through."

"Are you guys getting a divorce?" Poppy asked accusingly, her arms folded.

Almost certainly. Althea sighed. "I...don't know." She paused. "But I think...maybe."

Poppy made a harrumphing sound as she turned away, clearly not wanting to pursue that line of enquiry, which was just as well because Althea needed more time and emotional energy to sit her children down and talk it through. "Why is this place so...weird?" Poppy asked instead.

Her daughter had barely begun to see how weird this place could be. "Granny and Grandad are free spirits," Althea said with an attempt at a smile. "They always have been. It takes some getting used to, but there are some pretty cool things about living in a castle." Epic games of hide-and-seek, playing dress-up with actual outfits from the 1800s, discos in a ballroom practically the size of a football pitch… Yes, there had been some advantages.

There were also the downsides—draughts like winds from the Arctic, roofs that leaked, waking up with chilblains, a mouse infestation to rival the time of the plague…but you knew it was all part of the charm.

Even though Althea made no mention of any of this, Poppy looked understandably disbelieving. "I'll give you a tour tomorrow," she promised. "Show you all the nooks and crannies. Do you know Henry VIII slept in the four-poster in the master bedroom? At least we think he did. Passed down as part of the family legend, anyway." Poppy gave a little so-what sort of shrug and Althea sighed. "It's funny how you don't remember it. You were here for Grandad's seventieth birthday and that was only two years ago—"

"It was different then."

Yes, Althea supposed it had been. A big party out on the lawn, fully catered, the sun actually shining, and they'd stayed at the inn in Casterglass village because Jasper insisted on one-thousand-thread-count sheets and a fridge full of miniatures, neither of which he'd found at that humble establishment, but whatever.

And, Althea acknowledged, her parents could scrub up and act normally when pressed, her father full of genial bonhomie, her mother elegant if somewhat abstracted, and they had done so for that weekend, presenting a friendly, welcoming front to their guests—a motley crew of distant relatives and curious locals, along with the usual spattering of minor aristocrats and eccentric academics.

As Althea recalled that weekend in all its summery strawberries-and-champagne glory, she realised things at the castle might have slipped a bit more than usual. It was only two weeks before Christmas, and usually her father arranged for Alan, the local man who did the gardening, to festoon fairy lights over just about everything. This year he obviously hadn't. Was there even a Christmas tree in the entrance hall like usual? Somehow Althea doubted it. Her father's words, the ones she'd been trying not to think about since he'd said them, reverberated through her mind.

We're going to have to sell up.

Surely not. Everything in her rejected the notion, refused to give it so much as a single second's reflection. It bounced off her brain like a ball against brick. She simply could not let herself think about it, which was a little odd, considering how rarely she came to Casterglass, and how much dread she usually felt about making the journey, as memories of freezing bedrooms, ice-cold baths, and nothing to eat but her mother's soggy lentils or stale Weetabix, ricocheted through her mind. And yet it was home, more of a home even than the five-bedroom faux-Tudor manor back in Cobham.

She'd talk to her father after she got the children settled, Althea decided. Get to the bottom of things, if that was ever possible with her parents.

"There, that's you sorted." She gave the bedspread, ancient and threadbare as it was, an encouraging pat. "I'll bring you a hot water bottle in a bit. There are extra blankets in the chest at the bottom of the bed if you need them."

"In that?" Poppy pointed to the ornately carved wooden chest. "It looks like it holds Bluebeard's wives, or something."

"No, they're in the dungeon," Althea told her cheerfully, then gave her daughter a sympathetic squeeze of the shoulders when she saw her I-don't-know-whether-to-believe-you expression. "Don't worry, Poppy. I know it all seems a bit Gothic and grim right now, but it will be better in the morning." It probably wouldn't, but sunlight hopefully would make a difference. It would show up all the dust and cobwebs, at any rate.

She left Poppy to get Tobias settled, briskly making his bed as he slumped on a chair and played his iPad with a lethargic level of disinterest. She gave him the same pep talk, to which she received monosyllabic replies, and after kissing him goodnight she went in search of her father.

He was in the study, a wood-panelled room with curtains the colour of ox blood drawn against the stormy night. It had always been a comforting if messy room, with its leather-bound books and paper like parchment; her father was an extremely old-fashioned man. Althea's childhood had been marred by neither television nor computer. The castle had only had Wi-Fi put in—and very bad Wi-Fi at that—a couple of years ago.

"Althea." He rested his palms on the surface of his desk as he gave her a cheerfully appraising look. "The children are settled?"

"Yes."

"We're so glad to have you here, darling. I hope you know that."

"I do." A sudden, stupid lump formed in her throat. She knew her parents were scatty and strange, but she loved them and she knew—mostly—that they loved her.

A telling pause ensued, as her father waited for her to say something of why she'd fled London two weeks before Christmas without either her husband or any explanation as to why. She didn't.

"Ben is coming, as well?" he asked finally, and she nodded.

"He sits his last exam in a couple of days. He'll take the train from Durham."

"Good, good. Excellent. And your sister Olivia will join us in a few days, too."

"Not Sam?"

"No, no, he's in New Zealand this time, doing something for hospitals for the Maori."

"Of course." Her younger brother was out of the country ninety per cent of the time, usually doing something swotty and stupid like climbing K2 with a fridge on his back. He had made it practically a full-time job to do extreme sports for charity, in between his freelance work as a data analyst.

Another pause where neither of them made mention of Jasper.

"Dad, what did you mean about selling up?" Althea asked, finally grasping the nettle. She let out a laugh, inviting him to share the non-existent joke. "I mean, we've been in tight places before, surely…"

"I fear they're only growing tighter." Her father gave her a sorrowful smile. "I'm serious this time, darling. I'm sorry."

Althea sank into a chair as she stared at him dazedly. "But…you *can't*." Her father gave a little shrug, spreading his hands. "This castle has been in our family for eight hundred years."

"Darling, I know."

"But…" She shook her head slowly. She had never imagined so much as a moment when Casterglass wouldn't be here, waiting for her, even if the truth was she hardly ever came. "What will you do, if you sell this place?" She could absolutely not imagine her parents anywhere else.

Another shrug. "We were thinking of buying a little place in Cornwall, somewhere *slightly* sunnier." A lopsided smile. "We don't need much. A study, a few bedrooms in case any of you decide to visit."

"Of course we'll visit," Althea declared. She felt the hot press of tears against her lids and blinked them back.

"Well…" Her father paused, seeming to deliberate, before he said gently, "That hasn't always been the case, has it?"

Althea fell back on bluster. "What…what do you mean?"

"You haven't come back to Casterglass very often. Neither for that matter has Olivia, even though she's only over in York. And you know what Sam is like."

"What about Seph?"

"Persephone undoubtedly has her own plans, although she doesn't often see the necessity of making me aware of them." Her father smiled. "In any case, the real issue isn't how often you visit. It's the fact that there is no one who wants to *stay*." Althea's mouth opened and closed silently. "Being master of Casterglass is, I fear, a full-time job, and more importantly, a vocation. I know it most likely seems to you as if I don't do very much besides potter about in my greenhouse or write about the ghost orchid, but that's actually not the case. Taking care of the estate occupies much of my time, and it's not something I can bequeath to any of you without you understanding and wanting what you're taking on board."

A full-time job and yet it was *still* falling apart at the seams? Althea swallowed. "But you never said… Shouldn't we have a discussion first?"

"Naturally, that would be the ideal," her father agreed, nodding. "But we're so rarely all in the same place at the same time. I tried to broach the subject at my seventieth, but matters got away from us."

Althea vaguely recalled an impromptu, drunken game of

croquet, leading to an even more impromptu dip in the mere, which was more swamp than lake and had taken a certain level of non-fussiness about things like mud and leeches.

"But why now?" she asked.

"Because you're here, and so is Seph, and Olivia is coming for Christmas. And the cost of reroofing this place, which has become quite a pressing matter, is going to run to about two hundred thousand pounds. And that was the cheap estimate, given by a couple of shady men with a van and a ladder."

She swallowed. Hard. "But...surely we've run into these kinds of pickles before?"

"Yes, and there's always been more money in the pot before. But that has been steadily diminishing, and the stock market has been more or less like a whirligig, and the fact is I'm seventy-two, and I want to retire. I've got no one I can hand the reins to, so here we are."

"Sam..." Althea began, because she'd always thought Sam, as her father's only male heir and the next Baron of Casterglass, would one day take over, although the estate wasn't entailed like something out of *Pride and Prejudice*. Still, she'd assumed it would fall to him once he'd got the adventuring bug out of his system. A few more trips to Nepal and he's be good to go, surely...

"I spoke to Sam about six months ago," her father told her quietly. "When he was home between trips. He made it clear he didn't intend to make Casterglass his home, now or later."

"What!" Althea was strangely shocked and even hurt by this news. Wasn't that Sam's responsibility, if not his actual *raison d'être*? Besides, he was thirty-three. High time to settle down and make a go of it.

"It's his prerogative, darling. I've always made that clear. You've got to love this place, to want to stay here and battle through. It will never work otherwise. It is far, far too much effort."

"But I don't want you to sell it," Althea said, surprised by how much she meant it.

"Think of it this way. I spoke to an estate agent and if we can find a buyer, it's likely to fetch a good price. Three million, or thereabouts. Obviously there will be tax to pay, and your mother and I will want our bolthole, but there will be plenty left over for you lot. Far better to have that for your inheritance than a crumbling castle with a leaky roof and a haunted guard room."

"The guard room *isn't* haunted. Liv and I stayed up all night once to see if we could spy the ghost." The third baron had come to an untimely end during the English Civil War, and her mother insisted she'd seen him mournfully hoisting his sword in the guard room, days too late to come to the Royalists' aid in the Battle of Preston.

"Well, maybe he didn't want to make an appearance to you two, but your mother insists she can sometimes still hear the rattling." Her father smiled. "Anyway, it makes sense, as much as it pains me."

Althea didn't reply, because it did make sense, and yet she still hated the thought. She was suddenly finding herself besieged by memories—epic games of sardines in the old part of the castle, which was a warren of staircases and corridors and secret rooms; the solarium even had a priest hole by its chimney.

She recalled acting out the entire plot of *The Iliad*, complete with her mother's hand-sewn costumes, in the ballroom; pond dipping in the mucky mere; boisterous family meals in the kitchen; a childhood of rusty bicycles and muddy boots and afternoons curled up on the window seat as the rain pelted down and she lost herself in a book...

All right, she was romanticising everything more than a bit; half the time her parents had seemed to forget they had children, never mind that they needed to be clothed and fed. Winter was so cold that even with a hot water bottle and six blankets she'd *still* got chilblains. Boarding school at age eleven had pretty much been a seven-year nightmare and none of them had really got to know the locals here beyond hellos in the village, so she'd felt, until Jasper, completely unmoored, anchorless and drifting, longing for someone or something to keep her in place. And then, unfortunately, after her marriage she'd felt weighed down by a thousand-pound anchor she'd realised she hadn't wanted.

But to lose Casterglass? To never come here again—

never wander its rooms, or curl up in the library, or explore the seventy acres of wilderness, or make a den in the old potting shed? All right, she hadn't made a den in thirty years, but *still*.

"I'm sorry, Althea. Really I am. I can see this has taken you by surprise."

"It's just…" Her voice came out thick. "This is our *history*, Daddy. Our home."

"I know."

"Have you told the others?"

"Sam has known for a while. Persephone suspects, I think. I was going to tell Olivia at Christmas. Sit everyone down and spell it all out."

"All right." Althea swallowed, trying to dissolve the huge lump in her throat as she rose from her chair. Maybe things wouldn't seem so sad in the morning.

"Oh, and we're having all the neighbours over for a sherry on Friday night," her father said, his tone turning determinedly cheerful once more. "Bit of a farewell kind of do, although I haven't said as much to anyone, of course. We used to do it ages ago, do you remember? A Christmas knees-up for everyone?"

Vaguely Althea recalled the parties of her childhood, when the fires had been roaring and a twenty-foot Christmas tree had graced the front hall. They'd tapered off a long time ago.

"But we haven't even decorated for Christmas," she protested, and her father raised his eyebrows, bemused, surprised.

"Haven't we?"

"No. We can't have everyone with the place looking like…" She drew a breath. "Never mind. I'll sort it."

"I'm sure it will be fine—" Her father's words to live by, until, apparently, he'd decided it wouldn't be and was going to sell his family's estate.

"I'll sort it," Althea said, more firmly. If they were going to bow out, they would at least do it in style.

Chapter Three

ALTHEA WOKE IN the usual Casterglass sleeping position—foetal, knees to chest, hugging a now stone-cold hot water bottle, with the blankets pulled right up to her nose. Goodness, but it was freezing. And dark. She fumbled for her phone and blinked at the time—seven forty-five in the morning, but it looked and felt like the dead of a very long night.

As she pushed back the covers she experienced a full-body shiver that was more like a convulsion and then practically jumped into her dressing gown and slippers; she was already wearing flannel pyjamas, a fleece and wool socks. Everything seemed quiet, and she thought she was probably the first one up. Her children could happily sleep for hours yet, and her parents had never been early risers, although they'd pulled the occasional random all-nighter, lost in whatever project they had on the go—classics or horticulture. She still hadn't seen Seph.

She tiptoed downstairs and into the kitchen, standing close to the Aga's comforting warmth while she waited for the kettle to boil. Around her the house was starting to wake up like the living beast it sometimes seemed—pipes clanking, radiators hissing, wooden beams flexing and groaning as the wind continued to batter and blow. The kettle boiled and Althea made herself a coffee, giving the milk an exploratory sniff before she poured a splash in. She decided to take it up to the sitting room so she could watch the sun rise over the fells.

Darkness was beginning to dissipate into ghostly shreds as she stood by the window and sipped her coffee, gazing out at the view that revealed itself in increments. The gentle hills and sloping peaks of the Cumbrian fells—mountains, anywhere else in the world—emerged through a dawn fog, and Althea was able to identify Green Crag and Harter Fell, much to her satisfaction.

One summer when she'd been about twelve her father had decided they would hike all the Wainwrights, that was, the two hundred and fourteen peaks described in Alfred Wainwright's seven-volume *Pictorial Guide to the Lakeland Fells*, published in 1952. They'd managed five, which, all things considered, Althea thought quite impressive.

The sun had started to rise, a pale pink light creeping over the purplish-green peaks, some with a scattering of snow like a dusting of icing sugar. As the sun rose, the rose- and salmon-coloured sky was flooded with brilliance, and the vista before her was divided into stretches of light and pockets of darkness, an undulating patchwork of greys and greens that was so beautiful, Althea felt the sting of tears behind her lids.

She'd *missed* this, she realised, missed it all, even the chaos and the cold, although not projects like her mother's sourdough starter, to be sure. Recognising she might be feeling a tiny bit sentimental and maudlin due to her father's bombshell last night, Althea tried to organise her thoughts.

If her father did decide to sell Casterglass, it could certainly help to ease the financial pressure she was sure to feel once the divorce was finalised, assuming she did get divorced, which seemed more and more likely. Even if Jasper was willing to take her back, she was quite sure she didn't want to go.

Surely that long-awaited realisation was what had motivated her unexpected and entirely out of character explosion? She'd actually *thrown* things. She, who had accepted Jasper's infidelities with barely a murmur for nearly twenty years, because the alternative had been too dreadful to contemplate, had hurled a Waterford crystal vase at her husband's head. It had been thoroughly satisfying, even though it had missed, and Jasper's response had been one of stomach-crampingly cold fury.

Her stomach cramped again as she took bleak stock of her situation—she'd been a stay-at-home mother and wife for twenty years, had no career prospects whatsoever, and although her soon-to-be-ex-husband earned a mint, Althea doubted she would see very much, if any, of it, although at least the children would be provided for.

She'd signed a prenuptial agreement right before their marriage, and while she didn't actually remember the details of it, she was pretty sure they'd be spectacularly ungenerous. Back then, in a haze of twenty-one-year-old romantic delight and fairy-tale hope, she hadn't cared.

You would have thought, Althea reflected, that after nearly twenty years of marital disharmony and infidelity, she might have sneaked a peek at the prenup, but stupidly, she hadn't. Head in sand, that was her. Ostrich Althea until Jasper had forced the issue, or perhaps she had.

Althea drained the rest of her coffee as she determinedly pushed such melancholy thoughts away. She had more pressing issues to deal with—that was, getting some decent food in, and also decorating at least the on-show parts of the castle for their sherry evening on Friday night. How her parents could have invited everyone round and then not done a thing to prepare for it, Althea could not fathom, although by this time it was, unfortunately, completely in character.

Never mind. It was only a little bit after eight and she had a full day in front of her. Feeling brisk with purpose, Althea grabbed a quick shower—easy enough to be speedy since the water was barely a lukewarm trickle—dressed as quickly as she could while her body broke out in gooseflesh, and then, at half past eight, knocked on Poppy and Tobias's doors.

"Wake up, sleepyheads! We've got work to do!"

This cheery pronouncement was met with theatrical groans.

Still, she managed to drag them both downstairs for toast (there was half a loaf of fairly fresh shop-bought bread, thank heaven) and cups of sugary tea.

"Granny and Grandad are having a party tomorrow night, so we've got lots to do," she told them with sunny sternness. "The hall needs to be decorated, and we're going to have to find a Christmas tree."

"Plus you said we'd go shopping," Tobias reminded her hopefully. The poor boy was worried about his stomach. Althea understood.

"Yes, a big shop at Booths," she agreed.

"How are we supposed to find a Christmas tree?" Poppy demanded sulkily as she dabbed at toast crumbs on her plate. "Is it hiding under a bed?"

"We used to have the most enormous trees," Althea reminisced, ignoring her daughter's half-hearted snark. "Twenty feet tall at least. We'll have to downgrade this year, I suppose. Only eighteen feet." Neither of her children responded to her lame joke, both determined to be morose, and so Althea slapped her hands lightly on the table and stood up. "Right! You have fifteen minutes to dress while I hunt for the Christmas decorations, and then we're off to Ulverston. There's a garden centre there, so we should manage the tree all right. Okay?"

Before either of them could reply Persephone stalked into the kitchen, dressed in the baggy plaids and dirty jeans of a 1990s grunge band, and sporting a full head of waist-length pink dreadlocks Althea hadn't seen before. She gulped.

"Persephone," she managed. "Long time, no see."

"Yeah," Persephone agreed as she gave her niece and nephew a glance that was only mildly curious. "All right?" she asked with a voice that was the incongruous mix of half plummy posh and half Cumbria twang. They both nodded, awed into silence by their seemingly wild aunt.

"What have you been up to, Seph?" Althea asked in the jolly voice you used with children you didn't know very well and were slightly scared of. Persephone was her *sister*, but she didn't really feel like it. She never had.

Persephone had been her parents' surprise blessing when Althea had left for uni; she'd come back for holidays and been charmed by her cute baby sister, until she'd married when Seph had been only three—a flower girl all in pink tulle—and then Althea had had Ben, who was only three years younger than her sister, and somehow, in the busyness of her own family, Althea had half-forgotten Persephone growing up at Casterglass, although she'd tried to remember birthday and Christmas presents, had suggested visits that had never come to anything.

She had a feeling her sister had been forgotten by a lot of people—homeschooled by her parents, which, she knew from experience, meant a strange and decidedly patchy education, and Sixth Form at a local comprehensive because the money for the third-rate boarding schools Althea, Sam and Olivia had all gone to had run out. For the last three years she'd been living at home, working part-time for a local farmer, or so Althea had heard from her mother, during one of their infrequent and vague phone calls.

But despite knowing all that, she didn't actually *know* Seph. She didn't know what made her tick, or laugh, or feel afraid. Even though she was forty-one years old, Althea had to acknowledge she was intimidated by her sister who looked both scarily tough and, beneath the coolly indifferent veneer, somehow wounded and fragile. Or was Althea just transferring how *she* felt on to her baby sister?

"Not much," Seph said in answer to Althea's question. "You know."

But of course she didn't know. It seemed rude to point that out, however. "You're still working for that farmer?" Althea asked, as if she knew which one.

"Yeah."

"Cool." She hesitated as she thought about asking what Persephone thought about their father selling the estate, but then she remembered her dad had said only that her sister suspected. What did that mean, exactly? "I was thinking of getting the Christmas decorations out," she said instead. "You know about the do tomorrow night, I suppose?"

"Yeah."

A scintillating conversationalist her sister was not. "Fancy helping?"

Seph shook her head as she poured water from the kettle into a mug and then threw a teabag on top of it. Now that was just *wrong*. "No," she said, and Althea decided to leave it at that.

As it turned out, it was surprisingly easy to find the Christmas decorations, or at least some of them, stuffed into boxes and shoved into the first storeroom, one of a dozen small stone rooms on the top floor of the old part of the castle. All Althea had had to do was open the door. Breathing a sigh of relief that at least *something* was simple, she took them down to the great hall.

The great hall was exactly what it sounded like—an enormous medieval chamber with a high-beamed ceiling, whitewashed walls studded with heraldic shields, a minstrel gallery and a huge stone fireplace at one end of the room that took up a whole wall. It was the kind of fireplace you could roast a boar in, if you were so inclined. Althea was not.

There was a long, ancient trestle table taking up the centre of the room—it was five hundred years old but could, she thought, look at home in a school cafeteria. The centuries-old graffiti, some of it in Latin, was a conversation point, at least.

She put the boxes of decorations on the table and surveyed the room, her hands on her hips. Where to start?

Just then Poppy breezed in, her caramel-coloured hair ironed poker-straight, dressed in a red leather miniskirt and a tight, navel-skimming top.

"I'm ready to go to Ulverston," she announced with a flick of her hair. Althea thought her daughter must have higher hopes of Ulverston's social possibilities than she did.

"You look lovely, darling," she said as diplomatically as she could, considering how little Poppy was wearing, "but you're going to freeze your…" She paused. "Freeze," she finished, while Poppy glowered.

"Mum. I'm *fine*." She folded her arms with a theatrical huff while Althea suppressed her first sigh of the day. Her daughter was terribly spoiled, and that was at least somewhat her fault. Over the years it had become harder and harder to fight against Jasper's careless indulgence, followed by his even more careless indifference. The roller coaster hadn't been good for any of the children, and Althea had tried to compensate with unconditional love and affection. Unfortunately it had meant discipline had sometimes gone a bit by the wayside.

Could coming to Casterglass change any of that? Briefly she imagined Poppy learning how to cook at the big Aga, striding through mucky meadows in a pair of dungarees and well-used wellies, forgetting about her phone. Hmm. Maybe not.

"All right, then," she said. "As soon as Tobias is ready we'll head into town. Meanwhile I need to decide what to do with this lot." She gestured towards the boxes of decorations. "I want to make the place a bit more festive, considering we're having guests over."

"Hmm." Poppy narrowed her eyes as she gave the hall an assessing look. "I think you want to go with the less is more approach, and let the room speak for itself. Fresh greenery would do the trick—lots of holly and evergreen. You could twine it up there…" She gestured to the wooden railings of the minstrel gallery. "And over the fireplace, of course. If you get a few pillar candles in red and white you're sorted."

"You think so?" Althea gazed at her daughter in frank admiration. Poppy sounded as authoritative as the stick-thin, gel-nailed interior designer Althea had been intimidated by, who had decorated their house in Surrey, at Jasper's request while Althea had simply stood to the side, wringing her hands and trying to explain how she wanted a homey feel, which the designer had deliberately ignored.

Now she recalled demanding to know what Poppy was watching on YouTube, thinking it was something questionable, only to discover she was inhaling American home improvement shows with an admirable avidity. "Do you think you could take this on, Pops?" she asked hopefully. "You sound like you have a vision."

"Well…" Poppy looked startled, the insta-refusal on her lips, but then she paused, giving her phone a cursory glance-and-scroll. "Maybe."

That was as good as a yes in Althea's book. "Wonderful. I'm going to try to get a tree delivered from the garden centre in Ulverston—we used to chop one down from the estate but we haven't time now. And as long as we've got some sherry and mulled wine, we should be away." She checked her gold-and-silver watch, a present Jasper had given her, via his secretary, after Poppy's birth, and also an apology for the affair he'd had while she was pregnant. Maybe she'd get a new one, something cheap and plastic. "Now where's Tobias?"

"I'm here." Tobias sloped into the rooms, hands stuffed into the pockets of his jeans, shaggy head bowed. Althea gave him a smile, hoping to bolster his mood, although in truth she didn't know how he was feeling. Her youngest son kept to himself, his very still waters running incredibly deep. Either that or he was more concerned with the universes of Fortnite and Minecraft than anything that was going on in the real world.

"Right, shall we head off?" she asked brightly.

"Where are Granny and Grandad?" Tobias asked.

"I…I don't know." Althea supposed, in a parallel, normal universe, grandparents came to breakfast and asked how you were and just generally put in an appearance. Her parents were not like that. They wandered in and out like second-hand characters in a play, offstage half the time, occasionally making an appearance and sometimes forgetting their lines. But she could hardly explain that to a twelve-year-old.

"I'm sure we'll see them at lunch. If we go now, we can be back in time to make something for everyone." Not as if that was the most exciting incentive, but amazingly it motivated her children to turn and file out of the hall. She supposed they wanted, just as she had at that age, a certain degree of normalcy, so they could know what to expect. How many times had she wished—fervently, tragically—that her parents could be like other people's? That her life could be?

And then you went and tried to replicate what you thought a real life looked like, and see how that turned out?

"Come on, guys!" She was going full-on musical now, the last syllable ending in a fluting trill as she brandished her car keys like a trophy. This was going to be great.

Chapter Four

THE BOOTHS SUPERMARKET in Ulverston was an oasis of overpriced organic goodness; Althea glanced around happily at the familiar sights of bunches of beetroot, with their red-veined leaves, and compostable tubs of roasted red pepper hummus, bouquets of fresh-cut flowers and single orchids that cost twenty pounds. Her father would turn his nose up at the last one. *Common or garden*, she could hear him say with a sniff, *common or garden*.

As soon as Althea stepped through the door, she felt herself relax. This was a little slice of London in the Lake District, a supermarket that was elegantly packaged and extravagantly overpriced. Even Tobias and Poppy seemed to relax; *ah, observe. The creature in its natural habitat.*

"We needs loads of food, don't we, Mum?" Tobias asked eagerly, already reaching for a set of four chocolate muffins (organic, naturally) from the bakery aisle.

"Yes, we do," Althea answered firmly. She fully intended to stock Casterglass's larder to its ancient rafters. She had a debit card and several thousand pounds in her housekeeping account—yes, her marriage had been that pathetically old-fashioned and sexist, with Jasper giving her an allowance and Althea possessing no other bank account in her own name—and she intended to use a goodly portion of it this morning.

With a look of glee Tobias started chucking sugary things into the trolley. Even Poppy, whose relationship to food was complicated at the best of times, with periods of near-starvation followed by eating nothing but chocolate fondu and bananas, looked mildly interested at her mother's extravagant *carte blanche.*

Althea's heart lifted as she pushed her trolley down another aisle, tossing things in with abandon. She felt proactive and powerful in a way that was most likely ridiculous, considering she was doing nothing more than a food shop, but after the utter battering her self-confidence had taken for the last twenty years, often without her even realising it, she'd take her wins where she found them. A kilo of fusilli? *Yes.* Six organic chicken breasts? Bring it on.

"*Althea?*"

The note of wondering incredulity in the speaker's voice had Althea freezing, a jar of sundried tomato pasta sauce in her hand as she slowly turned around. A woman, short and ginger haired, was goggling at her in disbelief, and Althea had no idea who she was.

"Erm…yes?"

"Don't you remember me?" The woman let out a huff of laughter that sounded like a combination of amusement, scorn and hurt. "Obviously not. And here I thought we were BFFs forever." She put her hands on her hips as she shook her head slowly, a smile lurking around her mouth but not quite putting in an appearance.

BFFs…Althea's mind raced. She'd never had a best friend; she had always most definitely been in the lonely wannabe hanger-on category. Except…the penny finally dropped with a clunk.

"Jenna?"

"Got it in one." Jenna grinned, and Althea found herself smiling back. "I knew you couldn't forget me after our midnight high jinks during that residential trip to Eskdale."

"Oh my goodness." Althea let out an incredulous laugh of remembrance as her children looked on, bemused. "Jenna and I went to school together," she explained, and Poppy narrowed her eyes.

"I thought you were homeschooled."

"Well, I was, until Year Six." When she'd begged her parents to send her to the local primary because she'd been desperate to make friends, any friends besides her siblings. They'd relented reluctantly, and she'd spent a year feeling completely at sea…save for Jenna, who had been her one friend and much-needed life preserver. "It's so great to see you," she told her. "How have you been?"

As Althea waited for Jenna to reply, other memories were filtering through her brain. Coming back from boarding school for Christmas in year seven, to see Jenna hanging out with her cool friends outside the rail station in Casterglass, her gaze skimming away from Althea without so much as a flicker of acknowledgement. Going to the Casterglass pub with Olivia during uni, and seeing Jenna at the bar, a smugly superior look on her face as she watched Althea and Olivia huddle in a corner, away from the raucous gaggle of local Sixth Former and uni students they didn't know.

"I've been all right," Jenna said, and Althea forced her mind back to the conversation. "I've got the 2.1 kids and a house here in Ulverston. Husband and I called it quits last year, but what can you do?" She shrugged, the movement a little brittle.

"I'm sorry…" Althea began helplessly, and Jenna shrugged aside her sympathy.

"You're married?" Her gaze skated to Poppy and Tobias. "These yours, I presume, unless you nabbed a couple of kids from a Jack Wills advert?"

Althea tried to laugh, and Poppy glowered, while Tobias merely looked longingly at the muffins. She remembered how sharp Jenna could be sometimes.

"Ha ha, no, these are mine." She didn't answer the question about being married; that was far too complicated to explain in the pasta and rice aisle of Booths.

"Well, nice to see you…" Jenna began dutifully, taking a step back, and Althea felt a sudden, desperate urge not to lose the one person who had been fairly nice to her during her school days, sharp or not. "Look, we're having a bit of a

Christmas thing on Friday, seven p.m. Why don't you come along? Just sherry and mulled wine, nothing too fancy…"

"Inviting all the tenants?" Jenna asked, her voice too light to be considered actually jeering, but Althea flinched anyway.

"Just trying to be neighbourly," she replied a bit stiffly, and Jenna grimaced.

"Sorry, I didn't mean to sound so shrewish. The divorce has brought out the worst in me, I'm afraid." She smiled, so her eyes lit up and Althea felt reassured by her friendliness. "I'd love to come."

AN HOUR LATER they trundled out of Booths with an overflowing trolley, Althea feeling both exhilarated and exhausted. Next stop was the garden centre, where she paid an extortionate amount of money to have a ten-foot Christmas tree delivered to the castle that afternoon. Then it was back in the car, the boot full of food, to travel along the narrow, winding road that cut through the fells, all the way back to Casterglass.

As they drove through the village, with its pub, post office, tiny train station and a couple of houses, Althea wondered who would show up tomorrow evening. She felt a little bit ashamed that she'd forgotten the names of the villagers she had once known—who had run the post office when she and Olivia had managed the three-mile walk to look at magazines and buy sweets? Mrs Telford?

And the pub…lonely drinks during uni aside, she and Jasper had stayed there just two years ago, and she'd chatted to the owners, but she couldn't remember their names now. The Bartons?

She racked her brain to think of her fellow pupils at Casterglass Primary, run out of a Victorian-era brick one-room schoolhouse with a couple of hideous 1960s extensions, but her Year Six class had long ago blurred into a faceless sea of strangers, save for Jenna. She'd been too shy to make more friends, and everyone else had known each other since infancy, and most were second cousins once removed or something similar.

Well, perhaps tomorrow would be an opportunity to renew the acquaintance of some of those people. The thought made her feel a bit nervous; the relationship between village and castle had always been *slightly* tense, a mixture of curiosity on the part of the villagers about what life at the big house was like, along with a veiled hostility towards the so-called aristocracy and a more reassuring, open friendliness. Well, she would just have to make the best of it, Althea supposed.

By the time they'd unloaded all the groceries into the kitchen—Althea had given the larder a good scrubbing first—it was nearly noon, and her parents drifted downstairs, as if sensing food.

Althea started to assemble the lunches she remembered from her childhood—when her mother would put a bunch of random things in the centre of the table and they'd all graze like a herd of antelope.

"Oh, darling, it's so good to have you back," her mother exclaimed, positively beaming as she plucked an olive from a bowl Althea had put on the table. "I'm afraid I don't take very good care of your father when it's just us."

"And Seph, you mean," Althea said, and her mother shrugged.

"She rather comes and goes, doesn't she? And she makes her own meals—the most wonderfully complicated curries. They're quite delicious, actually, although the muesli she makes for breakfast is *ghastly*."

"And you do take wonderful care of me," Althea's father chimed in, slipping an arm around his wife's waist. Her mother gave him a loving smile in return while Althea gazed at them both with affection. There had never, even been any doubt in her mind that her parents loved each other. So, with that model in mind, how had her own marriage gone so disastrously wrong?

Another thought to push away as she concentrated on bringing more food to the table—sliced ham, cherry tomatoes, a wedge of good old Wensleydale. The sight of it all made Althea feel warm inside, almost happy. *Home.* This really was home, far more so than the five-bedroomed, million-pound executive house in Surrey that she'd tried so hard to be the welcoming bolthole she'd craved throughout her whole childhood.

The realisation jolted her. Was this yet more sentimentality because her father had said he was selling, or was it the real deal? Impossible to tell.

After lunch, Poppy decided, off her own bat, to begin decorating the great hall, and she enlisted Tobias's reluctant help. Althea was heartened by the sight of her children working together; popular Poppy usually had little to no time for her shy and goofy younger brother.

"So how long are you staying?" her mother asked as they stood at the sink together and washed dishes; the dishwasher had been broken for as long as Althea could remember.

"Umm…through Christmas, certainly," she hedged, because she could not see further ahead than that. Of *course* she had to go back to Cobham at some point; Tobias and Poppy had school, at the very least, starting the second week of January. They both went to eye-wateringly expensive schools and the fees had already been paid for the next term. She had a life, or she should have, but of course she didn't.

Not since Jasper had shown everything to which she'd been clinging was a lie. Although, Althea had to acknowledge, that hadn't been as much of a surprise as perhaps it should have been. Her friends had always been the fair-weather sort, wives of Jasper's friends and colleagues rather than people she'd met and befriended in her own right. She'd been intimidated by them all along, sensing their sharpened claws. Not one of them had texted her since she'd fled north.

"Well, you're welcome to stay for as long as you want," her mother said, putting one hand on her arm and giving her a surprisingly earnest, non-vague look. "I hope you know that, Althea."

"Ye-es," Althea answered, more because she could imagine a family of travellers taking up residence in the east wing of the castle and her parents not even noticing, never mind actually caring.

"When is Ben coming?"

"Tomorrow. I thought I'd pick him up from Lancaster to save him the agonies of the milk train." The train that trundled from Lancaster along the Cumbria coast was painfully slow; you could feel yourself ageing as it stopped approximately every three minutes at some tiny village or other.

"Good," her mother said absently, and it wasn't until she'd drifted back upstairs that Althea considered all the questions she *hadn't* asked—such as where Jasper was, and why they were spending Christmas apart, and why she didn't actually know how long she'd be staying. Had that been intentional, or simply more of her mother's muddledness?

The dishes done, Althea decided to check how Poppy and Tobias were getting on with the decorating. Her footsteps echoed on the ancient flagstones of the foyer, each one as big as a single bed, grooves worn into them by the passage of people and time. It never failed to amaze her, to consider how many of her ancestors had travelled these rooms, what intrigues, romances, tragedies and hopes had played out between these thick stone walls, time and time again, century after century. She rested one hand on the ornately carved banister of the staircase that led up to the castle's main bedrooms, all as good as museum pieces now, as sorrow swept through her again at the thought of losing it all.

If her father sold this place, what would happen to it? No doubt some chancer would turn it into a golf club or luxury hotel. She could picture it already—the admittedly debatable and tarnished charm polished into something that made Casterglass anonymously, inoffensively pleasant. She couldn't stand the thought.

"Mum, look!" Tobias came running out of the great hall, his face split into an uncharacteristic grin. "Come see what we've done!"

"What I've done, you mean," Poppy retorted, flicking her hair, but there was a hint of pride in her voice that made Althea smile.

"Let's see," she said, and then stopped into the doorway to the hall to survey their work. Considering they had only greenery to work with, it was impressive indeed. Slowly Althea looked around the room, taking in the boughs of evergreen and holly on the mantel, festooning the window-sills and heraldic shields. Poppy had even found an old pewter jug somewhere and filled it with a lovely arrangement of winter roses and clematis.

"Where did you find the flowers?" she exclaimed and

Poppy ducked her head, suddenly surprisingly shy.

"In the old walled garden behind the kitchen. Is it all right that I picked them?"

"Oh yes, of course." Althea hadn't been in the walled garden in ages, although when she was a child her father had kept a bountiful kitchen garden, along with his precious orchids in the greenhouse. She sighed, the sound gusting through her, as she was hit afresh with how much this house meant to her, how many memories it possessed. If she'd come back more often, would her father have reconsidered selling?

"Don't you like it?" Poppy asked, a tremor in her voice, and impulsively Althea gathered her daughter up in a hug, even though Poppy had exited the cuddly phase about five years ago.

"I love it," she said, and her voice came out thick with emotion.

After a few seconds of toleration, Poppy squirmed away. "I have to message Elise," she half-mumbled, and Althea knew she was embarrassed by her display of emotion. Jasper didn't do the warm, fuzzy stuff. Neither did her children.

Suppressing another gusty sigh, she turned to Tobias. "It's brilliant, Tobes. Really."

"Yeah." Tobias hunched his shoulders. "Can I play my iPad now?"

WELL, IT WAS a start, Althea told herself after her children had disappeared to their rooms to plug themselves into their personal matrices. Poppy and Tobias had worked together without killing each other, and there had been a small moment of familial bonding. It made Althea wonder if Casterglass could be some magical remedy, the kind you read about in a children's story or one of those soppy family films, where a crumbling castle became the miracle they hadn't even realised they were looking for.

She could already picture the hazy montage of family scenes, the warm-toned voiceover. *Coming to Casterglass seemed like a nightmare…but it turned into the castle of their dreams.*

She let out a snort as she shook her head. As if. It had been a touching moment, perhaps, but life didn't actually work that way. She had twenty years of experience to prove it.

She also had a lot of work to do if they were going to be ready for this knees-up tomorrow night. Glancing around at the greenery one last time, letting herself savour the moment, Althea turned and left the room.

BY FRIDAY AFTERNOON she was exhausted and running purely on adrenaline and stress. She'd done her best to clean up the castle's public rooms for the party—the foyer and great hall, the dining room and the library. Seph had, somewhat to her surprise, agreed to dust the floor-to-ceiling bookshelves and put away some of the stacks of books that had not made it to shelves, although when Althea had tried to engage her in conversation she'd been mostly monosyllabic. It would be nice to actually get to *know* her sister, but perhaps she'd save that for another day.

On Thursday afternoon she'd driven to Lancaster to pick up Ben, and while she knew she could hardly spare the time away from castle cleaning duties, it had been nice to have a break—and see her son, who at nineteen was wonderfully upbeat and cheerful.

"Mum!" He'd bounded over and enfolded her in his long, gangly arms, so Althea had closed her eyes as she'd revelled in her son's easy embrace. Of all her children, he was the most affectionate, although not, she acknowledged sadly, with his father.

Ben had only been at university for a term, and already Althea had missed his cheerfulness. Her oldest child had never been difficult, or at least not that difficult. She was probably romanticising it all because she missed him, but he'd certainly been a lot less work than Poppy, and he'd managed to escape inheriting Jasper's worst qualities—unvarnished ambition and a callous disregard for people he didn't consider useful, although her husband had kept those mostly hidden from his offspring.

"I can't remember the last time we've been to Casterglass," Ben had remarked as he'd slung his duffel bag into the boot of the car.

"We were saying the same thing. Grandad's seventieth, I think. But it's been a long time."

"Why don't we go more often?" Ben had asked as he settled himself in the front seat and Althea started the car.

She had given him a startled look, pausing before she'd spoken. "It's an awfully long way from Surrey. But perhaps we will more often now." Too late she'd realised she shouldn't have said that, if her father really was thinking of selling up. But what if he wasn't? Or, more to the point, what if Althea could convince him not to?

The idea had been germinating, like a stubborn little seed, since her father had given her the news. What if she could find a way to keep Casterglass?

Save the castle? Don't you need a white charger, Althea? Don't be ridiculous. You can't do anything like that.

She could almost hear Jasper's sneering tone as he shot her down, except it wasn't Jasper talking, it was herself.

"Where's Dad?" Ben had asked, his tone seeming deliberately, as well as deceptively, light.

Again Althea had hesitated. Poppy and Tobias knew Jasper had gone skiing, ostensibly for some networking thing, although she didn't think they knew about Miranda, the woman he'd invited along—one of Althea's so-called best friends, newly divorced and clearly on the prowl. "He's in Switzerland," she'd admitted. "Skiing. For work, really…"

"Yeah, right." Ben's normally amicable features had twisted with scorn for a moment before he turned to look out the window. "Don't worry, Mum, I don't mind."

Althea had not known how to respond. Jasper always presented his best, most charming front to his children, but she had sometimes wondered if, at nineteen, Ben could see beneath the polish. Or perhaps the polish was finally started to flake off.

She hadn't known whether the prospect relieved or worried her. Even if she and Jasper divorced, she wanted her children to have a good relationship with their father…didn't she? Was it even possible? Would it—could it—be a good thing, considering the man he was? Too many questions that she'd known she couldn't answer yet.

"I'm just glad to have you with us, Ben," Althea had said, deciding to bypass the whole Jasper conversation, and her son had seemed happy enough to do the same.

Now it was Friday evening, and guests were due imminently. When Althea had asked her mother how many people were expected, she'd simply raised her eyebrows and shrugged her shoulders.

"I don't really know, darling. Twenty? Forty? It was an open invitation to the whole village."

Althea had bought a case of cream sherry and another of mulled wine, as well as a hundred mince pies and vol au vents from Booths. In addition to Poppy's decoration of the great hall, Ben and Tobias had put the Christmas tree up in the entrance hall and she and Poppy had decorated it. Her father had come into the room when it was all over and beamed.

"Aren't you all so clever," he'd exclaimed, and Althea had wondered what her parents would have done if she hadn't come to Cumbria at the last minute. Perhaps her mother would have poisoned the whole village with some of her sourdough. More likely they would have winged it, as they always did, dragging cases of expensive wine from the cellar and tossing a bit of holly about. And somehow or other, it would have worked, because it always more or less did. It didn't stop Althea from wanting lists and schedules and organisation. She was a sucker for a Moleskine planner.

In any case, everything was more or less ready now, and she'd managed to find a suitable ensemble from the suitcase she'd packed in a matter of minutes, having flung a random assortment of clothes into it as tears of both fury and grief had streamed down her face. Jasper had already left by that point, indifferent to her agony.

Althea smoothed her hands down the front of her cran-berry cashmere jumper and wide-legged black trousers. She still looked a little haggard and shell-shocked; there was a certain blankness in her eyes that even three days at Caster-glass had not managed to dissipate.

"Hey, Mum." Poppy slipped into the room, dressed in a slinky dress of stretchy red jersey that looked to be comprised of just enough material for a headband. Althea knew better than to suggest her daughter put on something decent; it was a battle she'd lost a long time ago, when Jasper had sided with Poppy after a pitched argument about the length of her school skirt, which had been barely brushing her thighs. Somehow her husband had thought it reasonable for his sixteen-year-old daughter to look like she was making a music video rather than taking Further Maths.

Now she simply smiled as she met Poppy's gaze in the mirror. "Ready to go down?"

"I suppose."

For a second Poppy's expression looked morose rather than her usual icily bored, and Althea hesitated. "Everything all right, darling? I know this is strange…"

"I'm fine," Poppy said with some of her usual aggression, and Althea tried to find her smile again. Someday, she was sure, her daughter would stop acting as if she barely tolerated her. If Casterglass did have a little magic left, she hoped the castle would save it for her children.

Chapter Five

THE FRONT ROOMS of Casterglass Castle looked, Althea saw with a little frisson of pleasure, more than halfway decent. Candlelight and roaring fires in every fireplace helped loads, casting comforting, flickering shadows over the stone, and the greenery Poppy had brought in by the shed-load gave the air a fresh, festive scent. The tree, although not the massive conifer Althea remembered from her childhood, was still impressive, and she'd enlisted Poppy and Tobias to circulate with trays of drinks and hors d'oeuvres, while Ben was happy to meet and greet at the door. Maybe this would actually go off without too much of a hitch.

"Darling, you look beautiful," her mother exclaimed as she came downstairs, dressed in a sack-like dress of motheaten velvet and a long string of greyish pearls. "Isn't this dress divine? I feel like a flapper. It belonged to your great-grandmother, would you believe?"

Yes, she certainly would believe that, considering the state of it. "You look lovely, Mummy," Althea said, and kissed her mother's cheek.

"You've done such a wonderful job with everything," her mother continued to marvel as she took in all the decorations. "What would we have done without you?"

"I don't know," Althea returned honestly, but her mother had already gone to the front doors, smiling at Ben, before she flung them open to the night. A blast of icy air made Althea shiver, but then a few minutes later guests started trickling in, and she put her game face on as best as she could, even though she knew she felt too raw and tired to socialise successfully. She'd never been particularly good at parties anyway; in the last few years Jasper had stopped asking her to accompany him out, which had been more of a relief than a disappointment.

Her parents, however, were the surprising masters of small talk. As scatty as they were most of the time, they had the innate knack of being charming and loquacious when company demanded it. Give them a box of tatty costumes and a makeshift stage, and they could put on the entire works of Shakespeare, Althea thought with affection as she watched them circulate through the rapidly filling up room, chatting and laughing with ease.

Never mind twenty or forty, there had to be nearly a hundred people here, some of them vaguely familiar, most not. Perhaps everyone had decided to come up to the castle for its last hurrah. Although Althea didn't think her father would have told people his plans, in a place as small and remote as Casterglass, she suspected word might have got around. No doubt many of their neighbours wondered if her father would be selling up, and wanted to get the latest gossip—or craic, as they said in Cumbria.

She watched a corpulent man in full farmer's tweed toss back one sherry after another. At this rate she'd have to break into the Margaux '36 just to keep the booze flowing.

"So catch me up on the last twenty years of your life."

Althea turned around to see Jenna wearing a black velvet shift dress, her hair a halo of ginger curls springing about her face, smiling at her.

"More like thirty," she replied, meaning to joke but it came out sounding a bit accusing. It seemed that decades-old snub by the station still rankled a bit. Who knew?

"Has it really been that long?" Jenna shook her head wonderingly. "Well, have you got a few moments to chat, or do you have to hobnob with all the peasants?"

Althea decided to let the remark pass. "No hobnobbing," she told Jenna. "My parents are the experts at that. Let me just get a drink, if there's anything left."

"Great."

A few minutes later, armed with glasses of mulled wine, they tucked themselves away on a battered leather sofa in the corner of the library, the crackling fire casting cheerful shadows and much-needed warmth throughout the room.

"So, you married," Jenna announced as she took a slug of wine. "Happily?" There was a slight edge to her voice Althea didn't understand.

"No, not really." *Not at all* was the sad truth, but Althea couldn't bear to admit it.

Jenna made a moue of sympathy, curiosity sparking in her eyes. "Tell me about it?"

She hesitated, hardly wanting to go into all the gory details, and yet…a pressure built in her chest, a need to explain and even to vent. Still she felt uncertain. She hadn't seen Jenna in ages. She didn't know what kind of person she'd turned out to be, although that bit of snark in the shop hadn't given her that much confidence. But…Jenna was her only prospective friend in all of Cumbria at the moment, and she was willing to listen.

"Do you really want to hear about it?" Althea asked with an uneven laugh. "It's not pretty."

"Hell, yes. Then I'll tell you mine, although it's more boring than anything else. It's pathetic, isn't it, when tragedy becomes pedestrian? You can barely make yourself care." The way Jenna's lips trembled belied her statement, but Althea decided not to press. Jenna would tell her own story in time.

"I suppose so," she answered, wondering if her tragedy was pedestrian, a story told throughout human history until it became positively mundane. The scorned wife, the arrogant husband. She doubted she was the first Penryn damsel to have married an overbearing jerk and then regretted it. A few centuries ago it would undoubtedly have been much worse for her; Jasper would have been in chain mail, with a couple of snarling dogs and a stamping charger. She supposed that was some small commiseration.

"So, give me the lowdown," Jenna said, settling deeper into the sofa. "How long have you been married?"

"Twenty years."

"Crikey. You must have been a child bride. What, twenty?"

"Twenty-one. Fresh out of uni."

"How did you meet?"

"I did an internship at a consultancy in London in my summer after uni and met him there. He's seven years older than me, and he seemed very much the sophisticated man about town." Just remembering Jasper back then—debonair, light, laughing, exuberant—made a pang of loss ripple through her, not for what once was, but for what she knew now never had been. The front Jasper had shown her had been just that—a front. A façade. *Fake.* She simply hadn't recognised it as such.

The internship had been arranged through friends of her father's—it was occasionally helpful, to be a member of the minor aristocracy—and Althea had hated it from the start. She'd been overwhelmed and intimidated by all the high flyers and glamour girls; everyone had seemed incredibly intimidating. She'd only been to London a handful of times; they'd all grown up there.

They talked about charity galas and Ascot and the Cambridge-Oxford boat races in a way that had made Althea feel as if they all lived between the pages of *Tatler*. She'd had nothing to offer, and when Jasper had turned his attention to her, he'd felt like the proverbial white knight, rescuing her from the dullness of her job as well as the talon-sharp barbs of the other women working there. He'd wined and dined her in a flurry of luxurious evenings out that had made Althea's head spin.

"Sounds like a recipe for heartbreak," Jenna said with a nod of understanding. "Let me guess. He's overbearing, arrogant, inconsiderate and generally boorish?"

Althea let out a surprised, reluctant laugh. "If he was all those things off the bat, I would have been a fool to marry him."

"All covered by a slick patina of charm, of course," Jenna said, and Althea laughed again, although the comment felt a bit too barbed and on the mark.

"Yes, he definitely could turn on the charm. Still can, although he doesn't seem to see the point anymore, at least with me." She couldn't actually remember the last time Jasper had been genuinely pleasant to her. She simply wasn't worth the effort—something that made her feel sad. Why had she accepted such a terrible status quo for so long?

"So how long were you happy for?"

"Oh…" The single syllable came out in a long, wavery sigh, and quite suddenly, despite Jenna's jokey asides, Althea felt perilously close to tears. "Not very long, as it happens." Her voice wobbled a bit and Jenna dropped the attitude, leaning over to place one hand on Althea's arm.

"It stinks, doesn't it? It absolutely stinks. If I'm making jokes, it's because I don't want to break down myself. I'm the proverbial sad clown here, barely holding on to my smile."

Jenna smiled in sympathy, and Althea managed a rather watery smile back. "It's all right. I wouldn't mind injecting a bit of humour into the situation—it's just I feel so *pathetic*." She sniffed, dabbing her eyes as delicately as she could. The threat of tears was thankfully averted, at least. For now.

"Why? He's the arse, not you."

"Yes, but I married him. I stayed with him for *twenty* years—half my life—even though I knew he made me miserable." She shook her head slowly. "I don't think I actually realised it at the time. I got used to feeling that way, I suppose. Or perhaps I was like the frog in the cooking pot—I didn't realise how things got worse, bit by bit, until it was too late." Or until she had, without even realising it herself, decided she'd had enough.

"Tell me what happened."

Althea took a deep breath and let it out slowly. Where to begin? What to say? "I was bamboozled, is the long and short of it," she said finally. "Dazzled, really, by his charm and flash. Jasper was a lot of fun to be around back then—he threw money at everything, but in a nice, generous way." Or so she'd thought at the time. Later she'd wondered if his generosity had been mere boasting, an ego-stroking show-manship, to demonstrate just how wealthy he was. *Two hundred quid for a bottle of Bollinger they wouldn't even finish?*

No problem. A round for everyone at work? Of course.

Yes, Althea had been dazzled by that kind of extravagant generosity, because she'd grown up a certain kind of poor even though she'd pretended she hadn't, and to her twenty-one-year-old naïve self, money looked like love to her. How wrong she'd been.

"I think he married me because I was so compliant," she stated baldly. "Naïve and adoring. I can't think of another reason, really."

"Well, you are rather gorgeous," Jenna said dryly, and Althea blushed, embarrassed. All right, yes, she suspected her coltish, blonde, blue-eyed looks had appealed to Jasper back then; she'd maintained her pre-children figure and long blonde hair through a combination of dieting, exercise, and expensive hair salons, even though she disliked all three. She'd done it for Jasper, at first to please and impress him, and then later simply to avoid arguments or being run down by him in public. Coming to Casterglass would at least put an end to all that. She would no longer have to walk around with her stomach sucked in.

"Jasper could have had his pick of gorgeous women," she told Jenna. "Far prettier than me. But like I said, I think he liked how meek I was, and the whole thing about a title tickled him." She remembered how when they were dating, he would introduce her as Lady Althea at every opportunity, as if she were a princess. It had been embarrassing, because she wasn't even a lady; her title was the Honourable Althea

Penryn, if one was going to be particular, but Jasper hadn't seemed to care, and Althea had been too dazzled to correct him.

"Yes, the title and the castle are selling points, are they?" Again Althea detected a certain sharpness, but before she could let it bother her, Jenna continued staunchly, "You obviously had a lot going for you. But when did it start to go wrong?"

"Oh, right away, really," Althea replied with a shrug. She felt rather flat now; rehashing all this old history wasn't that helpful, after all. In fact, it made her feel worse, and Jenna's avid curiosity wasn't helping all that much. "As soon as the ring was on my finger the charm pretty much went. He still splashed money about, and he expected me to be the Surrey version of a Stepford wife, and I was so stupidly besotted and naïve that I did my best to accommodate him." Althea winced to remember the early years of waiting until Jasper got home so she could greet him in lipstick and pearls, cocktail at the ready, circa 1956. "Then I got pregnant, and after that I focused on the children." Which had been a relief. She'd started to suspect Jasper was playing away just a year into her marriage, when she'd been heavily pregnant with Ben, but she'd managed to convince herself she was imagining things until Jasper returned home one evening with a pair of panties stuffed into his blazer pocket. He hadn't even bothered to deny it, simply shrugging and saying 'so' as if their marriage vows counted for nothing, which apparently they did.

From then it had gone from bad to worse; he hadn't hid his affairs and Althea had done her best to pretend they weren't happening. He could still be charming, and he'd doted on the children in fits and starts, which had felt like enough. She'd cocooned herself in the world of her children, first with Ben and then Poppy, when she came along, and later Tobias; happy to stay at home and socialise only when necessary, suspecting everyone was laughing at her and trying not to notice.

"So what changed?" Jenna asked. "Because it seems you stuck with the status quo for a long time but now you're getting divorced? Did you just decide you had enough? Or did he?"

Althea glanced at her rather sharply; Jenna almost seemed as if she were enjoying this outpouring of woe. Well, who didn't like a juicy bit of gossip? "I *think* we're getting a divorce," she said and took another sip of wine, needing the fortification. "He came home five days ago and announced he was going skiing in Switzerland with a so-called friend of mine for Christmas. He'd been planning to tell me by text, but he needed his ski jacket."

"What a—"

"Yes. Quite." Strangely, Althea didn't want to start a bashing Jasper session. She'd done enough of that in her head, and it only made her feel stupider for staying with him. "Anyway, I flipped. I'm not even sure why. I'd been the meekest, mildest mouse of a wife until that moment, but something about his…utter indifference…just undid me." She took another sip of wine to steady herself. "He hadn't even been planning on telling me. I'd become that unimportant to him. Actually, I always had been." She shook her head slowly. "I think it was the children that did it for me. Ben was coming home for Christmas—he's in his first year at uni—and Jasper didn't even care. The house was all decorated, the presents were under the tree…and he wasn't even going to say goodbye to his own children." She let out a shuddery sigh, the emotion she'd been trying to suppress ripping through her again.

"Anyway, I flipped. I didn't even mean to—it just sort of happened." Twenty years of pent-up hurt and anger had come pouring out in a scalding rush, while Jasper had simply stared at her, bored.

"I threatened divorce," Althea continued after a moment, when Jenna hadn't said anything. She looked a little stunned by Althea's revelations. "I'm not sure why. I hadn't even let myself think of it for all those years, because of the children. Because I just…I don't know. I really don't. I was like a rabbit trapped in the headlights for two decades, and then I suddenly blinked the world into focus." Saying it out loud made her hate herself. She took another slug of wine.

"It's understandable that you wanted to keep your marriage—" Jenna began hesitantly.

"But I didn't even *like* him. I dreaded having him come

home." Now that Althea had started, she felt as if she couldn't stop. The words poured out of her in a rush of feeling. "We'd stopped…you know…ages ago. There really was nothing left, and yet it still managed to be a shock when he said; 'Fine, divorce me, you mad harpy.' And while I goggled he told me that never mind, *he'd* be the one to divorce me. He told me he'd call his solicitor the next day. And then he left."

Jenna was silent for a moment before she said quietly, "I'm so sorry, Althea."

She nodded mechanically, the pain of it still ripping through her, although it wasn't grief over Jasper's indifference, which she'd long ago got used to; it was sorrow at her own foolishness, as well as anger that he'd turned the tables on her, and made it his decision. And frustration too, that that realisation still stupidly hurt.

"At least you'll get a mint out of it, right?" Jenna said with an attempt at optimism. "What with no-fault divorces these days. You must be entitled to half of whatever he has. You'll be set for life."

"Mmm…" Althea replied, finishing her wine. She didn't want to admit to the prenup, whose details she still didn't know. Jenna could only excuse so much stupidity.

"Now you've got to tell me about yours," she said, desperate to switch subjects. She was feeling emotionally drained and definitely fragile, and she needed to focus on someone else. "What happened?"

"Oh, nothing much, really." Jenna clearly wasn't going to be as forthcoming as Althea had been, vomiting up all her heartbreak. "We grew apart. He met someone else. The end."

"I'm sorry…" Althea said helplessly, wishing Jenna had shared as much as she had. Now she felt even more stupid, as if she'd been dancing around naked while Jenna was buttoned up in a chin-to-ankles overcoat.

"I really did love him, though." Jenna's voice was brittle. "That's the stinger. And I still do." She tilted her head back to drain her wine glass. "How about another?"

"I'll get them," Althea said, reaching for her glass. She needed to clear her head, and she also wanted a few moments to recover her composure. She was still feeling uncomfortably fragile, especially since it clearly wasn't going to be a tit-for-tat in the sharing department. Talking about Jasper had been like stirring the cauldron of her soul. All sorts of unappealing bits had come bubbling up to the surface, ready to spill over, and she was definitely not ready to deal with the mess.

Jenna nodded her thanks and Althea headed out of the library, dumping the empties on a forgotten tray before collecting two more from Poppy, who gave her a suspicious look.

"Mum, are you…*drunk*?"

"Of course not," Althea replied with dignity, although she might have slurred a bit. The wine, on an empty stomach, had gone straight to her head, and combined with all the excess emotion, it threatened to be a disaster. When she got back to Jenna, she'd change the subject from their divorces. Talk about something innocent. Er, innocuous. Goodness, she couldn't actually be *drunk*. She hardly ever drank alcohol, which was perhaps part of the problem.

"Are you sure?" Poppy asked, still sounding incredulous, and Althea gave her what she hoped was a haughty look.

"Of course I'm sure. What an idea," she replied sniffily, only to whirl around and run smack into somebody, spilling the sticky, spicy mulled wine over them both.

Althea let out a little shriek of surprise while the person—a man, she saw, tall and rangy—stepped back, swiping ineffectually at his now-stained and soaked jumper.

"Why didn't you watch where you were going!" she burst out shrilly, when what she'd meant to say was: *I'm so sorry, please forgive me for bumping into you and dousing you in wine.*

The man understandably looked at her in disbelief. "Watch where *I'm* going?" he repeated in a distinctly Cumbrian burr.

"Yes," Althea said, sounding truculent now, and horrified at herself. *Why* was she acting this way? Was it because she felt so raw, so dangerously close to tears or worse, and this man looming in front of her, stranger that he was, made her think of Jasper—all quiet, brooding arrogance?

Except, of course, this man was nothing like Jasper at all. He looked like a farmer, for a start, with a shock of brown hair lightly peppered with grey, hazel eyes glinting beneath shaggy brows, and a face full of creases and wrinkles that reminded Althea of Stick Man in the children's story, although she didn't think he could be too much more than in his mid-forties. He was dressed in a now-drenched jumper of heather grey and a pair of battered cords, both pieces of clothing looking at least a decade old. No, this man was no Jasper, and she'd just been inexplicably, insufferably rude to him because she was off-kilter and at least several sheets to the wind.

"I'm sorry," she blurted, and he merely raised his eyebrows, clearly nonplussed by the bizarre situation as well as unmoved by her apology. Then, to her horror, Althea burst into tears.

Chapter Six

WELL, THIS WAS embarrassing. She was blubbing, actually *blubbing*, in front of a complete stranger who had every right to be incredibly annoyed with her. And somehow she couldn't stop.

Through the haze of her tears Althea saw him reach for her, and realised he was taking the now-empty wine glasses out of her hands. Out of the corner of her eye she saw Poppy watching, amazed and appalled, and her heart lurched as she started crying even harder. What would Poppy think? How could she be falling apart *now*?

The man had taken her by her arm, and somehow or other Althea let him lead her away from the hall and the milling guests; when she wiped her streaming eyes she saw he had led her to the guard room, with its stacked shields and gruesome-looking halberds and maces lining the walls. At least it was private.

"This room is meant to be haunted, you know," she managed to get out, and then hiccupped.

"A ghost might be a good thing right about now," the

man replied dryly. "Although it seems as if you've already had a shock. Would another help?"

"I haven't had a shock," Althea protested, as she tried to mop her face. She felt ridiculous. She smelled like cinnamon and wine. And she was, amazingly, still crying. Tears leaked from her eyes as if she were a broken tap. *Something* in her was broken, clearly.

"No? Well, you know what they say. Don't cry over spilled milk...or spilled wine. Or stained jumper, for that matter."

As Althea's vision finally cleared, she saw that he was smiling wryly down at his ruined jumper, and she felt a weird mix of affection and guilt. He seemed so *friendly*, and yet she'd behaved like an utter shrew.

"I really am sorry about your jumper," she said. "Although I know I didn't sound like it at first. It's just been..." She released a pent-up breath, not wanting to go into just what it had been. "Quite a day. But don't worry, I'll buy you a new one..."

"Or have me send the dry-cleaning bill to your butler?"

The sudden, slight sharpness in his tone had her blinking. What had she been thinking, that he was friendly? Now, as he appraised her with narrowed eyes, he looked shrewd and somewhat unimpressed. Perhaps she'd been imagining the friendliness. Admittedly, she had behaved badly at the start, but...

"I wouldn't advise dry-cleaning it," she replied coolly,

startled into reserve, "but a good handwashing should do. I'd be happy to do it myself, if you'd rather." She met his gaze with a haughty challenge she didn't feel, but something about his slightly jeering tone had got her back right up. She was really rather tired of the whole poor little rich girl sarcasm that so often came her way. *Oh poor you, you live in a castle. Boohoo.* She knew very well that she'd grown up privileged, but that didn't make some parts of her childhood any easier to have dealt with. And this man didn't know her from Adam, or Eve, for that matter.

Something flickered in his eyes, but Althea couldn't tell if it was admiration or annoyance, or something else entirely. "You obviously know who I am," she told him after a moment, trying to sound level if not downright friendly. "But I'm afraid I can't say the same."

Another flicker in his eyes, like a shadow in water. His expression remained uncomfortably appraising. "You can't? I'm John Braithwaite. I own Appleby Farm."

"Oh." He'd spoken as if she should have known both his name and his farm, but she wasn't familiar with either. Back in her childhood she'd had a very passing acquaintance with the local farmers and their families, but the knowledge had slipped to the far reaches of her mind long ago.

"It used to be Casterglass Farm," he supplied, his tone still holding that hint of sharpness. "My ancestors were tenant farmers of the castle's estate. Probably serfs, once upon a time."

Oh, so *that* was the chip on his shoulder? And he was blaming her how? "I see," Althea said, her tone turning as cool as his.

"The tenth baron of Casterglass—your great-grandfather, I believe—sold the farm to mine about a hundred years ago. We've been running it ever since."

"So we're neighbours," Althea said, determined to get this odd conversation on more civil footing. "I'm sorry I didn't realise, but I haven't been able to come back here very often."

"Is your father selling the place?" John Braithwaite asked abruptly, and Althea tensed.

"Why do you ask?"

He shrugged. "Because news gets around, and I'd like to know."

"News gets around?" She knew news got around, but she wanted to know how, at least in this instance. Her father had said he hadn't told anyone yet.

"Word was some locals gave him an estimate for the roof replacement, and he went pale and started muttering to himself." He spoke carelessly, even coldly, and Althea flushed in both embarrassment and anger.

How on earth had she thought this man was friendly, even for three disorientating seconds? Her poor father. He must have had such a shock, and he hadn't told any of them. "Thank you so much for your concern," she told him in decidedly chilly tones, "but our family's business has nothing to do with you."

"Actually it does, since my farm is adjoining the property." She detected a slightly sneering undercurrent of anger in his tone that made her start to actively dislike him. "So if your father decides to allow this place to be turned into a golf club or a hotel, it will certainly affect me."

"How?" Althea flung at him, and a look of scorn passed over his face.

"Because a developer might want to acquire the land adjacent, or put up a bloody big car park, or have day trippers traipsing through my fields and terrorising my sheep, that's how."

"And how is that my concern?" Althea asked, folding her arms, wondering how they'd managed to get into such a stand-off so suddenly.

"Obviously it isn't, it's mine," John Braithwaite retorted, his face darkening with anger. "But if your father could let us lowly locals in on the plan, it might help us to prepare."

"Prepare to fight, you mean? Wreck any potential sale? How helpful of you."

He took a step towards her, looming over her in a way she didn't like. "Unlike some people, we live here and we care about Casterglass, not just as a castle, but as a village. You know, the lowly peasants you forget about?"

"One minute you're asserting your independence and the next you're saying you're peasants who need to be taken care of?" Althea snapped, hardly daring to believe her audacity, and yet it felt *good* to come out swinging for once. "Which is it, then?"

"All I'm saying is, there's more to Casterglass than the castle. And people who live here actually care about the community—"

"Oh, and we don't, I suppose? You've got it all sussed, have you?"

"Like you said," he replied evenly, "you don't even seem to find the time to come back."

"Oh for heaven's sake, you're such a snob," Althea exclaimed, fury, hurt and wine acting together to loosen her tongue. How dare this stranger make judgements about her life, her very self, without knowing the first thing about any of it?

John Braithwaite stared at her in disbelief. "*I'm* a snob?"

"You don't know anything about me or my life," Althea raged, "or what I've been up to for the last twenty years, yet you seem perfectly willing and even eager to point the finger and assume I don't care about my own home. Well, let me tell you, Mr Braithwaite, I *do*." For emphasis, she jabbed her finger into his chest, surprised at how hard and muscled it was, and then even more surprised when he grabbed her hand, his long fingers wrapping around her wrist, skimming her pulse.

Although his grip wasn't tight it still jolted her, and Althea caught her breath as an entirely unexpected and unwelcome warmth stole through her. Of all the reactions to have right now… It had to be because of the wine.

Slowly he loosened his grip on her wrist, drawing her arm down to her side, making Althea realise how close their bodies were. She felt the heat emanating from him, and a shiver went through her, again not unpleasant. *How* could she be responding this way to such an odious man? She couldn't remember the last time she'd felt attraction for *anyone*. This was absolutely ludicrous, and yet she still felt it, a treacherous warmth seeping through her veins, embarrassing and infuriating her because it was so inappropriate. Hopefully John Braithwaite hadn't realised.

He gazed at her evenly, the coolness in his hazel eyes disconcerting her all the more, especially considering the warmth in her own body. His face was still friendly in a rugged and craggy way; it was the face of someone she *wanted* to like, but definitely didn't. The animosity so clearly rolling off him in waves made her respond by yanking her arm out of his grasp and taking a much-needed step back.

"I'll send you the dry-cleaning bill," he told her, and her mouth dropped open before she snapped it shut.

"Handwash," she managed to sputter, before he strode out of the draughty guard room, leaving her alone with a lot of armour.

A choked sound escaped her, something alarmingly close to a sob. Having some pointless altercation with a stranger was something she had definitely not needed right now. Plus, in addition to having ruined John Braithwaite's jumper, she'd also stained her own cashmere one, which *was* dry-clean only.

Biting her lips to keep another sob-like sound from escaping her, Althea squared her shoulders and headed back into the fray—or, rather, the party. But first she needed to change her jumper.

"Are you okay, Mum?" Poppy asked, sounding more accusing than concerned, as Althea, in a new jumper, went to fetch another glass of wine for Jenna. She'd decided she had definitely had enough.

"I'm fine," she managed, forcing her trembling lips into the approximation of a smile. "Why?"

"Because you, like, burst into tears a few minutes ago?" Poppy raised her eyebrows in incredulity. "I mean, what was that about?"

"I think I'm just tired. It's been a long few days." She'd forgotten Poppy had seen that alarming little episode. "I'm sorry if I worried you, Pops. I'll be okay."

"You didn't worry me," Poppy replied in scathing tones. "But it was, like, *really* embarrassing."

"Oh." Althea tried not to let this all too honest remark flatten her further. "Well, I'm sorry for that too, I suppose. I'll do better about keeping myself together."

Poppy eyed her uncertainly, looking like she wanted to ask more questions but wasn't sure if she wanted the answers. Or maybe that was just the way Althea was feeling herself. She couldn't bear to think about the future, and yet she knew she had to.

"I'm sorry for all the upheaval, sweetheart," she said quietly, determined to make an effort with her daughter. "I know it's been hard. And not being at home for Christmas with your friends…"

Poppy hunched one shoulder as her gaze skated away. "It's okay," she mumbled, which Althea knew was as close as she would get to tender compassion.

"Well, I do understand," she said, patting her daughter's arm. "Truly. And I'm hoping we can still have a really nice Christmas here at Casterglass."

Her voice wobbled at the end and Poppy mumbled something unintelligible in reply, and then moved off with her tray of depleted drinks. The sherry was holding out, but probably not for too much longer.

Althea headed back to the library in search of Jenna, but when she came into the room she found it empty. Jenna must have got tired of waiting for her, something that dispirited her further although she supposed it shouldn't have. It was just she was feeling so very raw.

As she turned back to survey the crowds milling about the foyer and great hall, she realised she couldn't see a single person she knew. Her parents, Seph and her own children were not in sight, and she really didn't know the locals anymore, if she ever had, but the unsettling truth was, like John Braithwaite, they all seemed to know her. They knew her and judged her, she thought, recalling John's unfair remarks.

Her family had never had a butler, or even a maid, but of course everyone assumed they were living with at least three silver spoons sticking out of their mouths. *Why* had she had such an affection for this place, anyway?

She moved through the crowds, offering people vague smiles without making eye contact, feeling weary right down to her bones. No one spoke to her or stopped her, and she felt almost invisible as she slipped through the rooms into the kitchen, which was quiet and empty save for the rumble of the Aga, and then, recklessly now, out through the back door.

She had no idea where she was going, only that she felt a need to escape it all for at least a few minutes. Escape herself, even, but unfortunately she couldn't do that, and so she'd make do with leaving the party behind, just for a little bit.

It was freezing outside, the air sharp and clear, the sky scattered with a thousand stars glinting high, high above. Althea started walking towards the walled garden with its twisty brick paths and flower beds, but then at the last minute she veered away from the wooden gate built into the stone wall and headed across the terraced lawns, now tufty and damp, down to the rolling, wide open fields that went on straight to the sea, about a mile away.

It was a foolish thing to do, because her high-heeled boots sank deep into the muddy turf, and the hem of her trousers was soon soaked and dirty. Something else to be dry-cleaned, Althea thought morosely. Oh help, but she was driving full steam ahead into self-pity mode, and she was too tired to keep herself from it. She wanted to *howl*.

Why had she married a man like Jasper, who had seemed so confident and kind, and had turned out to be an utter tosser? Why had she let him chip and chip away at her confidence until there was almost nothing left? She hadn't even realised for so long, desperate to make excuses and amends, make it *work*, because she wanted a family, a home, a hearth, and she'd clung to them all even as they had slipped away.

Why hadn't she developed her career, even a part-time job, *anything* that would make her life more viable now? And why had John Braithwaite had to be so irritating and downright mean? Not, Althea acknowledged with a sigh, that she'd been much better, blaming him for her accident, but still. He'd seen how overwrought she'd been. Couldn't he have been a bit more kind?

She continued to walk through the grass, even though she was in parts ankle-deep in mud, and her Ted Baker boots were probably ruined. She felt the need to keep moving, even if she had no destination in mind or sight. At least it felt vaguely productive, going somewhere physically if not actually in life.

Ten minutes later, out of breath and shivering from the freezing cold, she finally stopped in the middle of a muddy field, the sea a stretch of black in the distance. She turned around to see Casterglass Castle glimmering far away, its stone walls darker against a dark sky, a few lights glinting in its windows. Her father must have put up fairy lights on the drive, she realised, as she caught sight of the twinkle of tiny lights all along its tree-lined sweep. She hadn't noticed. Perhaps he wasn't quite so lackadaisical as she had thought.

An icy wind blew right through her and she wrapped her arms around herself. What was she actually doing here? Not out here in a field, which was questionable in the extreme, but at Casterglass at all? The sentimental affection she'd been feeling in the wake of her father's announcement had faded, leaving a cold, depressing realisation that even if this had been her childhood home, it wasn't her home now. She didn't know anyone here, and her memories of the place were a grab bag of good, bad and horrendous. Why was she thinking about staying?

Because you have nowhere else to go.

The realisation flooded her with despair. She *couldn't* return to Surrey. There was nothing left for her there, hadn't been for years. Her friends were the wives of Jasper's friends; she'd tired of the whole moneyed set years ago, had stopped trying to impress or even show up awhile back, and now it showed.

Besides, what on earth would she do for money? She didn't think Jasper would be so cruel as to cut his own children off, and in any case she knew there was such a thing as child support, but she doubted he'd spare her much. The thought made her shiver in a way that had nothing to do with the arctic wind.

What was she going to *do*?

Althea closed her eyes tightly, as if she could will all the issues away. Tobias and Poppy would expect to return to Surrey; they had friends, after all, although Tobias interacted with his mostly online and Poppy's friends weren't necessarily the type of people she wanted to base life decisions on. What if her children didn't mind staying here? Althea suspected Tobias might be all right with it, but Poppy would probably have six fits.

Even so…

She opened her eyes and gazed at the castle, her home—yes, her home. The only one she'd ever had, and walking away from it felt like failure, even if the money she might receive—assuming the castle actually sold—would certainly help. But Althea realised she didn't want to give up. She'd rolled over for the last twenty years, letting Jasper behave as he liked as long as she had the house and the children. Convincing herself it was enough.

Well, now she had a house *and* children, and she wanted to keep both. She would.

Straightening her shoulders, letting the wind blow through her, Althea started back through the mud to Casterglass.

As she slipped into the kitchen, cold, muddy, and tired, she was surprised to see her father there, sitting at the table alone.

"Daddy?"

"Oh, darling, thank goodness." Relief flashed across his face as he rose from the table. "I was worried."

"I'm sorry. I didn't realise I'd been gone for so long. Has everyone left?"

"Yes, they all satisfied their curiosity, I think, and trotted off full of the delicious sherry you'd bought. I will repay you—"

"No, no—" Althea insisted, and he smiled.

"Nothing like good old Bristol Cream. The others are up in the sitting room watching some dreadful reality TV show, where a bunch of so-called celebrities are trapped in a jungle. I couldn't bear to watch."

Althea smiled at that, and her father cocked his head. "Is everything all right, Althea?" he asked quietly, his tone so gentle she had to blink back tears. Again.

"Not really," she admitted with a wobble in her voice. "But I'm hoping it will be, you know, eventually." He nodded, waiting for more, and Althea confessed in a rush, "Jasper and I...we're getting a divorce. I think. No, I know. We are." She nodded mechanically several times.

"Oh, darling. I'm sorry." Her father came towards her, his arms closing around her as Althea rested her cheek on the satin lapel of his velvet jacket, the one he always wore at Christmas even though it made him look like a third-rate magician.

"It's all right," she told him with a sniff. "It's for the best, really. He…he wasn't that great a husband, as it turned out."

"Oh, Althea." Her father's voice was filled with sadness.

"It's all right," she said again, meaning it more this time. She hesitated, took a hitching breath. "But, Daddy…" She lifted her head to look at him. "I know what you said about the roof, and it's most likely halfway to impossible, but I still want to try."

Her father frowned, although his eyes were warm and kind. "Try?"

"To keep Casterglass," Althea blurted, her tone turning both insistent and pleading. "Somehow. Some way. There's nothing for me back in Surrey. I could move back here permanently, with the children, to make a go of it. We've got to try…" She trailed off at the look on his face; his eyes were bright and he looked suddenly and alarmingly near tears. When he spoke, his voice choked a little.

"Oh, Althea," he said as his arms came around her again. "I was so hoping you would say that."

Chapter Seven

ALTHEA WOKE WITH a headache and a stomach that seethed, thanks to indulging in too much mulled wine, but even so she was energised with purpose. *They were keeping Casterglass!* Or at least they were going to try. She had no idea how, but she intended to start formulating a plan today, with the help of her father.

She showered and dressing quickly, grimacing at the muddy mess of last night's clothes, a necessary evil, perhaps, for it had been out on the moors like Cathy in *Wuthering Heights*—or was it Heathcliff who roamed the craggy clifftops? Althea had only seen the adaptation on the telly. Still, the mood felt right—determined and wintry.

Downstairs she found Ben, Poppy, Tobias and Persephone all sitting round the table, eating big bowls of porridge. It was such a homely scene that Althea immediately felt heartened.

"Good morning," she sang out, and Poppy eyed her warily.

"Are you better today?" she asked, and Althea flushed in

remembered regret.

"Yes, I'm fine. I was a bit emotional last night… Sometimes it gets to you, I'm afraid." She gave them all a grimace of apology that Ben at least returned with sympathy.

"It's okay, Mum. We understand."

"So what shall we do today?" Althea asked brightly as she filled the kettle at the sink. In the bright light of day, with sunlight streaming through the dusty window, she felt both full of optimism and yet completely at a loss as to how to start, well, anything. Should she tell her children her plan? Did she even have a plan?

"Seph is giving us a tour of the castle," Ben said. "I'm sure I've seen it all before, but I can't remember. And then we were going to play sardines."

"Sardines," Althea said, smiling. "Sounds like a fabulous plan." She glanced at her sister, who stared rather sullenly back. She didn't look all that enthused, but perhaps she'd liven up once they got going. Perhaps it was just Althea she had a problem with, although why that would be Althea didn't know.

"Yeah, well," Ben answered with a laugh, "you only live once, right?"

"And it's not like there's anything else to do," Poppy muttered as she picked up her phone and started scrolling with determination, her pretty face falling into familiar, discontented lines.

"Sardines sounds like loads of fun to me," Althea answered as lightly as she could. "Perhaps we could do some Christmas shopping at some point? Your aunt Olivia is coming by train tomorrow, to Kendal. We could all go to meet her and do some shopping on the way."

"In *Kendal*," Poppy said in something like disgust.

"I don't think you've ever been," Althea returned mildly. "It's really quite pretty."

All the reply she got was a shrug, and Althea did her best not to sigh. Before the blow-up with Jasper, Poppy had been asking to go to some Christmas party that everyone in the Sixth Form was desperate to score an invite to. No doubt she was fuming at being left out. At that age, Althea was sure, missing a party felt like a death sentence. Admittedly, when she'd been sixteen, there had been little to no chance of being invited to any such an event, but she knew Poppy had aspirations to the in-crowd.

Their porridge finished, the children headed off for their tour, Persephone leading the way, and Althea took her cup of coffee to the sofa at the far end of the room, along with her laptop, which she'd dug out of her bag.

She had to move several piles of papers and books to find a place to sit, but with the sunlight coming through the windows and the Aga rumbling away it really was a lovely spot. She took a sip of coffee and then flipped open her laptop, her fingers poised over the keys. Where to start?

After a few seconds of vague pondering, she typed in *how to save family home*. The first result she got was *how to save money by living with your parents.* She let out a strangled laugh. *Check.* Scrolling down the list of results, she didn't see anything particularly helpful. Tips about inheritance tax, which her father had thankfully managed to pay when his father had died when Althea was in her twenties, and how to keep the family home during a divorce. *Ha.* Unlikely.

Taking another sip of coffee, she went back to the search bar and typed in *ways to make an ancestral estate profitable.* The first result was an article about 'Fun Ways to Keep the Castle'. With her heart skipping a small, hopeful beat, Althea clicked.

From glamping to folk music festivals, marmalade making to safari parks, discover the offbeat ways estate owners turned entrepreneurs are making a living off of their family home.

With excitement quickening through her veins, Althea scrolled through the article. She felt a wave of empathy for the people she read about—people, who, like her, had left the family home to go to university, have jobs, marry. (Well, she hadn't done the job thing, but still.) They'd returned to their estates—a fortress-like castle in the Highlands for one, or a seventeenth-century manor house in the Cotswolds for another—and decided to somehow make a go of it.

Althea read about jousting festivals, adventure playgrounds, safari parks, glamping sites, renting out estates for weddings or film shoots… The possibilities seemed endless, limited only by her imagination and perhaps some hard work and money, if she was being practical. None of this would be at all easy.

"All right, darling?" her mother asked as she wandered into the kitchen, looking around as if she didn't know how or why she'd arrived there.

"Yes…" Althea looked up from her computer screen, blinking her mother into focus. "Mummy…what if we turned Casterglass into a…a tourist attraction?"

"Hmm?" Her mother was opening and closing cupboard doors seemingly at random.

"A tourist… Are you looking for something?"

"Hmm, oh, yes. What was it?" Her mother paused, tapping her chin with one finger, while Althea looked on with bemused exasperation. *"Coffee,"* she finally exclaimed with something like delight. "Yes, I came down for some coffee."

"I'll make it for you," Althea said, and went to fill the kettle once again.

"What were you talking about, darling?" her mother asked as Althea spooned coffee granules into the cafetiere. "Something about tourists?"

Althea was amazed her mother had listened that much. "Daddy told me how he felt he had to sell Casterglass," she began, and her mother let out a long, woebegone sigh.

"*So* hard to imagine—"

"But I was thinking we wouldn't have to," Althea continued in a rush. "If we could make this place…viable."

Her mother wrinkled her nose. "Viable? Darling, what can you mean?"

"Well, I don't know exactly, not yet, but you know some people open their estates to the public?"

"Well, we've always been happy to give tours," her mother replied generously, "but that's hardly going to fill the coffers, is it?"

"I'm not talking about just putting up a few flyers in the village. We'd have to turn Casterglass into a proper venue." As she said the words, Althea felt another leap of excitement. Surely this could work, if they all came together.

"A venue," her mother said dubiously, as if she'd never heard the word before.

"Yes…you know, *offer* things, not just a tour to someone who happens up the drive." Althea's mind raced as she recalled the article and all of its intriguing possibilities. "We could do glamping, for example."

"Glamping?" That clearly was a word her mother had never heard before.

"It's camping, but luxurious. In yurts or pods or—whatever." She didn't actually know much about it. Jasper wouldn't touch glamping with a ten-foot barge pole.

"Yurts…" Her mother sounded dreamy now. "I stayed in a yurt, once, when I was a girl. It was really quite muddy, darling. Not at all luxurious."

"They wouldn't be *actual* yurts, Mummy," Althea explained patiently. "They'd be kitted out with carpets and air mattresses and things." At least she thought they would be. She'd certainly have to look into it more.

"Well then, they wouldn't be yurts, would they?" her mother returned so very reasonably. "The one I stayed in had its walls reinforced with yak dung. Surprisingly effective, but I hardly think someone wants to pay for the experience, and in any case we don't have any yaks here, unless you were thinking of starting a yak farm? Now that would be interesting…"

"No, I don't want to start a yak farm," Althea said on a sigh as she handed her mother a cup of coffee. Although safari parks were apparently a thing. Still, it wasn't really possible to have a measured, logical discussion with her mother about, well, anything. She'd have to talk to her father about it, and her sister when she arrived, although Olivia had inherited some of their mother's dreaminess. If only Sam were coming home for Christmas. Apparently he wasn't returning from New Zealand until February.

Althea supposed she should discuss the possibility with Persephone, but the fact was she was still a bit scared by her youngest sister. She couldn't imagine her being enthused about the idea, although in truth she couldn't imagine Seph being enthused about anything. Still, it was worth a shot, surely? She wasn't going to fall at the first hurdle.

While her mother wandered back upstairs with her coffee, Althea went into the front hall in search of Seph and her children. She paused at the bottom of the stairs, one hand on the ornate newel post, as a burst of laughter echoed through the upper chambers of the old part of the castle. Ben said something, and Seph said something back, followed by more laughter. Clearly they were all having a good time, and Althea was reluctant to disturb it.

Besides, she probably needed to do a *bit* more research. From her admittedly brief discussion with her mother, she realised how little she knew. Skimming one article that a haphazard internet search had thrown up was hardly due diligence.

Another burst of laughter sounded from upstairs, making Althea smile. Already she was imagining a blissful alternate reality where her children bonded and grew into themselves out here in the wet and windy Cumbria countryside…

Although today the sun was shining, and with that in mind, Althea grabbed her coat and boots—not the Ted Baker ones, but a pair of ancient wellies from the clutter that took up permanent residence in the boot room—and headed outside to inspect the estate from an entrepreneurial perspective.

The day was clear, the grass speckled with frost, as she pulled on a pair of gloves and lowered her head against the brisk wind. She took a step from the castle and tilted her head to look up at it in all its majestic, medieval glory.

Originally a Norman-era fortress, its square stolidness presented an imposing front while the higgledy-piggledy nature of the additions lent the back of the property a certain charming eccentricity, kind of like its occupants.

But what about the rest of the estate? Althea followed the

gravel drive around to the back and the assortment of falling-down outbuildings that cluttered the landscape. In addition to the greenhouse her father still made good use of, there were several potting sheds, a Tudor-era tithe barn whose roof had caved in, and several low-roofed stone buildings whose purposes had long ago been forgotten—a dairy? A creamery? The octagonal tower by the barn had been, Althea knew, a dovecote, although it had long ago been left empty, like so much of the estate. Everything had been falling down when Althea was a child; it was much worse now.

Could she really do this?

With some elbow grease and a hard wrench, she managed to open the door into the walled garden, which was an acre of twisting paths and neatly tended flower beds. At least it *had* been. Now it was a tangle of dead shrubbery and clumps of nettles, the remnants of rose bushes and herb patches barely visible in the encroaching nettle-filled wilderness, yet with a few beautiful flowers poking through all the thorns—the winter roses Poppy had found, or what was left of them.

Althea picked her way along the path, trying not to feel dispirited. The garden alone was going to take a massive amount of work and more money than they had. And what about the roof? The barn? They'd have to sink a fortune into repairing the place before they even thought about investing in new initiatives like a glamping site or a safari park.

As she turned back to the gate, she heard the crunch of

wheels on gravel and wondered who was approaching the castle. By the time she'd come round to the front, a very battered Land Rover was already heading back down the drive, towards the rusted iron gates that hadn't been able to close in over a century.

Althea turned to the front doors, forgetting that they could no longer be opened from the outside, thanks to the rusted ring that had fallen off upon her arrival. As she turned to go back to the kitchen, she saw a parcel lying on the steps, wrapped in old-fashioned brown paper and string, like something out of *The Sound of Music*.

Curious now, Althea picked it up, and saw, with a frisson of surprise, that it was addressed to her in a bold, scrawling hand.

She carried it round to the kitchen, mystified and more than a little curious as to who had sent her something, never mind what it actually was. She unwrapped it at the kitchen table, letting out a small gasp of surprise as the paper fell away to reveal a turtleneck sweater in soft blue cashmere. A card had fallen out as well, and Althea picked it up to read:

This really is dry-clean only. I realised your jumper needed replacing as much as mine did, and yours was far nicer. This isn't the same colour, but I thought it matched your eyes. —JB.

Chapter Eight

KENDAL WAS LOOKING quaint and festive, bedecked with Christmas lights, as Althea drove into town the next afternoon, intent on a day's Christmas shopping before it was time to fetch Olivia from the train station. Ben was in the passenger's seat, Tobias and Poppy in the back; Seph had declined to come along, even though Althea had invited her. Never mind. She'd try again.

She'd spent the last twenty-four hours in a ferment of both ideas and anxiety, for a variety of reasons. There was Casterglass, of course, and her children's well-being, as well as her parents and Seph, and then there was the sky-blue jumper she'd put up in her bedroom without telling anyone about it, disposing of the paper wrapping like you would the dead body of someone you'd murdered, with great secrecy and trepidation. The last thing she wanted was speculation about John Braithwaite's gift, and yet that was exactly what she was doing.

Why on earth had he sent her such a lovely and expensive gift? What could it possibly mean? It almost seemed flirtatious, the way he'd mentioned her eyes, and yet surely that was a ridiculous notion. She didn't even know if he was married or in a relationship or anything like that, and it shouldn't even matter if he was. She'd broken out in a hot flush just thinking about those questions, never mind their answers.

Perhaps it didn't mean anything, and he was just being nice because he'd been such a grumpy sod the night before. Knowing she could spend hours thinking about it and getting nowhere, Althea had tried to put it to the back of her mind and focus on the present—that was, getting ready for a Christmas at Casterglass.

She'd wanted to talk to her father about her potential plans for their ancestral home, but he'd spent the entire day outside with a tree surgeon, trying to sort out some rotten oaks on the edge of the estate. Managing Casterglass really was a full-time job, Althea had realised with an uncomfortable prickle of awareness. Was she mad, to think of taking it all on? There was only one way to find out. Hopefully she'd have an opportunity to talk to her father before too long.

Now her mood was determinedly ebullient as they parked near Blackhall Yard, with its quaint mix of artisan shops and independent boutiques.

"What about all our Christmas presents at home?" Poppy asked sullenly as they headed towards the main courtyard lined with shops.

Althea tried not to wince at the accusation in her daughter's tone. As upset as she'd been when they'd left Surrey, she had forgotten to pack all the presents currently residing under their bedecked Christmas tree.

"They'll be there when we get back," she said, although the thought of returning to Surrey made her cringe inwardly. Of course she had to go back at some point, but she didn't like thinking about it.

"Yes, but we won't have them for Christmas," Poppy complained.

"Which is why we're Christmas shopping now."

"Oh, and somewhere in Kendal sells Prada?" her daughter retorted sarcastically, folding her arms. "Because you know I wanted those biker boots."

Which were currently sitting wrapped under the Christmas tree in Cobham. Althea took a deep breath to keep from saying something unhelpful, like Christmas presents were not just an order you put in. She wanted Poppy to get into the spirit of the holiday, but she knew she wouldn't achieve that by haranguing her.

"There are some lovely things here," she said instead, as diplomatic as ever, although part of her felt like shaking Poppy by the shoulders. *When did you get so spoiled?* She wanted to ask. *And how do I undo the damage?*

"Come on, Pops," Ben said mildly. "Don't be boring."

Poppy puffed up with indignation. *"Boring—"*

"You get exactly what you want for Christmas every single year. Let this year be a bit different."

"Well, I'm certainly not getting what I want *this* Christmas," Poppy huffed, and strode ahead, her body bristling with affront.

"Ben," Althea said quietly. "You know this is hard for her."

"She's acting like a spoilt little madam," Ben replied without so much as a flicker of repentance. "Why doesn't she think about someone else for a change? It might do her some good."

"It's hard for her," Althea said again, a bit helplessly, and Ben gave her a look.

"You let her off the hook way too easily. Just saying, Mum."

"Noted."

Tobias tugged on her sleeve, distracting her from the Poppy problem. "Can I go in there?" he asked eagerly, pointing to a fantasy gaming store that made Althea smile with its windows full of wizards and dragons.

"Yes, although you can't spend the whole afternoon in there. We do have some shopping to do, you know."

"I'll go with him," Ben offered, who was not opposed to a bit of gaming himself. As they happily trotted off, Althea paused in front of a boutique that sold stained glass ornaments and jewellery, each piece startling in its simplicity and colour. Heading into the shop with a reluctant Poppy, she browsed earrings and bracelets made of glass as Poppy kept her arms folded, doing her best to look bored.

"Poppy, you can't be having much fun, keeping this up," Althea said as gently as she could. "Why not just relax into it? We're here for now, and you don't want to spoil your whole Christmas by being in a mood."

"I'm not in a mood."

"I'm sorry, I didn't mean that as a criticism." Althea decided to try a different tack. "What do you think about these earrings? I think they'd look fantastic on you, with your colouring." Poppy had the same chestnut hair—currently highlighted to caramel—and hazel eyes as her father, and was, Althea thought without too much bias, an absolute stunner.

She held up the green and blue stained glass earrings to Poppy's ear, and with a sound of impatience Poppy tried to twitch away, before the beauty of the earrings lured her in.

"They are nice," she admitted grudgingly, and then gave Althea the barest glimmer of a smile. "I mean, they're *okay*."

"High praise, then." Althea glanced at the price tag—thirty pounds. Not cheap, but not outrageous, either, although she supposed she should be thinking about money a bit more sensibly now. "Well, I'll keep them in mind." She put them back, fully intending to go back and buy them when Poppy was engaged elsewhere.

"Mum, what happened with Dad?" Poppy was staring fixedly at a display of bracelets, running her fingertip along the bangles, as she waited for Althea's answer. "I mean, really."

Althea stared at her, at a loss. She hardly wanted to have a conversation of this magnitude in a shop with a hopeful sales assistant hovering nearby, but she didn't want to prevaricate, either. Her daughter deserved more. "We had a big fight, Poppy," she said carefully, "but it had been coming for a while. I suppose." She swallowed, almost choking on the words. "The truth is, we grew apart." She wasn't willing to admit her husband's infidelities right then; no matter how insensitive and heartless Jasper had been to her, he still had a relationship with his children to maintain, and she needed to figure out a sustainable way forward in that regard.

Poppy slid her a challenging look. "What does that even mean, 'you grew apart'?" She paused, her eyes wide, her teeth sinking into her lip before she blurted, "Did he…did he have an affair?"

Althea forced herself not to look away. "Poppy…" she began, and then trailed off because she didn't know what to say.

"*Did* he?"

Althea bit her lip, wondering what exactly was motivating her reluctance to come clean on this subject. Sensitivity for her children's relationship to their father, or her own stupid pride? "Why are you asking?" she said as Poppy turned away to examine some stained glass coasters, picking one up at a time and squinting at each in speculation as if she was about to make a very important purchase.

"Because I want to know. This is my *life*, you know?"

"The reasons for the divorce aren't as important as the divorce itself—"

"They are. Like, don't you think I want to know if my dad is a total douchebag?" Tears glittered in Poppy's eyes as she flung down one of the coasters she'd been examining, causing it to shatter, the sound making them both jump while the sales assistant whipped her head round, eyes narrowed. Poppy bit her lip again as a tear slipped down her cheek. "I'm sorry, Mum…"

"It doesn't matter." Heedlessly Althea pulled her daughter into a hug, grateful when Poppy reciprocated, holding her tightly, her face buried in her shoulder. "I'm so sorry about all of this, Poppy. I really am."

"It's not your fault, though, is it?" Poppy returned, her voice muffled against her coat.

"Even so."

Poppy pulled away, her nose running, her face blotchy. "It's true, isn't it? He did have an affair. Is he in Switzerland with someone, then? Some tart?"

Althea hesitated before she nodded. "He is with someone, it's true." She couldn't lie to her daughter, not for Jasper's sake, although she'd ignore the tart remark. "I'm sorry."

"Don't be. I don't like him, anyway."

"He's your dad, Poppy—"

"Only when he feels like it," Poppy retorted with more emotional astuteness than Althea had expected. It was true,

Jasper could turn the interest and affection on and off like a tap. She'd just hoped her children hadn't really noticed, accepting that he was busy and distracted with work, if not other women, and basking in his attention when he chose to give it. But that was no way to live, was it? It certainly wasn't a relationship.

The sales assistant chose that moment to sweep down on them. "I'm sorry," she said, sounding genuinely regretful, "but we have a policy of customers having to pay for any breakages. With stained glass being so fragile…"

"I understand," Althea said quickly, not wanting to make a big deal of it. "We'll pay for the coaster, and can we take these earrings, as well?"

"Mum—" Poppy protested, and Althea shot her a quick, smiling look.

"Early Christmas present. Because we forgot the boots."

"I don't care about the boots," Poppy mumbled as she scuffed her shoe along the floor. This was progress, Althea decided, of a sort.

She handed over her credit card, trying not to blink at the cost of the coaster—fifty quid!—and telling herself it was worth it, for the brief heart-to-heart she'd had with her daughter. She felt closer to Poppy now than she had in a long time.

"I'm sorry, ma'am, but your card has been declined."

"I—what?" Althea blinked at the assistant who was handing back her card with a cringeworthy mixture of apology and censure. "Declined? Are you sure?"

The woman nodded while Althea took back her platinum credit card as a hot, prickly flush stole over her body. "Maybe it was something with the magnetic stripe…" she mumbled as she fumbled with her purse to find her debit card. "Here. You can use this."

The woman plucked the card from her fingers while Althea waited, trying to look unruffled.

"I'm sorry," the woman said after an endless few seconds. "This has been declined, as well."

"But that can't be!" Althea burst out as she felt Poppy becoming tense next to her. "Both my cards…" She didn't have any other ones. She had no other recourse to funds of any kind, and no money save for the cash in her purse. The realisation left her feeling panicky and faint.

"Mum…" Poppy whispered, sounding more scared than embarrassed, which panicked Althea further.

"I'll pay with cash," she blustered, flinging a few twenties on the counter that the woman scooped up efficiently.

"Would you like the earrings wrapped?" she asked politely, and Althea shrugged the question aside.

"No, that is, thank you, we'll just take them as is."

A few blessed seconds later they had left the shop, Althea's cheeks scarlet with mortification—and alarm. Why had *both* of her cards been declined? The answer, she feared, was one she could barely stand to consider—Jasper had cancelled them, cut her off without a single penny, simply out of spite. She really needed to have a look at the prenup she'd signed when she'd been little more than a kid.

"Mum, what happened in there?" Poppy asked, her tone turning urgent. "Why were your cards cancelled?"

"I…" Althea's head swam. She couldn't keep hiding from the truth. "I think your father cancelled them," she admitted.

"But why?"

"To—to punish me, I suppose." No doubt Jasper was angry that she'd confronted him about his affair. She didn't usually; she was as compliant and docile as a trained seal. The realisation revolted her now.

"To punish you?" Poppy looked disgusted. "What on earth for? I mean, how messed up is that? He's the one cheating."

Althea managed a weak smile and a shrug. She had no answer.

Then Poppy squared her shoulders, her eyes flashing. "I bet he hasn't cancelled my card," she said, fishing in her bag. Althea had forgotten Jasper had given both Ben and Poppy credit cards when they'd turned sixteen, an easy way to curry favour.

"Poppy, you don't have to—"

"I do," Poppy insisted, holding the card up triumphantly. "We're going Christmas shopping, aren't we?"

Althea managed a small smile. "This could infuriate your father," she warned her, and Poppy gave her a glittering look.

"Good."

TWO HOURS LATER they were laden down with bags of presents for everyone and Althea was trying not to feel too guilty about having put it all on Poppy's card. Ben had, she'd discovered, cut up the card as soon as Jasper had given it to him, making Althea want to ask about a dozen questions, but deciding she could do it later.

She didn't want to think about Jasper now, or worry about what he could do; she wanted to enjoy the afternoon with her children which had, despite the bumps, been rather brilliant.

Dusk was already falling, like a violet curtain being drawn across the sky, as they piled back into the car, Ben squeezed in the back seat with the others, to pick up her sister Olivia from the train.

Althea was looking forward to seeing her sister; although they were very different, they'd always got along, and Althea had tried to message her once a week or so, just to check in. Yet as she pulled into the station's car park, she realised those messages had dropped off in the last few months, and she wasn't sure if that was because of her or Olivia.

Life sometimes had a way of slipping away from you, she reflected, without you even realising it was happening. In her determination to keep an even domestic keel, she'd let a lot of relationships slide—Olivia, Seph, her parents, even Sam.

She barely kept track of what mountain or marathon he was tackling next anymore. And as for other friendships…well, the truth was, there had never been very many, but she had made a few decent friends in uni who had fallen off after she'd married Jasper. Perhaps it was time to start reconnecting. She'd start with her sister.

"Olivia!" Althea found herself shouting her sister's name as she came off the train, looking as lovely and ethereal as always, her pale golden hair piled up messily on top of her head, a beat-up leather holdall slung over one shoulder. She was swathed in scarves and an old patchwork coat, the hippy-dippy kind of clothes that Olivia somehow made look fashionable, while Althea suspected if she wore them she would appear homeless.

"Althea." Olivia smiled as she hugged her. "I didn't realise you'd come home for Christmas. And the kids, too." She paused, sliding a questioning, violet-eyed glance towards Althea who gave a little shrug. No Jasper. It didn't even need saying.

"How are you? I meant to text to tell you I was home but time got away from me. We've only been here a few days."

Ben manfully took Olivia's bag as she hugged the children in turn and they started walking back towards the car.

"I'm all right." Although Olivia spoke lightly enough, something in her sister's tone made Althea give her a second, more thorough, look. Her sister had always been slender and waif-like, but there was a fragility to her that Althea hadn't seen before. Violet shadows the same colour as her eyes darkened the skin under them, and she looked away quickly from Althea's scrutiny.

"Oh," Althea said in a tone of big-sister ominous neutrality, making sure Olivia knew she wasn't pulling the wool over her eyes.

Olivia managed a small smile. "I'm sure I'll get a grilling later," she said, and then turned to ask Ben about uni, and Poppy about her A levels, before engaging Tobias about some computer game that Althea knew nothing about.

Her sister had always been amazing that way, connecting to people with seeming effortlessness while Althea's attempts felt stilted and too much like hard work. Maybe she overthought things too much, while Olivia, simply and artlessly, responded. Sort of like their mother did, but thankfully with a tad more self-awareness and sensitivity, although sometimes she could be as scatty as their mum.

As they all piled in the car to head back to Casterglass, Althea did her best to push away all the things that were picking at her—the cancelled cards, the sky-blue jumper, the fate of her family home. It was enough, she told herself, as she listened to Olivia answer Ben's questions about her job at a garden centre in York, to be with her family. To make the small steps she knew could seem like so little, but meant so much.

Putting the key in the ignition, she started the car and then headed for home.

Chapter Nine

S HE SHOULDN'T HAVE walked. Even with a pair of mud-caked wellies rather than the now-ruined Ted Baker boots she'd had on the last time she'd decided, on a whim, to walk through a muddy field, walking across the estate to Appleby Farm had not been a good idea.

It had seemed like it, when the sun had been shining twenty minutes ago as she'd started out, and she'd convinced herself that having a good meander around the property would help in her discussions with her father, which still hadn't happened yet.

"It's Christmas," he'd implored when she'd cornered him in his study that morning. "Let's enjoy the holiday as a family. We can sit down to business after, I promise."

"All right," Althea had agreed a bit grudgingly. She was the type of person who liked to sort things out sooner rather than later, unless it concerned her marriage, in which *never* was the preferred choice. Although never was looking a lot like now, especially with Jasper having cancelled her credit and debit cards. Who knew what else he had done?

Althea knew she needed to call their solicitor and find out where she stood in regards to the prenup, but she was reluctant to make what was sure to be an unpleasant phone call, since Edward Fotheringhay was most definitely Jasper's solicitor, not hers.

Surely that phone call could wait. It was Christmas, after all.

So she'd decided instead to tackle another thorny problem—that of John Braithwaite and his jumper. When they'd been in Kendal she'd bought a reciprocal jumper, wanting to be on an even footing with a man she really wasn't sure about, and she'd wrapped it in Christmas paper and included a card with a watercolour of the castle on it that her mother had painted decades ago. Her father had had hundreds printed out as a birthday present, but they were hardly ever used.

She hadn't exactly thought out her plan in heading over to his farm, but she hoped they'd be able to put the altercation the other evening to rest, and be on an equal, friendly footing as neighbours. After all, if she was thinking of turning Casterglass into a going concern and actually living here, she needed to be on good terms with the locals.

Unfortunately now, having scrambled across the wooden stile and drystone wall that separated Casterglass's property from that of Appleby Farm, she was now ankle-deep in dark, sucking mud, clutching the sweater to her chest, and eyeing several dirty, irascible-looking sheep with some alarm while rain started to spatter down.

She wasn't *scared* of sheep, not precisely. Having been born and raised in Cumbria, such a fear would be ridiculous. But she did, Althea realised as she came eye to eye with a curly-horned ram, have a healthy—and wary—respect of the creatures. They were bigger than you expected them to be, somehow. And the beady look in that sheep's eye was making her distinctly nervous, especially when several other sheep ambled up to it, all of them giving her the same distinctly fixed look. They were also blocking her way forward, although she supposed she could skirt round them, if she dared.

She didn't.

More sheep joined the growing flock, so she was staring down a round dozen, her heart starting to beat alarmingly fast. This was silly. They were *sheep*. And yet…

"Are you going to move?"

The shout from afar had Althea stiffening, and then narrowing her eyes as she raised a hand to shield her face from the rain, she saw John Braithwaite standing at the gate on the opposite end of the field. Great.

"I'm just waiting for these sheep to move first," she shouted back, trying to sound light and wry and, she suspected, failing miserably. She glanced back at the sheep and one actually lowered his head, horns and all. Did sheep charge people? Was that even a thing?

She felt herself going both hot and cold with embarrassment as she realised John Braithwaite was witnessing this whole absurd episode. All right, she'd show him, then. She'd just…walk…between the sheep. Show them who was in command. It would be easy.

"Go on, shoo," she called, flapping one hand as she clutched her lumpy parcel with the other. "Get out of here. Go on. *Move.*"

The sheep simply stood there and stared. Stupid creatures. She willed herself not to glance at John, still standing by the gate. He was probably laughing at her. Or maybe he was angry with her for being in his field. She hadn't even considered that when she'd started across, but now she recalled his comment about day trippers traipsing through his fields, terrorising his sheep. Whoops.

She took a step forward, and then one of the sheep—the one that had lowered its head in that rather menacing way— let out a loud, bawling baa, making Althea jump and then nearly fall down.

To alarm her further, she suddenly heard the excited barking of not one but several dogs, and when she looked up she saw two black and white Border collies racing towards her, looking practically rabid in their excitement. She definitely wasn't scared of dogs, not nice dogs anyway, but these ones were barking quite a lot.

She took a step back, slipping in the mud, and then, with her hands windmilling helplessly, both she and the parcel went flying. She heard the splat as she fell bottom-first into the mud, while the two collies rounded up the sheep and herded them to the far corner of the field. Oh, so that was what they had been doing. Naturally.

"Are you all right?"

Althea blinked through the rain that was now falling steadily to see John Braithwaite, dressed appropriately in all-weathers, extending a hand to her. She felt rainwater trickle into her ears and mud seep into her jeans and she knew her humiliation was complete. This was so not how she'd wanted this to go. *Mistress of Casterglass, flat on her arse.* Perfect.

"I'm fine," she said, her voice stiff with wounded dignity.

"Let me help you up."

Knowing she needed the help, she grasped his hand, which was miraculously both warm and dry considering the downpour, and let him haul her to her feet.

"Your parcel got a bit muddy, but it looks all right." He reached down for the wrapped jumper, the wrapping paper now covered in mud, and handed it to her.

"Thank you," Althea said in that same, stiff voice while John looked at her in bemusement.

"Were you coming to see me?"

"Well…yes," she admitted, reluctant to say as much even though she could not fathom another reason why she would be out there in a muddy sheep field.

"Well, let's get back to the warm and dry," John said, and whistling for the dogs, he headed across the field, leaving Althea no choice but to follow.

It wasn't until she'd reached the five-bar gate and gone through it, John holding it open for her, that she realised what that meant. A mud-splattered quad bike was parked by the gate, and was clearly their mode of transport.

"Er…"

"You can hop on the back," John said easily. "It's too far to walk, especially in this rain. A good mile."

Still Althea hesitated, and John rolled his eyes. "I haven't got a limousine, I'm afraid."

"Oh, please, enough with the poor little rich girl remarks," she retorted tartly. "I thought that's what the jumper was an apology for?"

He laughed, his eyes crinkling up at the corners. "Right you are. It's a bad habit of mine, I'm afraid. Come on, then. Hop on."

He climbed on first, straddling the bike easily, and after a second's agonising indecision Althea finally clambered on behind him. Goodness, but this was awkward. She pressed the parcel against her chest so it was cushioned between their bodies, and then, closing her eyes against the embarrassment, she put her arms around his waist as lightly as she could.

"Hang on," he advised as he started the bike, and when he took off down the rutted, muddy road, the dogs barking and running alongside, Althea had no choice but to do so for dear life.

The bike bumped and rattled its way down a mile of rough track, with Althea's eyes clenched shut and her mouth open in a silent scream. She was clinging to John Braithwaite like a limpet, and even in the midst of her terror, some subconscious, animalistic part of her brain was registering his washboard-like abs, particularly impressive on a man who had to be approaching his mid-forties.

By the time John had pulled into the muddy stable yard by Appleby farmhouse, every part of Althea had been jolted and shaken. Her ears were ringing and her teeth felt as if they were rattling around in her head. She extricated herself as quickly and gracefully—that was, not at all—as possible from the bike, and tottered towards the front door, still clutching her precious parcel. John followed at a more relaxed pace, moving past her to open the front door that led directly into the farmhouse's kitchen.

"After you," he said graciously, and Althea mumbled her thanks as she stepped into the long, low-ceilinged room. Although it was much smaller, it reminded her of the castle's kitchen, with many of the same trusty set pieces—the battered Aga, the big wooden table, a shabby sofa at one end that was piled with papers. She laughed out loud, and John gave her a questioning look.

"It just looks so much like the kitchen back at the ca—at home," she said and he raised his eyebrows.

"Seems like we have something in common, then."

"The only thing, perhaps," Althea replied, meaning to tease, but it came just a bit too sharp. He really was going to think she was a shrew.

"Perhaps," John agreed dryly, and she was glad he hadn't taken the opportunity to spare her yet again. "Tea? Coffee? A splash of whisky?"

"Tea, please." She drew a shaky breath. "With a splash of whisky in it, if you're offering."

"Sounds like my kind of drink." He stripped off his waterproofs, revealing a toned and tanned glimpse of stomach before he pulled down his jumper, a holey Aran one that looked about twenty years old.

Althea watched him as he headed to the kettle, before she realised she was dripping dirty water onto the floor. She was soaked and muddy and starting to shiver.

John glanced back at her. "If you want to change, I can give you some clothes." His tone was mild, deliberately so, but Althea blushed away. How had she managed to get herself into this situation? Oh, yes. By being stupid and walking.

"Um…"

"You'll freeze if you stay in that," he told her bluntly. "You're absolutely soaked. Don't worry, I don't have any nefarious intent. You're about the same size as my daughter. I'll get you some of her clothes."

He had a daughter? "Er…all right. Thank you." Althea didn't know how to refuse politely, and she didn't really want to, anyway. She was absolutely icy.

John ducked through a low doorway and then Althea heard the thud of his feet up the stairs. She put her parcel on the table, and then peeled off her coat and hung it on the back of a chair.

A few minutes later John came down, holding a T-shirt, fleece, and a pair of jeans. "Will this do?"

"That's great, thanks—"

"You can change through there, in the loo." He nodded towards the doorway from which he'd come, and with more mumbled thanks Althea headed through.

Her curious gaze skimmed over a messy, comfortable sitting room—age-blackened beams over leather sofas, a coffee table piled high with magazines and books, and a fireplace that spanned the width of the room. The door to the bathroom was ajar, and she stepped inside, locking the door behind her, curious about even this small room for it clearly bore the stamp of someone with personality.

Postcards from every corner of the world, corners curling, photos fading, formed a floor-to-ceiling collage of colour. Althea paused as her gaze drifted over the place names—Sweden, Finland, Italy, Greece, Bali, Thailand. Who were they from? Who had done all that travelling? She turned away abruptly, strangely disconcerted. She needed to change.

Her freezing fingers fumbled with buttons and zips as she stripped off her wet things and then, feeling acutely self-conscious, slipped on his daughter's clothes. The jeans were a little snug over her three-pregnancies tummy that no amount of Pilates could touch, but the fleece fortunately covered the inevitable muffin top.

She ran her fingers through her damp hair, made a face at her reflection, and then drawing in a fortifying breath, she headed back to the kitchen.

John was just adding a generous splash of whisky to two steaming mugs as she came into the room, noting the two dogs sprawled in beds by the Aga, and the papers that had been whisked off the sofa and dumped onto a Welsh dresser.

"Thank you," she said as he handed her a cup of tea. She took a sip, trying not to grimace as the whisky hit the back of her throat.

John laughed, noting her expression even though she'd tried to hide it. "Not a whisky drinker?"

"Not often," Althea admitted, and took another sip. Already the alcohol was stealing through her veins, warming her right through. "I didn't know you had a daughter."

"Why would you?" He spoke without any rancour but she still felt a bit chastised. She should have known. She should make it her business to know, at least, now that she was thinking of staying.

"I suppose I wouldn't," she admitted, deciding to be candid. "How old is she?"

"Sixteen."

"Same as my Poppy." He nodded, and she wondered if he'd already known that. It was disconcerting, not knowing how much someone knew about you. Her life, or at least what was known of it, might have been raked over in the village pub every weekend for years, and she had no idea.

Although perhaps it was arrogant, even to wonder if that were the case.

"And your wife?" she asked brightly, and something almost like amusement flashed in his eyes even as his mouth tightened and he looked down quickly.

"I'm...widowed."

"I'm sorry," she said, even as the pause between the two words made her wonder. Had he been going to say something else? You were either widowed or you weren't, right?

"Thank you. It was a long time ago." A pause. "Six years."

"Oh. I see." Although she didn't, really. "That must have been tough."

"Yes. Laura was..." He stopped and then shook his head. Clearly it was too painful to talk about. They both sipped their tea in silence for a few moments while Althea tried to think of something else to say.

"So to what do I owe the pleasure of your company?" John finally asked, and Althea nearly winced. She *had* invited herself over in the most obvious and overbearing way.

"I wanted to thank you for the jumper," she told him stiltedly. "It wasn't necessary, but...thank you."

"You're welcome."

She met his gaze, and then had to steel herself not to look away. His eyes were hazel with flecks of gold, his expression composed and unwavering. After a few uncomfortable seconds Althea finally couldn't keep from glancing away as she gulped her tea, the whisky scorching her throat once more.

"I brought you this," she said once she'd swallowed it down. "Since you didn't bring me your jumper to wash."

"I figured it was a lost cause. It was old, anyway."

"Even so." She put her mug down as she reached for the muddy parcel. "I realise I was rather rude when I first spoke to you, back at the party." Her voice sounded far too high and thin. "Things have been a bit…well, it doesn't matter." She practically thrust the package into his arms, and he took it, bemused.

"Let me guess. A jumper?"

"You're clever, aren't you?" She hadn't meant to sound flirtatious, but somehow she had, and as a result she blushed.

John smiled, a quirk of his mouth that seemed to skitter along her skin. Goodness, she really needed not to respond this way. Not to drink whisky, perhaps, in the company of a handsome man. She was married, after all, even if the divorce papers might already be winging their way here and she hadn't actually been *intimate* with her soon-to-be ex-husband in—well. Never mind.

"I am clever," he replied, his mouth quirking all the more. "Or at least I like to think I am." He tore a strip off the wrapping paper. "Let's see this jumper, then."

And just like that, Althea felt nervous. Would he like it? Was it too much? Why had they bought each other jumpers, after all? And why did she care?

"Ah. Very nice." He shook it out, inspecting it thoroughly. It was nothing special, Althea told herself, just a plain wool jumper in moss green.

"It matches my eyes, just like yours does," he said, looking up, those very eyes crinkling at the corners. "We can be twins."

Althea had no idea what the look on her face was—embarrassed, appalled, perhaps—but whatever it was, it caused John to let out a shout of laughter.

"Was that unintentional?"

"Er…"

"Never mind." He bundled the sweater up and put it on the top of a basket of clean washing. "Drink up your tea and whisky, and tell me what you're really doing here in Casterglass."

Chapter Ten

"WHAT I'M REALLY doing?" Althea repeated a bit stupidly. Her mind was racing, although perhaps trickling was more the word, thanks to the whisky. She felt as if her thoughts were wading through treacle. "I'm here for Christmas…" John merely raised his eyebrows, waiting for more. "What are you getting at?" Althea asked, with an attempt at bluster that clearly failed.

"Only that you weren't expected for Christmas—that much was clear. Your mother told Mary at the post office that you'd emailed rather suddenly to say you were coming."

"Oh, she did?" Althea didn't know whether to bristle or groan at this news.

"And Mary's sister is Ruth, who cleans the church."

"Of course she is."

"And my daughter Alice does a spot of flower arranging in the church," John finished, as if it were all so very simple. "That's where she heard it from, and she told me."

"Your sixteen-year-old does flower arranging?" Perhaps she'd have something in common with Poppy's interior design aspirations.

"It's part of her community service for her Duke of Edinburgh Award. She's going for gold."

Althea heard the note of pride in John's voice, and it caused a welter of feelings in her. None of her children had done the Duke of Edinburgh Award, the prestigious program of camping, community service and general all-around excellence for secondary school students. Ben had tried for the bronze, but had given up when his hiking team had fallen apart. Poppy had point-blank refused. The fact that John's Alice was going for gold shouldn't affect her at all, of course, and yet…

It didn't take much these days to make her feel like a crap mother.

Althea pulled out a chair at the table and sat down, cradling her mug between her hands. "So I decided to come for Christmas. What's the big deal?"

John shrugged. "Just seemed a bit sudden, that's all. And you've dropped a few hints yourself about things being a bit…never mind?" He tossed her words back to her with a smile that held a touch of sympathy, as well as a dose of amusement.

Althea had no idea why he was fishing. Idle curiosity? Concern for Casterglass? She remembered how he had berated her for not caring about the village and she wasn't sure she wanted to offer up her personal tragedies for his— and no doubt the whole village's—consumption.

And yet, she realised, it wasn't exactly something she could hide.

"I'm getting a divorce," she stated baldly, deciding to be blunt. "I don't know if you recall my husband Jasper… He's visited a few times…"

"I know him."

The grimness of his tone made her give him a sharp look. "You do?"

"He's hard not to notice. Made a fuss over everything, as I recall. I was in the post office when he had a barney over not being able to buy the *Daily Telegraph* there. Seemed *The North-West Evening Mail* wouldn't cut it."

"Oh, dear." Althea sighed and shook her head. "That sounds like him."

"And the sheets at the Plough and Star weren't soft enough, or so I heard."

"Good grief." She gave a not-so-pretend wince. "Is there nothing this village doesn't know?"

"A few things, I'm sure."

She sipped her tea, realisation trickling through her. All the villagers must know what an arse Jasper was, and they'd judged her for being married to him. It made sense, but it also hurt.

"I'm sorry you're getting divorced," John said quietly. "It can't be easy, but…good riddance, I say."

Wow. Blunt. Althea took another sip of tea, needing the hit of whisky. "Well, I'm not divorcing him because of any of that," she felt compelled to tell him. The whisky was definitely loosening her tongue. "I know he could be fussy and rude and arrogant, but the reason we're getting divorced is because he was—is—a serial adulterer."

"Ah." John nodded, looking all too unsurprised.

Something like horror flashed through her, and everything inside her cringed. "Don't tell me you knew that, too?"

A pause, all too telling. *Oh, no.* "Suspected," John admitted finally. "He made a call on his mobile in the foyer of the pub last time he was here. A few of us overheard. It was clearly to someone…"

"His bit on the side?" she filled in flatly. John nodded. Althea looked away, suddenly feeling winded, and also as if she wanted to cry. Everyone in Casterglass knew she'd been made a fool of. Everyone probably thought she was pathetic. It shouldn't really matter, and yet… She took a deep breath and willed the tears back. John Braithwaite had certainly seen enough of them. "It's good to know the whole village is talking about me," she managed in a rather brittle voice. Maybe she *was* going to cry. She certainly sounded like it.

"It's not like that," John told her, his voice roughening. "People here care."

"Oh, right, *I'm* the one who doesn't." She slapped her hand against her forehead, and realised her fingers were trembling. "Silly me." The ache in her throat warned her she was seconds off letting a sob loose.

"I shouldn't have said that. The jumper was meant to be

an apology for being so rude." Althea nodded jerkily, not trusting herself to speak. John sighed as he raked a hand through his hair. "Look, I've clearly handled this all wrong. I'm too blunt, I know. It comes from being on my own for too long. Alice always tells me I'm putting my foot in it."

"Those are wonderful excuses," Althea managed in something close to a snap, and that lovely little smile quirked his mouth again.

"You're right, they are excuses. Will a simple and heartfelt I'm sorry do?" His gaze held hers, and once more she had to look away.

"I don't know." She passed a hand over her face, willing the threat of tears to subside completely; she could still feel the pressure gathering behind her lids, in her throat. "I hate the thought of everyone picking over my personal business."

"No one means it badly but that's village life, I'm afraid."

"I suppose it is."

"Anyway." He paused. "It won't much matter, will it, if you're back down south by New Year's?" The lilt of a question in his voice had her swallowing hard.

"Well, I…I might not be," she said after a moment. Part of her brain was frantically reminding her not to spill her fragile, barely formed dreams to this man, who would no doubt have it all over the village by Tuesday, and yet…

She wanted to know what he thought. If he thought she was crazy for keeping Casterglass, well, so be it. It would be no more, or really no less, than she expected. But if he didn't…

"What do you mean?" he asked.

"I'm thinking of staying here," she stated, something like challenge in her voice. "Living here. Turning Casterglass Castle into a…a viable enterprise."

John had been standing, one hip braced against the Aga rail, but now he pulled out a chair and sat down in it, all without breaking her gaze.

"Oh?" he asked, his tone what Althea suspected was deceptively pleasant. She didn't know whether scepticism or derision lurked behind that innocuous syllable. "How do you plan to do that?"

"I'm not going to be building a roller coaster on the front lawn, if you're worried about something like that," she told him, slightly annoyed by his evasive manner. She realised, somewhat to her shame she'd wanted him to be excited. *Oh thank goodness, you're going to save the day.* Ha. As if.

"I never said—"

"You didn't have to. You've got 'stupid southerner thinks she's going to turn Casterglass into an amusement park' written all over your face."

He opened his mouth to argue, and then laughed instead. "All right, I admit it. I was having nightmares of giraffes terrorising my sheep."

"I'm the only one terrorising your sheep so far," Althea returned with a small smile, heartened that he hadn't doubled down on his ire. He was a man who could admit when he was wrong, and that was very refreshing.

"That's true," he answered, giving her a look that was considering, and for some ridiculous reason it made Althea go all funny and warm. It had to be the whisky. "So what is your plan, then?"

"Well, I don't really have one yet. This is all very new. I didn't realise my father was thinking of selling until I came home."

"So he is thinking of selling."

Althea groaned. "Please don't spread that around the village just yet—"

"I don't gossip," he replied, affronted yet smiling. "Ruth does."

"And Mary."

"You're learning fast."

Was this banter? Were they actually...*flirting*?

"I need to learn fast, if I'm going to try to keep this place," Althea told him seriously, doing her best to ignore the little flutters that had started low down in her belly. "Right now I just have a handful of half-baked ideas."

"Such as?"

"Well..." Her mind raced as she thought about the ideas she'd read about as well as the ones she'd been mulling over. "Whatever we do, I want it to be authentic to the surroundings." John arched an eyebrow, looking slightly sceptical. "No safari parks or roller-coaster rides," she told him with a small smile. "Maybe some glamping," she admitted, suddenly feeling embarrassed. Telling him this much made her feel weirdly vulnerable. She couldn't bear if he poured scorn over it all, at this early stage.

"I can see that working," he said after a moment, and that was enough to keep her going.

"Whatever we might plan, I want it to look…organic. Natural, I mean, part of countryside and estate, not some eyesore or monstrosity." He nodded encouragingly, and emboldened, Althea continued. "Some of the old outbuildings and barns could be turned into little shops, I thought, or maybe even a tea room. Perhaps some workshops for local artisans…"

"Getting local people involved would be ideal," John agreed as he took a sip of his whisky-laced tea. "In a perfect world, the castle and village would have a symbiotic relationship."

"Symbiotic…" She hadn't considered the notion before. "How do you mean, exactly?"

He lifted his shoulder in a shrug. "The castle employs local residents and recommends, for example, the pub in the village. The village sells tickets to the castle, puts its brochures on the post office counter. That sort of thing, having it all be mutually beneficial."

"Yes, I can see that…"

"What we wouldn't want," he continued, a sudden, implacable note entering his voice, "is for loads of tourists to come to the area and *only* spend time at the castle. As the major landowners in this corner of the world you have a responsibility to encourage industry and tourism in the whole area."

Althea bit her lip to keep from retorting something unhelpful. A few days ago he'd been sneering at her for being too lady-of-the-manor, and now he was acting like the vassal he claimed he wasn't, demanding Casterglass take responsibility for the local residents. Which was it?

Still, she understood the gist of what he meant, and of *course* she wanted to help the whole area, and not just the estate. But with two hundred thousand pounds to find for the roof not to mention a host of other things she hadn't even thought of yet, she wasn't about to put the pub or the post office first.

"Naturally I want to be supportive of the village and its businesses," she told him after a moment, "but at the same time my priority has got to be the estate."

"Well, that's the idea behind it being symbiotic. Hopefully supporting the village *will* be supporting the estate, and vice versa. You've got to have local people on your side, especially when you have an emergency call-out for a plumber at two o'clock in the morning."

Althea gave a not entirely mock shudder. That scenario was all too plausible. "The way you're talking," she said slowly, "it's as if that hasn't been happening." She glanced up at him, unsure if she wanted to ask this question, yet knowing she needed to hear the answer. "You're a local, and your farm borders the castle. Do you feel my father hasn't been…attentive…to the village?"

John didn't answer for a long moment. He leaned back in his chair, stockinged feet stretched out in front of him, his mug held in one large, capable-looking hand while the other rubbed his jaw. "He used to be," he finally answered. "As I'm sure you remember yourself. Back in the day he employed more people…a couple of lads to mow the lawn, old Alan to do the gardening."

"I remember Alan." She hadn't actually realised her father didn't hire Alan anymore, although when she thought of the unmoved lawn, the garden that was little more than a tangle of weeds, she supposed it was no big surprise.

"It was nice, opening the place up for a Christmas do the other evening, inviting everyone," John continued. "That hasn't happened in a long time."

"My parents are getting older," Althea told him, a bit defensively. "And the money isn't there anymore, the way it once was."

"I know." John leaned forward, his look frank yet sympathetic. "It's hard. I do understand that. Appleby Farm is a twentieth the size of your estate and the truth is I've struggled to keep it going."

"You have?"

"Sheep farming doesn't pay what it once did," he acknowledged with a wry smile. "Just like being lord of the manor doesn't, either. I've had to diversify."

"How?"

He shrugged. "I keep bees and make honey, supplying some local shops as well as Booths."

"Wow…"

"It's not much, but it helps."

Althea nodded slowly, her mind starting to tick over. "What if…what if the castle had a local shop, to offer all the things people in Casterglass make? Your honey, even the lamb from your farm…we could have a little butcher's shop…local vegetables…crafts…" Her mind was starting to race ahead now.

"It all sounds amazing," John said dryly. "But it's a lot of work, and I mean a *lot.*"

"You don't think I can do it?"

"I didn't say that. Just that it's a lot to take on, and you're in a precarious position—soon-to-be divorced, three kids…"

"Yes." Althea slumped in her seat, that momentary flicker of excitement already on its way to being extinguished. "And the money isn't there."

"There are business loans for this sort of thing."

"I suppose…" Money made her think of Jasper, and those cancelled cards. How could she be contemplating anything, when she didn't have so much as a penny to her name? She'd spent the last of her cold hard cash on a stupid stained glass coaster. The earrings had been worth it, though. Poppy had been wearing them this morning.

"What is it?" John asked, his surprisingly gentle voice breaking into her thoughts. "You look as if someone just told you your dog had died."

"No, nothing like that." Althea tried for a smile. "Just the usual woes and worries. Quite boring, really."

"You're not talking about the castle now, I take it?"

"No." She paused, not wanting to moan about her situation or even to reveal it, and yet something about John's open, friendly look made her blurt, "My husband—soon to be ex, I think—has cancelled my cards."

John's eyebrows rose in an almost comical look of surprise. "Cancelled them? But aren't they in your name?"

"Yes, but they're his accounts. He held the purse strings quite tightly all through my marriage." She flushed, aware of how pathetic this made her look, like some 1950s housewife. Why had she taken it for so long?

"You're saying you don't have any of your own money?" He sounded scandalised, and Althea tried for a bit of light-hearted bravado.

"Not a penny. I spent the last of it in Kendal yesterday, Christmas shopping, before I realised he'd cut me off completely." With belated horror, she realised he could think she was fishing for a loan, or something ridiculous like that. "I'll be fine," she said quickly. "It's just an irritation, really. I'll be absolutely fine."

"But…" John was frowning as he slowly rubbed his jaw with one hand. "When you do actually divorce, you'll get a good settlement, won't you? I mean…he'll have to support you and the children?"

"Well…" A lump was forming in her throat as she looked away. She didn't want to have to admit to the prenup she'd signed, and yet she was longing to share the burden with someone. But with this man she'd barely met, a man she suspected would be scathing of her stupidity?

"Althea?" It was, she realised, the first time he'd said her name. "That's right, isn't it?"

"I'm…I'm not sure. I signed a prenuptial agreement before we married, when I was twenty-one and desperately, deeply in love, or at least I thought I was. I was stupid, basically. Stupid and naïve. I don't even remember what it said, but based on the twenty years of experience I've had since, I doubt it will be very generous."

John's eyebrows drew together to form a ferocious shaggy line. "Well, you need to find out. Why don't you call your solicitor?"

"Because he's Jasper's crony and I don't want to talk to him."

"That might be, but he has a legal obligation to furnish you with the particulars. You should at least know what you're dealing with."

"I suppose…" She really did not want to endure a moment of Edward Fotheringhay's patronising snark.

"Call him right now." John reached for the receiver of a very old-fashioned-looking landline telephone. "Don't waste another moment."

"What?" Althea was so surprised she had to fall back on bluster. "No, I mean, I—I *will*, but that's, you know, it's not exactly…" She trailed off helplessly as John held the phone out, unmoved by her stammering protests.

"Do it," he said, his tone firm but kind. "It's better to know what you're dealing with."

She stared at him, wanting to argue, yet knowing he was right. She'd been Ostrich Althea for too long. She'd wanted to start taking control of her life, to feel empowered to do more than buy a trolleyful of groceries at Booths. She wanted to save a castle, for heaven's sake. She could do this.

"All right," she said as she took the phone. "But I don't know his number."

"Easily found." John retrieved a battered laptop from the pile of papers that he'd whisked off the sofa earlier. He opened it up, and then, hands poised over the keyboard, gave her an enquiring look. "What's the name?"

"Edward Fotheringhay, of Fotheringhay and Blackwood Solicitors."

"Sounds like a right toff."

"He is." Althea grimaced. "It's his father's firm. He and Jasper went to uni together." John raised his eyebrows, and Althea gave a rather shamefaced smile. "At this point you must be wondering why I married him in the first place…"

"It's not my business," he said quickly, turning back to the laptop, and she felt strangely rebuffed. No, it wasn't, but for a little while there she'd thought they'd been becoming friends. Clearly not.

"Right." He cleared his throat. "I've found the number."

"Okay." Althea didn't think she was imagining the slight tension that had suddenly sprung up between them when she'd mentioned Jasper. She didn't understand it, but she felt as if she'd been put in her place.

John read out the number, and with her trepidation growing by the second, Althea dialled it. She really didn't want to hear Edward's plummy, disparaging tones, treating her like a backward child or a bit of fluff; he'd done both in the past, the few times she'd had to interact with him at parties and the like.

The phone rang, and a snooty-sounding secretary answered. Sounding as forthright and imperious as she could, Althea asked to speak to him.

"May I ask who's calling?" the secretary asked with a sniff.

"Althea Fowler."

"Lady of Casterglass," John whispered, and Althea rolled her eyes as a nervous laugh trembled on her lips.

"You make me sound like the Lady of Shalott, or something," she whispered back after the secretary had asked her to hold.

"Well, you've got your four grey walls, and four grey towers," he quipped, and Althea stared at him in surprise, for she realised she hadn't expected him to know the Tennyson poem.

"Four grey walls, and four grey towers, overlook a space of flowers," he quoted. "And the silent isle imbowers—"

"The Lady of Shalott," Althea finished, and they both grinned at each other. "That's one of my favourite poems," she said quietly.

"Mine too."

For some reason this information made her feel like shivering. Before she could process it, Edward came on the line.

"Althea. I thought I might be hearing from you," he said, a slight sneer to his tone that made her tense. "Have you received the papers?"

Althea blinked, already on the back foot. "The papers...?"

"The divorce papers. I believe the court served them yesterday."

Chapter Eleven

A LTHEA BARELY HEARD what Edward said after that. She saw John's eyes crinkling in concern and he mouthed something but she didn't hear that either. Her mind was suddenly full of a buzzing blankness and her vision was actually starting to tunnel. *Divorce papers.* This was really happening. She shouldn't be surprised, she knew, and yet she was. She felt blindsided.

"Althea?" Edward's voice, definitely sounding impatient now, broke into her swirling thoughts. "I'll email you a PDF of the prenuptial agreement?"

Had she mentioned that to him? She must have. Her mind was in a complete daze. "Okay, thank you," she managed after another few seconds of spinning silence, and somehow she managed to finish the call in a semi-coherent manner. Hopefully.

Numbly she handed the phone back to John, who was frowning at her. "Althea? What's wrong?"

"I...no." She shook her head. Why was she so shocked? She'd been expecting this, and yet...somehow it felt different. It felt worse. Her marriage really was over. That was a good thing, but right then it felt like failure. A tragedy.

"No?"

"Edward told me the court served me divorce papers yesterday. It's not exactly a surprise, of course but…" She trailed off, shaking her head, unsure what to say, or even how to feel. Was she bereft? Relieved? A bit of both? Gobsmacked, really, although she knew she shouldn't be. Jasper had *said* he was going to contact Edward before he'd left, after all. Yet it had been a careless remark thrown over his shoulder, and somehow Althea had, despite telling herself and everyone else she was getting divorced, not really believed it, until now.

She felt John's hands on her shoulders, surprising her, because she hadn't seen him move.

"I'm sorry, Althea," he said, squeezing her shoulders lightly, not quite a hug but something close.

She tried to smile. "I'm not upset," she assured him, although her voice sounded a bit too wobbly for that to be entirely true. "I'm just surprised. And…I don't know." She shook her head again. "Twenty years down the drain. If I'd been smarter, I wouldn't have married him at all, but then I wouldn't have my children."

And just like that, she suddenly felt as if she could sob. And this man had already seen her sob once. She really did not need a repeat, and she doubted he did, either.

She lurched up from the table, nearly knocking over her

chair. "It's getting late. I should go."

"I'll drive you back," John replied immediately. "Not on the bike this time." He gestured to the windows. "It's already dark."

"Is it?" How long had she been here? Hours, probably. Everyone would be wondering where she was. "Where's your daughter?" she asked abruptly, and he smiled.

"Took the train to Lancaster to do some Christmas shopping with friends. She'll be back in an hour or so. Plenty of time for me to drive you to the castle. Let me just get my keys."

Althea nodded dumbly, everything in her still reeling. As he passed by her, he gave her shoulder another squeeze. He needed to stop doing that, or she really would start to cry.

They didn't speak as they headed outside into the on-coming night, the air sharp with cold. John opened the passenger door for her before walking over to the driver's side, another small gentlemanly gesture that made her like the man all the more. Her initial instinct had been right; he was someone she could like. *Did* like. And in truth she needed a friend right about now.

"Look, about your plans for the castle…" he said after they'd been rumbling down the dirt track that led from his farm to the B road for a few minutes. "Why don't you come to the Christmas fete the village is putting on tomorrow evening? It's not much—Santa does a little visit, and they turn the lights on the big Christmas tree on the village green, but I think everyone would appreciate someone from the castle making an appearance, and it might be a way for you to get to know the people here a bit more."

"That sounds like a good idea," Althea agreed a bit woodenly. She was still thinking about those wretched divorce papers, but she appreciated his suggestion. Going out would be a welcome distraction.

Already the castle was coming into view, its lights glimmering in the distance. Without her having to say, John pulled his muddy Land Rover around to the kitchen door rather than the front.

He put the car in park, and then turned to look at her, his face barely visible in the darkness.

"It will get better, you know."

She nodded jerkily. "Thanks." Although she supposed he didn't really know what getting divorced felt like, since he'd been widowed, which had to be worse. "I'm not sad," she felt compelled to him. "Not like that, anyway."

"I know." He hesitated, and she had the sense he wanted to say something important, but then he just smiled in a farewell sort of way. "See you tomorrow, then?"

"Yes," Althea agreed as she clambered out of the car. "Tomorrow."

"WHERE HAVE YOU been?" Poppy demanded theatrically as soon as Althea stepped into the kitchen. "And whose car was that?"

"Our neighbour's," Althea answered, on autopilot. "I was talking to him about—" She stopped suddenly, because she hadn't told anyone but her father about her plans to keep Casterglass.

"About?" Poppy asked, eyes narrowed, hands on hips.

"Something about the estate," Althea finished a bit lamely. "Nothing important." She felt the beginnings of a headache start to hammer her brain. "How has everyone been here?"

"Poppy's been in a *mood*," Tobias offered. He was sitting at the kitchen table, crunching his way through a bag of crisps. "But Olivia and Ben and I all played an epic game of Risk. She found it upstairs. It was, like, properly vintage."

"That sounds nice." Althea glanced back at Poppy, who was still glowering. "Everything all right, Pops?"

"Yeah, fine, I just didn't feel like playing stupid Risk," Poppy snapped, giving her even more aggro than usual, and making Althea wonder what was going on in her daughter's world. She watched as Poppy slipped her phone from her pocket, scowled at it, and then put it back in.

"How are all your friends doing?" she asked, and Poppy rolled her eyes.

"They're having fun," she practically snarled, and then she stomped out of the room.

"She's been like that all day," Tobias informed her. "After she saw something on her phone."

Althea's parental antennae immediately perked up. "On her phone?"

"Yeah, a message or something. She gave a noise like this—" he did a theatrical gasp "—and then she disappeared for hours."

"Hmm." That did not sound good. In the past, Althea might have made her daughter a cup of tea and tentatively asked if she was okay. Poppy would have shouted at her and she would have tiptoed away. She wanted to take more control now, but her head was aching and life felt pretty overwhelming as it was. She promised herself she'd talk to Poppy at some point that evening.

"I suppose I should make something for supper," she said on a sigh, and Tobias looked at her eagerly.

"Burgers?"

Althea smiled. His stomach was her son's number-one priority. At least that felt simple. "Burgers it is," she agreed.

She'd just taken a package of mince out of the fridge when Olivia came into the kitchen, her forehead creased with concern.

"This came for you today."

Althea knew what it was before her sister handed her the big brown envelope, with Fotheringhay and Blackwood Solicitors stamped on the top left corner. Her stomach clenched.

"Do you want to talk about it?" Olivia asked quietly.

"Maybe later tonight, over a bottle of wine, just the two

of us?" Althea did her best to smile. Perhaps then she'd get to the bottom of whatever was causing the violet shadows under her sister's eyes, never mind lamenting over her own woes.

"It's a deal." Olivia smiled, her eyes lightening to lavender. "I'm going to hold you to it," she warned.

"Good." After putting the envelope aside, Althea cracked an egg into the mince and started to mix. "I'm counting on that."

The next few hours thankfully passed in a blur of activity; Althea made dinner and served it out, listening as attentively as she could to Tobias and Ben talking about the game of Risk they'd played, and keeping an eye on a morose Poppy, to make sure she ate. She tried to engage Seph, but once again her sister went monosyllabic, while her parents kept the conversation and wine flowing in their genial and absent-minded way.

Ben offered to do the dishes, corralling Poppy and Tobias, and with her parents disappearing to their prospective studies and Seph agreeing to help the children, there was nothing to keep Olivia from grabbing a bottle of wine from the cellar—not the Margaux '36, but something equally delicious—and two glasses, and summoning Althea.

"Where are you going?" Althea asked in half-hearted protest as she followed Olivia from the usual set of rooms where the family lived to the old castle with its stone-flagged floors and draughty corridors. "Olivia, we'll freeze."

"I've got it sorted," Olivia tossed over her shoulder, past

the bedroom with the four-poster and its moth-eaten hangings that had once held Henry VIII's large form, and several others that had similarly dubious claims to fame.

"Where…" Althea began, only to stop when Olivia opened the iron-banded door that led to the castle's one and only turret, an addition from the 1700s that was more folly than fortress.

Its deep diamond-paned windows had seats built into the stone, and a fire blazed in the hearth, giving the room a cheery, welcoming warmth.

"Did you set this all up?" Althea exclaimed, for there were blankets on the seats to wrap up in, and the little room had clearly been recently cleaned.

"It didn't take long." Olivia curled up on one end of the window seat before brandishing a corkscrew and opening the wine bottle. "I've always loved this room," she said as she pulled the cork out with a satisfyingly loud *pop*. "It's so cosy with the fire going, and the bedroom up above." She glanced at the spiral stairs that led to the room above, which Althea suspected was full of useless stuff, like most of the castle was.

If they ever did manage to turn Casterglass into a tourist attraction, they'd have to catalogue a *lot* of junk.

"So." Olivia gave her a frank look as she handed her a glass of wine. "What was that envelope about, then?"

"Can you guess?" Althea managed a wry smile. "Ben or Tobias must have let something spill during your epic game."

"No, they were focused on battling it out over South America. Ben launched an assault from Egypt to Brazil." Olivia pursed her lips, her thoughtful gaze sweeping over her. "I can guess. I think. But I don't want to."

"Divorce papers," Althea confirmed heavily. "Honestly, it's a relief. I don't know how much you know or have guessed about Jasper…" She paused, fortifying herself with a sip of wine. "He was a cheater. Loads of women. And I'd finally had enough, but he filed first." She gave a what-can-you-do sort of shrug, even though she still felt like bursting into tears.

"Oh, Althea." Olivia laid a hand on her arm. "I had no idea…I mean about the other women." She bit her lip, looking almost guilty, which didn't make sense. "I'm sorry."

"Not your fault," Althea said as breezily as she could. "I came back here because of the massive row we had, and the fact that Jasper had swanned off to Switzerland with his latest, someone who was *supposed* to be my friend. Anyway." Another sip of wine, this one more of a gulp. "It *is* a relief. It's just getting the papers was more of a shock than I expected." And she still had the PDF of the prenup to face. Perhaps she'd leave that for tomorrow.

"That's understandable."

Olivia still looked vaguely guilty, and Althea narrowed her eyes. "Why are you weirdly looking like this is somehow your fault?"

"No…" Olivia began, but she sounded so alarmed that a

sudden, horrible thought stole upon Althea, making her stomach churn.

"You…you didn't…" she began faintly, and Olivia stared at her in confusion.

"Didn't…"

"You…you…" She could barely say the words. "You and Jasper…"

"What!" Olivia's squeal of outrage was enough to have Althea sinking back against the window seat's pillows, awash with relief.

"Sorry, sorry. Of course you didn't." She'd been mad even to consider it, but it felt sometimes as if life was throwing her every curveball it could. "It's just…for a second you looked *guilty*…"

"Of course I wouldn't do that," Olivia exclaimed, flushing. "Never in a million years. Really, Althea!" She shook her head, her indignation leaving her in a gust as she slumped back against the pillows, as well. "Although the truth is I can't really talk." Guilt flashed across her features once more. "I'm a bit of a hypocrite that way."

Althea tensed all over again. "What do you mean?"

Olivia sighed. "I don't want to get into it right now, but trust me, it has nothing at all to do with Jasper." She glanced over at Althea. "So how are you feeling about the divorce?"

"I don't know. It doesn't feel real, somehow." She thought of her life back in Surrey—the executive house, the designer clothes, the fake friends. She realised, with a sense of surprising liberation, that she wouldn't miss any of it. Not a single thing. And while that made her feel free, it also left her with a deep sorrow, far greater than that she felt about actually leaving Jasper—or, rather, Jasper leaving her. "I feel like a failure," she said after a moment. "Not because my marriage didn't work, but because it happened in the first place. I more or less wasted twenty years of my life."

"You didn't," Olivia protested. "Because you have great kids. And you're still young, Althea. You could meet someone else."

John Braithwaite's craggy face flashed through her mind, making her blush and look away. "Maybe," she half-mumbled. "But still…I should have left him years ago, after Tobias was born, maybe. Then I would have my kids and have been free when I was thirty. That would have been a much better scenario than this one."

"You weren't in a place to make that decision then," Olivia replied staunchly, "and you are now. Don't waste any more of your life on regrets."

"So you do think I wasted it!" Althea half-joked, and Olivia wrinkled her nose.

"No, no, I didn't mean…"

"I know you didn't." Althea sighed and sipped some more wine. "Tell me what's going on in your life." She needed a break from thinking about her own. "I feel like I've lost touch with you a bit recently." She shook her head ruefully. "Life has felt weirdly consuming, yet in an empty way." Burying her head in the sand took effort.

"There's not much to tell, really."

Althea thought her sister sounded evasive. "How's the job?"

"The same. Pretty slow in December, once the rush for poinsettias and Christmas trees has passed."

"You still like it?"

"Yes, I love gardening, but some of it is a bit dull. Repotting five hundred clematis can only give you so much of a thrill."

"You should do something with the garden here," Althea suggested, and Olivia looked nonplussed.

"This place could use half a dozen full-time gardeners, I'm sure, but I live a little too far away to pop over and weed a few flower beds."

"Yes, I know…" But Althea's mind was racing. What if Olivia came back to Casterglass too? It was a long shot, of course, because her sister undoubtedly had a life in York, unlike her own lack of one back in Surrey. And yet, if Olivia could manage the gardens…

"What are you thinking about?" Olivia asked with a laugh. "You look as if you're doing massive sums in your head."

"Just having thoughts." It was a bit too soon to ask Olivia to up sticks and move, but she felt as if she'd just had a tantalising glimpse of what could be. What if saving Casterglass could be a full family effort, with everyone coming together and getting involved? Her, Seph, Olivia, even Sam, once he traipsed back from New Zealand. Why not? *Why not?*

"Althea?" Olivia prompted, sounding concerned. "What kind of thoughts?"

"Oh…just thoughts," she hedged, reaching for the wine and topping up both their glasses. There would be time to tell Olivia her plan later, after she'd talked to her father. After she figured out whether any of this could actually work.

Yet for the first time since coming home real, proper hope fizzed through her, as if she was full of bubbles. *I want this to work*, she realised afresh. *As half-baked as it might seem, I really, really want this to work.*

Chapter Twelve

THE VILLAGE OF Casterglass was little more than a hamlet, a tiny square of green with a red pillar box opposite the place's only pub and B&B, which was next to a post office shop. A dozen houses, a Victorian schoolhouse and a parish church with a squat Norman tower completed the small scene. If you drove through it in a car, it was a blink-and-you'll-miss-it kind of place, but as Althea walked up to the green, with its Christmas tree towering in the centre, she realised she held this little village in almost as much affection as the castle itself, never mind that she didn't really know the residents.

Everyone had been amenable to the idea of coming to the village fete, save Poppy. When Althea had bearded the lioness in her den after her chat with Olivia last night, Poppy had been sulkily dismissive.

"Mum, please don't try to bond with me, okay?" she'd said after Althea had attempted to ask about what was happening with her friends, and then sympathised about not being in Surrey for Christmas. "It's so cringe."

"Okay," Althea had answered after a moment, doing her best not to feel stung. "Sorry." She'd tiptoed away, determined to try later, but by the next evening as they'd headed into Casterglass, that moment had not come. At least Poppy had agreed to come along, even if she was determined to sulk the whole way.

Still, Althea did her best to be cheerful, for her own sake as well as everyone else's. She had yet to open the envelope for Fotheringhay and Blackwood, or look at the PDF Edward's secretary had sent, but she would. She wasn't sticking her head in the sand anymore, just…waiting until she was ready. There was a difference.

In the meantime, she intended to enjoy the evening, and perhaps even meet a few new—or old—friends. There was a crowd of about thirty people on the village green, waiting for the lights to be turned on, and while Althea vaguely recognised some of them, she didn't see either of the people she knew best, John or Jenna.

She hadn't had any communication from Jenna since the sherry evening, which made sense because they hadn't exchanged mobile numbers, but Althea had been hoping Jenna would make an appearance tonight so they could stay in touch. And, she knew, she wanted to see John, although she didn't probe the why of it too deeply.

A little booth had been set up at the edge of the green, where a woman was doling out paper cups of mulled wine or hot chocolate. Someone else was setting up speakers to play

Christmas music, and the overall feel was homegrown and friendly, without any of the expensive polish a similar event in Surrey would have. Althea liked it all the more for its lack of pretension.

"Shall we get a drink?" she suggested to her crew. Everyone from the castle had come, with Seph, Olivia and her parents piling into her father's ancient Volvo estate while Althea had taken her children in the Rover—the car, she had realised as she'd driven into the village, was in Jasper's name. She wondered how long it would be before he reclaimed it.

They headed over to the booth, and Althea fished out a couple of pound coins to pay for their drinks while the woman doling them out gave her a squinty-eyed stare.

"Althea Penryn! I haven't seen you in donkey's years."

"It's Fowler now," Althea said before she could think better of it. It wouldn't be for much longer.

"Is it?" The woman sniffed, and it took her a moment to realise who it had to be... Mrs Telford, who had sold her snotty-nosed childhood self sweets, several decades ago. She was still running the post office shop and probably half a dozen other things besides. Althea almost wanted to laugh.

"How long are you staying this time?" Mrs Telford asked with a sniff, and once again Althea answered without thinking.

"Maybe forever."

"Wait—what?" Poppy's horrified double take had Althea cursing herself.

"I mean, who knows?" she backpedalled quickly. "It's Christmas." As if that made a difference. Poppy was still looking shaken and Mrs Telford decidedly sceptical as she handed out hot chocolate to everyone.

"Well, it would be nice to have children in the castle again," she said. "And a bit more life in the place—not that your parents don't do their bit, as best as they can." She gave Althea a surprisingly sympathetic smile. "Come down to the shop when you have a moment, love, and we'll have a good old natter."

Althea couldn't actually imagine having anything close to a natter with Mrs Telford, with her gimlet stare and broad bosom, but she appreciated the sentiment, even though she suspect it was born out of curiosity rather than compassion.

"Thank you," she said warmly. "I'll do that."

"What do you mean, forever?" Poppy demanded once they'd moved on from the booth and were standing on the fringes of the crowd, waiting for the lights to be turned on the tree.

"I didn't mean anything by it, Poppy. I was just..." She couldn't quite make herself say *joking*, because that felt like a lie. "Would it be so bad?" she asked a bit desperately, and Poppy gave her a look of utter disbelief.

"Are you serious?"

Usually by this time Althea would be scuttling backwards, tripping over herself to placate or sympathise. Now she reminded herself she was trying to grow a backbone, and so she gave Poppy a direct look.

"Yes, actually I am. I mean, I could be." All right, she needed a little help with said backbone. "It's worth thinking about, anyway."

"What?" The single syllable erupting out of Poppy's mouth was scathing.

Althea glanced around at her family, who were listening in various degree of curiosity—Ben avid, Olivia a little less so, Tobias focused on his hot chocolate and her parents completely out to lunch. She sighed.

"Poppy—"

"Are you kidding me? This place is the back of—"

"Poppy."

"I think it would be kind of cool." The words, so quietly spoken by her youngest son who clearly had been listening more than she realised, had the surprising effect of silencing both Althea and Poppy.

"You...do?" Althea said after a moment while Tobias wiped the whipped cream from his upper lip.

"Yeah. It's cool here. I mean, how often do you get to live in a castle?"

"Too often," Poppy snapped, but she looked a little shaken by her brother's admission. She turned back to Althea. "You don't mean it, do you, Mum? Not really?"

"I..." Why on earth had she thought it was a good idea to broach this serious subject here, in the freezing cold, in public? Clearly her brain had been disengaged in that moment. There was being proactive, and then there was just being stupid. "I don't know," she admitted. "I suppose I feel like this could be a good time to…reconsider…our priorities."

This earned her a snort of disgust, which Althea could hardly fault. It had sounded pretty lame to her, too.

"I cannot believe this," Poppy declared, furious and tearful, as she whirled away. Althea decided to give her some time to cool off before she attempted to make amends.

"Are you serious?" Olivia asked in a low voice when Poppy had stomped off.

Althea shrugged. "Like I said, I don't know."

"For a second there, it sounded as if you did."

"Well…I'm thinking about it. I don't really want to go back to Surrey."

"You don't?"

Althea shook her head. "There's nothing for me there."

"There's nothing for me in York," Olivia returned, and Althea couldn't tell if she was joking or not.

"What do you mean?"

Olivia shrugged. "I've made some bad decisions. I don't really feel like facing them."

"I'm not sure that's a reason to stay away," Althea said as gently as she could. "What kind of bad decisions, Liv?"

"I can't talk about it now." She glanced meaningfully at the children surrounding them; Tobias had finished his hot chocolate and was clearly still listening.

"Okay, but I'm going to hold you to it, just like you held me to it last night."

Olivia gave her a rather unhappy smile in return, and Althea vowed to get to the bottom of what was bothering her sister—as well as her daughter. Poppy had been in a bad mood ever since yesterday afternoon, and she still didn't know why. She needed to find out, never mind the argument they'd just had.

"Hello there," a familiar voice rumbled near her ear, making her jump a little.

She turned around, her stomach leaping at the sight of John standing there, dressed for the season in a winter parka and bobble hat, a dark-haired, slender young woman standing next to him.

"Oh, hello," she answered, trying to sound natural and light and feeling she'd failed. She glanced at Olivia and saw that her sister had already raised her eyebrows in obvious speculation.

"This is Alice," John said, touching his daughter's arm. She gave Althea a fleeting, uncertain smile and murmured hello. "I thought perhaps she could show Poppy around a bit."

"Oh. Er." Althea hoped her daughter wasn't in so much of a strop that she would be rude to someone trying to be nice, but she knew she couldn't guarantee it. "That's a lovely idea. Let me go get her." She gave Alice an encouraging smile before she hurried over to where, a dozen feet away, Poppy was disconsolately flicking through her phone.

"Poppy, our neighbour's daughter here is your age and she'd like to show you around—"

"Oh, and now I'm six?" Poppy cut her off with some serious snark and an eye-roll. "You have to organise my play dates?"

"Poppy, please. She's right over there. She's nice."

"Fine." With a long-suffering sigh Poppy shoved her phone into her pocket and slouched towards John and Alice, fluttering her fingers at them in a way that looked almost mocking but Althea hoped wasn't. She felt embarrassed both for Poppy's sake and her own. Right now her daughter was not exactly being a credit to her, but surely things could only improve.

"Sorry, was that too obviously awkward?" John asked once Poppy and Alice had gone off to inspect a booth that was selling homemade Christmas ornaments, and Olivia was off chatting with their mother. They were, in the middle of a crowd, more or less alone. "Alice told me it would be, but as usual I didn't listen."

"I'm afraid Poppy's in a bit of a bad mood. Something to do with her friends at home, I think. Trust me, it's no reflection on Alice."

"Well, hopefully it won't be too excruciating for the pair of them." He smiled in the way Althea liked, with his eyes crinkling at the corners. "Tell me, how did you end up with the name Althea, anyway?"

"Oh…" She laughed, and then foolishly blushed. "Well, my mother picked it out. It's from Greek mythology, although the Althea of old is not all that admirable. She was the daughter of King Thestius and she was known to be ruthless, causing the death of her own son." She tried to give a what-can-you-do kind of laugh while John rocked back on his heels.

"Wow."

"I know. I don't think my mum was thinking about that when she named me. She said she thought it sounded elegant."

"Well, you are that," John told her, seeming to mean it, so Althea was at a loss for words.

"Oh…but I'm not really," she said, and he raised his eyebrows.

"Are you kidding?" He laughed, sounding genuinely in-credulous. "You look like you stepped out of a spread in *Country Life*."

Somehow this did not *quite* seem like a compliment. "That's not who I am," she insisted, because she suddenly had a terrible feeling that John thought she belonged in Jasper's world, the moneyed world of arrogant privilege and careless ease that she'd always, *always* felt on the fringes of. She'd wanted to be part of it, it was true, back in boarding school when she'd never been one of the cool girls talking about their ponies or skiing trips to Switzerland, and then in university, when she'd drifted towards the same kind of group because she didn't know any others.

But twenty years on, twenty years of living as that kind of hopeless hanger-on, and she knew she didn't want to anymore. And she didn't want John Braithwaite to think she did.

"I'm really not like that," she said quietly, and John frowned.

"It wasn't an insult."

"I know." Yet it felt like it had been, a little bit, even if he hadn't meant it to be. *You're not like me*, he'd been saying. *You never will be.*

Or was she just being ridiculously oversensitive, because she felt so fragile?

"Look, Althea," her mother called, making Althea turn away from John, which was something of a relief. "The lights!" Her mother looked as delighted as a child as the tree flickered and then glowed with multicoloured lights. Even Althea, with the jumble of confused feelings making her feel so mixed up, could not keep from giving the prerequisite 'Aah.'

"Hey, Seph," John said, and she turned back to him as she watched him greet her sister, who actually smiled and waved.

"You two know each other?" she said dumbly, as they both gave her well-duh looks. Of course, Seph lived here. She knew the locals far better than Althea did.

"Seph works for me," John explained.

"Wait—what? Why didn't you tell me?"

John, understandably, looked a bit surprised by this question. "Tell you? It never came up. And...I suppose I thought you already knew."

Of course she *should* have known, if she knew anything about her sister. Althea didn't reply as she shoved her hands in her pockets. She was starting to feel seriously out of sorts, and she knew it was her own fault.

She hadn't made enough effort to get to know Persephone, or Casterglass, or anyone or anything here. She wanted to change that, and coming here tonight had been a part of that, but she hadn't realised how out of her depth she might feel, how on the fringes, as she always did. She didn't like the feeling, but it was up to her to change it. No more being an ostrich, although Tobias had informed her recently that ostriches didn't actually bury their heads in the sand; that was just a myth. Well, now neither would she.

Yet as Seph and John exchanged pleasantries, Althea realised, with a lurch of uncomfortable self-awareness, that part of her had been expecting to rock up to the village like the Lady of Casterglass and have everyone pleased and even awed to see her. Good grief, what was *wrong* with her, that she could have those stupid expectations without even realising it?

Then she thought about how yesterday John had lectured her about her responsibility to the village, and she wondered if they both had hang-ups about their age-old roles. She wasn't the lady of the manor, and he wasn't the tenant farmer or peasant or whatever. Of course not.

He was different, just as she was, and maybe they both needed to make an effort.

"I didn't realise it was John you worked for, Seph," she told her sister, who gave her the same flat look she always did, as if Althea was wasting her time. "What do you do exactly?"

"Stuff."

Wow, thanks, Seph, that's really helpful. Althea kept her smile in place. She was trying, at least. "What kind of stuff?"

A shrug was all the answer she got before Seph sloped off. Althea couldn't keep from letting out a growling sound of frustration.

"She's a quiet one," John said after a moment and Althea tried to sound joking as she replied, "That's one thing I do know about my sister."

"I suppose she's a lot younger than you."

"Nineteen years younger. I was already at university when she was born." John didn't reply and she confessed in a rush, "I don't really know her, actually." She winced. That sounded worse out loud than in her head.

"I suppose if you stay at Casterglass, you could remedy that."

"Yes, I hope so. Right now it all feels a bit pie in the sky, to be honest."

If she'd been hoping for the kind of compassion she'd

received yesterday, she didn't get it. "Well, the only way to change that is to act," John told her robustly. "It's not going to happen by itself, you know."

"I know," Althea returned with a shamefaced smile. She could tell from the glint in his hazel eyes that he'd recognised her obvious bid for sympathy and was calling her on it. Over John's shoulder she caught sight of Jenna chatting with another woman, and her heart lifted. "Oh, there's Jenna. I was hoping I'd run into her."

"Jenna? You know Jenna Bancroft?" John sounded surprised.

"Yes, we were friends in primary, and we've recently got back in touch."

"You have?"

Why did he have to sound so disbelieving? "You must have gone to the school as well," she realised out loud.

"Before your time, I'm sure. I'm forty-three."

"Not that much before." But since she'd only joined in Year Six, they wouldn't have crossed paths. But the conversation made her realise something she should have before, that they could have—would have, even—known each other as children. Seen each other in the village, at least, or at those Christmas parties she barely remembered. Why couldn't she place him? Admittedly it had been a long time ago, but she wished she had more history behind her. More memories.

"I think I'll go say hello," she said, and murmuring her farewells, she headed over to Jenna.

"Althea!" Jenna looked surprised and a bit discomfited to see her, which Althea supposed she should have expected, considering how their conversation had been curtailed the other night. "Sorry I ran off at the party," Jenna told her. "I had a massive headache."

"It's all right. I had a bit of a wobbly myself. It's good to see you again." Althea gave her a megawatt smile, determined to start with her anti-ostrich campaign. "I thought maybe we could go for a coffee sometime?"

"Oh…uh. Yeah. Sure." Jenna smiled back, but only after a second, making Althea feel a bit uneasy. Were all her relationships at Casterglass going to be awkward? Hopefully only at first.

"So where are your kids?" she asked as she glanced around at the people milling on the village green. "You have two, right?"

"Yes, two boys, Jamie and Will. They're twelve and fourteen, over there." She gestured towards a stand of oaks where some teens were clustered. Althea couldn't make out their faces.

"Tobias is twelve," she said. "Perhaps they could meet up."

"Oh. Right. Yeah, maybe."

Jenna was definitely sounding lukewarm. Althea told herself not to take it too personally. It had been a long time, after all. She glanced around the green and saw Poppy and Alice laughing together, a sight that brought her a sense of relief mixed with hope.

See, this could work. It would just take a bit of time…and effort.

"I should go check on them, actually," Jenna murmured, starting to move away, and Althea reached for her phone.

"Let me get your number first."

"Oh…right."

A few seconds later she had her number, and Jenna had gone. All right, that had been a bit strange, but Althea decided not to be put off by Jenna's seeming reticence. She needed to make friends. She was going to be proactive.

"They seem to be getting along," John remarked as Althea walked back to where he, Tobias, and Ben were all standing by the hot chocolate booth. He nodded towards Poppy and Alice, who were still chatting.

"Yes, that's amazing," Althea answered with heartfelt relief. "I think Poppy could really use a friend. A proper one."

"Listen…" John looked uncharacteristically uncertain as he scratched his jaw and didn't quite meet her gaze. "Why don't you come round for a meal before Christmas, if you have time? You and your three? Alice can tell Poppy and Tobias about school, if you really are serious about staying, and…well, it could be nice."

Was John Braithwaite actually *blushing* a little? The possibility had Althea's stomach doing somersaults. "That would be lovely," she said, keeping her tone firm. Proactive. See, she told herself, this was all going to work wonderfully.

Chapter Thirteen

THE KITCHEN WAS full of the smell of cinnamon and sugar as Althea put the last tray of shortbread in. She was feeling remarkably festive and upbeat, two days after the village fete. She'd cleaned the kitchen, organising all the papers and books that had been piled everywhere, and had spent the morning with sacks of flour and sugar and half a dozen mixing bowls as she tried to do all her Christmas baking in one go.

Poppy and Tobias had helped her for a bit; Poppy seemed to have snapped out of her dark mood at least a little. Ben had gone out with Seph; her parents were, as usual, occupied in their separate pursuits; and Olivia had disappeared after her morning coffee. But with several roaring fires going, the castle didn't feel quite so freezing and Althea was almost starting to imagine it feeling like home again.

Tomorrow night they were going over to John's for supper, and the day after that was Christmas Eve. 'Ding Dong Merrily On High' was blasting out of her iPhone speakers, and really, everything was starting to feel quite Christmassy.

It helped that she'd done her best not even to think about the divorce papers or the prenup. She'd save those for after Christmas. She simply wanted to enjoy this time with her family, the possibility that was unfurling inside her.

"Hey, Mum."

She glanced up to see Ben strolling into the kitchen, snatching a freshly baked shortbread from the cooling rack before Althea could so much as protest. He paused with it halfway to his lips.

"Do you mind?"

"No, of course I don't," she told him with affection. He looked impish and cheerful, and her heart expanded with love. "I thought you were out with Seph?"

"Yeah, but she had some stuff to do."

"Oh." Althea turned to the sink to start the washing up. "You seem to be getting along, though," she remarked, hoping she sounded casual enough.

"Yeah, Seph's cool."

"She seems very cool to me," Althea said on a laugh. "I'm a little intimidated by her, to tell you the truth."

"It's the dreads," Ben agreed as he snuck another shortbread. "She got them to look tough."

"She did?"

"Yeah."

Her son knew more about her sister than she did. "Why did she want to look tough?"

He shrugged. "Just, you know, because."

"Hmm." Althea starting scrubbing out a bowl. "I wish I knew her better. I never really had the opportunity." Or perhaps she simply hadn't taken enough of one.

"Seph is pretty quiet."

"Yes, I've gathered that."

"I think she's shy."

"Shy?" Somehow this had not occurred to Althea. Her sister always seemed so *sullen*. Her silence had felt like a choice, an aggression, but what if it wasn't? "You really think so?" she asked Ben, and he shrugged.

"Yeah, I mean she never went to school until Sixth Form, and she said she hated it. And you and Aunt Olivia and Sam were all practically grown up by the time she was born. Sam left for uni when she was only about seven."

"That's true." She paused, bracing her forearms on the edge of the sink as she gazed out at the weed-filled walled garden. "She told you all this?"

Another shrug. "Pretty much."

She really did need to make more of an effort, Althea decided. In all sorts of ways.

"Mum...is it true you're thinking about staying here? Not going back to Cobham?"

The hesitation in Ben's voice had Althea turning to face him fully. "I'm thinking about it."

"What would you do here? I mean..."

"I'm thinking of trying to make the castle into a going concern. Not a tourist attraction, not exactly, anyway, but something like it." She met his gaze head-on, wondering what he thought about that. She valued his opinion as much as anyone's, if not more so. Ben had always had a good head on his shoulders.

"That's so cool." His face brightened. "I think it's a great idea."

"You do?"

"Definitely."

"It might come to nothing," she warned him. "It will take a lot of work, and, well, money."

"I know, but you're not afraid of work, Mum, and as for money…" He shrugged. "There's got to be a way to get some, surely? I mean, this place is chock full of antique stuff. I bet some of it is worth a bomb."

"I never even thought of that," Althea said slowly. She didn't know how her parents would feel about selling some of their debatably priceless treasures, but it was definitely an idea worth considering.

"We should ask *Antiques Roadshow* to come and do a special on the castle," Ben only half-joked. "Who knows what they'd find?"

"How would you feel about me not returning to Cobham?" Althea asked, bracing herself. Ben was easy-going enough, but she knew she was asking her children to give up a lot. "Dad will still be there, I think…"

Ben shrugged. "I don't much care."

"Ben, he is your father," Althea told him gently. "I want

you to have a relationship with him—"

"Why?"

The question took her by surprise. "Well, because, like I said, he's your father. Your dad."

"He's also an arse," Ben said bluntly. "I know he's been messing around for years."

"You do?" Had all her children suspected? Here she'd been, thinking she was keeping up a good front for their sakes, and everyone, absolutely *everyone*, had known what was going on.

"It was obvious, Mum. Besides…" He hesitated, and Althea steeled herself.

"What is it? Tell me?"

Ben looked away, unable to meet her eye. "Dad used to…joke about it with me."

"What?" She stared at him in horror as she clutched the edge of the table for support, her stomach starting to churn.

"Only in the last couple of years, but he acted like we were in some stupid boys' club together. It was gross."

"I can't believe that." She spoke numbly, her mind reeling. It seemed there were no end of surprises, no disgusting depth her husband hadn't been able to descend to. "I can't believe he *joked*…"

"Yeah, it started after my sixteenth birthday. Like it was some initiation or something. I mean, what the actual…? Sorry, Mum, but I don't want a relationship with him."

With a shaky hand Althea pulled out a chair and sank

into it. Now that she looked back, she recalled Ben going a bit cool on Jasper a few years ago…right around the time he'd cut up that credit card, most likely. She'd just assumed it was normal teenager stuff. Now she knew.

"I'm sorry, Ben. That must have been awful."

"*You* don't need to apologise," he exclaimed. "I'm just letting you know why I'm not much interested in being around Dad."

Althea dropped her head into her hands and closed her eyes. She felt a deep sadness, deeper even than when Jasper had said he was skipping Christmas, or when she'd been sent the divorce papers, or at any point, really, when she'd realised her marriage was over.

"Mum…?" Ben asked quietly as he sat down beside her and put one hand on her shoulder. "Are you okay?"

"Yes." She took a deep, shuddery breath. "It's just…I stayed with your father for so long because I thought it was best for everyone. The stable home, the two-parent family. It wasn't just for your sakes," she continued quickly. "I did it for mine, as well, because I was scared of facing the world on my own. But I never thought that staying with him could be worse for you all than leaving. Even after coming here, I thought this was the lesser option for you and Poppy and Tobias."

"But now you know it isn't." Ben's voice was gentle. "We're much better off here, Mum. I mean, we do live in a castle."

She let out a wobbly laugh as she peeked at him between her fingers. "A broken-down castle with a leaky roof."

"Still."

"Yes. Still." She dropped her hands from her face. "That is something."

"Maybe I should have told you I knew earlier on. I just didn't want to hurt you."

"It doesn't matter, Ben." Althea took another steadying breath as she rose from the table to take the shortbread out of the oven. "I don't mind that you told me. Please don't feel guilty about that. And I don't want to waste any more time looking back over the past and wondering what if. We're at Casterglass, and we're going to stay here." She let the words reverberate through her, meaning them. "We need to look to the future now. All of us."

A LITTLE WHILE later, still feeling a bit battered by the knowledge Ben had given her, but determined to remain upbeat, Althea took a mug of coffee and a couple of shortbread on a plate up to her mother, who was working in her study.

For as long as Althea could remember, her mother had used the observatory as her personal office. Built on the top floor of the Victorian addition by the ninth baron of Casterglass, it was a funny, added-on room accessed from a single set of narrow stairs, and had gabled windows of nearly floor-to-ceiling glass that gave it an amazing airiness. Apparently the ninth baron had been something of a stargazer. His telescope was still positioned in the window, now draped with a couple of gauzy scarves.

"Darling!" Her mother looked up from her pad of foolscap—her mother, like her father, was absurdly old-fashioned—with a delighted smile. "Is that coffee for me? You're an *angel*."

"I thought you'd been working rather hard," Althea said as she handed her the mug and plate.

Her mother grimaced in apology. "I'm being a rather terrible hostess, aren't I? I should be down with you all, baking cookies and the like."

Althea could not recall a single instance of her mother baking cookies. "Don't worry, I've got that covered," she said.

"These are *marvellous*," her mother said as she bit into one of the shortbread. "Really, Althea, you have a gift."

"How's the Catullus going?"

"Catullus?" Her mother looked rather predictably blank. "Oh, I finished that yesterday. No, it's Ovid now, I'm afraid, and how Catullus influenced him. Terribly interesting, of course."

"I'm sure," Althea murmured with a smile.

Her mother put down her mug. "How are you, darling?" she asked. "Really?"

"Well, I'm getting a divorce," Althea answered with a

shrug and a smile.

"Yes, I thought you were. Condolences, of course, but I must confess I really rather thought he was a bit of an arse."

A surprised laughed bubbled up out of her. "That's what Ben said. That's what *everyone* has said. How did everyone know, Mummy, except for me?"

"Well, you know, we all have a bit of distance, haven't we? And of course the value of hindsight. I can't say I thought he was such when I first met him." Her mother tapped her chin thoughtfully. "As I recall, he was quite charming, in a blustery, overblown sort of way. A bit of a showy Uriah Heep. He did like to spend money, didn't he?"

"Yes," Althea recalled on a sigh. "He did."

"I suppose that's what drew you to him, at first. When you haven't had much of it, money can look like love."

"Yes, that was part of it, I think." Her mother's astuteness astonished her. How could a woman who spent most of her life studying ancient Greek poetry and had not been able to remember her children's birthdates when asked at the doctor's have such a sudden, sensitive perception?

"I'm sorry about that," her mother said as she took a sip of her coffee, her face drawn into uncharacteristically sorrowful lines. "Perhaps you were too sheltered growing up. Or perhaps I should have been the sort of mother who sits you down and tells you these things, but I wasn't. I lost my own mother when I was just a baby. I don't suppose I ever really knew how to do it properly, the way you have with your three. They're a credit to you, Althea."

"Oh, well, thank you…" Althea mumbled, blushing. She thought of how Tobias spent too much time on screens, and Poppy's spoiled stroppiness, both things she could control better if she just tried harder. Still, they were good kids, at heart. She did believe that. And she was going to be a better, more proactive mum.

"I never really thought about you losing your own mum," she told her mother. "That must have been very hard."

"I didn't know anything else. And your grandfather, bless him, was not exactly father material." She let out a fond laugh that was tinged with sorrow. "He was even more absent-minded than I am. He completely forgot about me sometimes." Her mother sounded affectionate rather than bitter. "I suppose I should have tried to do better myself, and in all honesty I think I did, if only a little. But I loved the wild freedom of my own childhood, most of the time, anyway. I wanted to give you four something of the same." She glanced at Althea, a surprisingly vulnerability visible in her face. "Do you think I was wrong?"

Althea swallowed hard. "Not wrong," she said after a moment as she tried to untangle her own complicated feelings. She wanted to be honest, but she didn't want to hurt her mother. And right now, remembering her childhood, she realised how fortunate she'd been. She'd had some amazing experiences, even if she'd longed for the more normal ones. "Sometimes it was hard," she said finally, "but everything is hard, at one time or another. I don't regret it." Not all of it, anyway.

"You're lovely to say so, darling. I do think I should have been better about things like dentist appointments and birthday parties."

"Oh, I don't know." In that moment Althea didn't think she'd change anything about her scatty, strange, lovable mother. She wished she'd thought more about how her mother's upbringing would have affected her, how perhaps she was trying her best, just as she was, and sometimes best didn't look all that great, but that's still what it was.

"How would you feel if we all stayed at Casterglass, Mum?" she blurted. "For good?"

Her mother reached out one slender, beringed hand to grasp Althea's. "Oh, darling, I'd love it. Of course I would."

"I want to turn Casterglass into something of a tourist attraction. Did Daddy mention it to you?" *She* had, but she doubted her mother remembered that conversation in the kitchen.

"Oh, he might have done, darling, but you know what I'm like."

Yes, she did. Althea squeezed her mother's bony fingers. "I just hope I can do it."

"Well, it's not all up to you, surely. And in any case, you've always been so fearless, Althea—"

"Fearless?" Althea let out a hollow laugh. "Me?"

"Remember when you were Hector in *The Iliad*?" Her mother's eyes sparkled as Althea recalled performing a version of the epic scripted by her mother when she was fourteen or so. They'd all been cast in it and it had lasted hours. "You were magnificent! Striding out from the gates of Troy—in the ballroom, do you remember—to fight Achilles. 'And he fell on the fight like some fierce tempest that swoops upon the sea,'" her mother quoted. When she started on *The Iliad*, she could quote for hours. "That was you, darling. Absolutely majestic."

"It was acting," Althea protested with a laugh.

"Which shows you have it in you," her mother returned with serene logic. "Why does it matter whether it is acting or not?"

"Well…"

"And in any case, it wasn't *just* acting. You were always so capable, Althea. Organising everyone. Do you remember you taught Sam his GCSE maths? I was hopeless, I'm afraid, but he got a B, thanks to you."

Yes, she did remember that. Their homeschooled education had been patchy indeed.

Her mother squeezed her hand before turning back to her tea. "All I'm saying, darling, is don't sell yourself short just because your husband did. You're perfectly capable of saving Casterglass on your own, but in any case you don't have to. You've got your family, darling, remember." She gave Althea a fleeting smile that put a lump in her throat before turning back to her manuscript, utterly absorbed within seconds. Still feeling emotional, Althea tiptoed out of the room.

She decided it was as good as ever a moment to find Poppy and try to get to the bottom of whatever was bothering her daughter. Taking a deep breath and whispering a wordless prayer, Althea tapped on her daughter's bedroom door before pushing it open.

"Pops?"

Poppy was lying on her bed, glaring at her phone, but she flung it away from her as Althea came into the room.

"What?"

Althea perched on the edge of her bed as Poppy scowled at the ceiling. "I just wanted to check in," she said gently. "It seems as if something has been upsetting you these last few days…"

"*Everything* is upsetting me," Poppy retorted as she rolled onto her side so her back was to Althea. "*Obviously.* I mean, what are we actually doing here?"

Althea decided not to answer that question just yet. "What about your friends?" she asked. "Did something happen, Poppy? Tobias said you saw something on your phone and you let out some sort of gasp—"

"Oh, so what, he's spying on me?"

"No, not at all." She paused, feeling as if she were wading through treacherous quicksand, every step a danger. "I just want to help, Pops. If something's happened…"

"Nothing's *happened.*"

Just then the screen of Poppy's phone lit up with a new message and Althea's gaze moved automatically to where she'd flung it next to her on the bed. Even from where she was sitting she could see the all-caps message: NO ONE CARES, LOSER.

She let out a soft gasp as Poppy snatched the phone, angling the screen away from her even though it was too late.

"Poppy..." Althea said softly, and her daughter's face crumpled. The question she'd been about to ask died on her lips as she wordlessly held her arms out to Poppy, and after only a second's hesitation, her daughter flung herself into them.

Chapter Fourteen

APPLEBY FARM'S DRIVE was strung with multicoloured Christmas lights, the house lit up like a welcoming beacon, as Althea bumped her Land Rover up the drive, her children looking out the window in varying degrees of curiosity. They'd all been more or less amenable to the idea of coming to supper at the Braithwaites', something that had filled Althea with hope. Life could work out here. They could make friends, find a way. It was already starting to happen.

She glanced in the rear-view mirror at Poppy, who had her arms wrapped around herself as she stared out the window with a bleakness that tore at Althea's heart.

Last night they'd had a painful, humbling heart-to-heart that had made Althea feel both regret and relief in equal measure. Now she knew what had been troubling her daughter, but it caused her so much pain, because she knew—from her own hard experience—just how Poppy felt.

Poppy had submitted to Althea's hug for only a few seconds before she'd pulled away, wiping her streaming eyes, her shoulders hunched.

"Who sent you that message, Poppy?" Althea had asked gently. Her daughter hadn't wanted to answer, merely shaking her head as she turned even farther away from Althea. "Whoever they are…" she'd said quietly, "they're not really your friend."

"Obviously," Poppy had replied in an attempt to sound scathing, but her voice had been too clogged with tears for it to work.

Althea had stared helplessly at her daughter, wishing she knew the right words to say. Every attempt at bonding seemed to alienate her, which is why, over the years, she'd let so much slide, or tried to show her love in other ways—like buying ridiculously expensive Prada boots. But her mother had been right, Althea had realised then. Money wasn't love. At twenty-one she'd confused the two, and she'd done the same as a mother without fully realising that was what she'd been doing.

No, love was a lot harder than buying something from a shop. Love was tough and enduring; it held on even when it would be so, so much easier to let yourself be shaken off and walk away.

Love stayed. Love hurt. Love won.

"Poppy," Althea had said slowly, feeling her way through the words, "I've had friends like that before. When I was in school, and even after, when we moved to Cobham. When I was growing up I wanted to be like everybody else. It was what I wanted more than anything else in the world. Just to be…*normal*. You've seen the castle. You know what it's like."

"But living in a castle is cool," Poppy had said with a sniff, and Althea had to smile. Her daughter thought it was cool now? Well, that was good news.

"Yes, but I didn't see it that way back then. I just felt different all the time, and I wanted to fit in. And so I tried, hanging on to the edges of the cool crowd even though I wasn't really like them. I accepted whatever scraps came my way—and trust me, they were scraps—because it seemed better than nothing."

Althea had lapsed into silence then as awareness trickled through her. Why, for so long, had she been willing to accept so little? First from her friends at school, and then from Jasper. Why had she set her sights so *low*?

The easy option would be to blame her parents, their scattiness and seeming neglect, but Althea knew it wasn't that simple. Yes, she'd struggled sometimes with the way she grew up, but she'd never truly doubted that her parents loved her.

Her lack of self-confidence was more inbuilt and fundamental than that, and as she'd gazed at Poppy's tear-streaked face she became determined to root it out of both of them.

"So what happened?" Poppy had asked after a moment, her chin tucked low so Althea couldn't see her face. "With your friends?"

"I realised they were no friends at all. After we finished

Upper Sixth, they all planned a holiday to Greece—you know, the usual kind of thing, parties on the beach and all that." The memory of it caused an ache of regret, not for missing it out, but for wanting to go in the first place. "They didn't invite me," Althea had continued quietly. "They didn't even ask. But what was worse, they'd talk about it while I was there, without even a shred of apology. I realised it hadn't even *occurred* to them to invite me. They didn't see me as their friend at all, the way I'd been so desperate to see them, all along."

Poppy had winced. "Ouch."

"I know, right?" Althea had given a wry laugh. "It hurt unbearably at the time, but looking back I wish I hadn't tried so hard to be friends with them. The cool girls. There were plenty of other people I could have been friends with, girls who just wanted to be nice. I wish I hadn't wasted so much time trying to fit in, and instead just been myself."

Poppy had been silent for a long moment. After a while, she'd tucked a strand of hair behind her ear and given a sniff. "Alice is nice," she'd said, and Althea decided to leave it at that for now.

"Yes, she is, and we're going to dinner at the Braithwaites' tomorrow night, so hopefully that will be fun." She'd leaned over and kissed Poppy's forehead; to her daughter's credit she hadn't tried to resist. "I love you, Pops."

Poppy had given her a fleeting smile. "Thanks, Mum."

Now, as Althea pulled the car up to the farmhouse, she

prayed Poppy would have a good time tonight. Her daughter needed a friend, the kind she could trust. She still hadn't got to the bottom of that awful message on her phone, or what exactly had happened, but she would. And in the meantime she hoped Poppy could take some small positive steps here.

"Welcome, welcome," John said as he opened the door and they trooped into the kitchen, the dogs sniffing around them excitedly. Alice hung back a little, offering them a shy smile.

"You've done some decorating," Althea remarked. The kitchen smelled of cinnamon and in the sitting room there was a Christmas tree in the corner, weighed down by a plethora of homemade ornaments.

"Alice was on the job," John replied. "I'm afraid I let things slide sometimes, but she keeps me on the straight and narrow."

He fetched drinks for everybody while they milled around, the children all looking at each other slightly askance, as teenagers tended to when forced into socialisation. Long gone were the days where she could send them off with a cheery "Go and play" and they'd be constructing a complicated den in the sitting room within seconds.

John, however, did not seem to have that problem. "Scat, you lot," he told them amiably as he waved his hand as if shooing away a fly. "Alice, go show the kids the TV room. You can play the Wii or Monopoly."

"You have a Wii?" Tobias said somewhat incredulously.

"Yes, circa 2004. We're old-school. But you can play Mario Kart on it, and that's all that matters."

Dutifully the children trooped out, and Althea met John's laughing eyes with a smile of her own. "That was blunt."

"It's the only way. Either that or beating them off with a stick. Wine?"

"Thank you."

As he opened a bottle of red, she felt a surprising frisson of pleasure—and excitement. This almost, but definitely not quite, felt like a…a *date*. Which, was, of course, ridiculous. There was no way this was a date. There were four children in the other room loudly debating the merits of Funky Kong versus King Boo, and in any case, she was still married. It was far too soon to be thinking romantically about anyone.

She knew that, and yet as John handed her a glass of wine, his fingers brushing hers, she felt a shiver go through her and had to work hard not to let her reaction show in either her face or her body.

"So, have you looked over the prenup yet?" he asked.

Wow, way to kill the mood, she thought as he settled in a kitchen chair and Althea took one opposite.

"No, not yet."

"Althea." She couldn't help but like the way he said her name, without stumbling over it, without it being weird. Like he actually *knew* her.

Which, of course, he didn't, not really.

"I thought you weren't burying your head in the sand anymore. You want to take control of your life. And you need to know what you're dealing with."

Had she said all that to him? Or had he just discerned it? Perhaps he did know her, after all.

"You're right," she said after a moment. "I wanted to wait till after Christmas, but…" That had really just been an excuse.

"No time like the present," John said briskly, holding out his hand.

Althea stared at him blankly. "Wait…what?"

"Give me your phone. It was emailed, right? I'll forward it to my email and then print it out." For a second his no-nonsense manner faltered and he gave her an uncertain and abashed look. "Unless I'm being completely nosy and inappropriate and then you can just tell me to bugger off."

She let out a surprised laugh. "I'm not going to do that. You're good for me, John." Whoops, that sounded a bit too intimate. Althea blushed as she fumbled for her phone and unlocked it with a swipe of her finger. Another few swipes and she had the email with its PDF attachment on the screen. "Here you go."

A few minutes later John had forward the email and printed out the prenup. Althea listened to it rattle out of what sounded like a very old printer in the nook adjacent to the kitchen that served as John's study, and then he had it in his hands and was giving it over.

She still didn't want to look.

"Come on, Althea." John's voice was low, warm. "You can do this." He took the seat next to her, his thigh nearly brushing hers, as she gazed unseeingly down at the sheaf of papers.

"Yes." She nodded rather mechanically. "I can." And then she refocused so she could actually read the words on the page.

It was, at first glance, a lot of legalese gobbledygook, at least to Althea's untrained eyes. *All property which belongs independently at the date of the agreement to each of the parties…*

She scanned down, her heart bumping in her chest, while John sat next to her, solid and steady.

All assets…all investments…all possessions…

She swallowed hard.

"Well?" John asked gently after a few minutes had passed, and she'd managed to get to the end of the wretched document.

"Well, it's just as I'd thought." Her voice came out high and bright. False. "I get nothing."

John frowned, his eyebrows drawing together. "Nothing?"

"The children will be provided for, at least. There is provision for 'any issue'."

"Well, of course the children will be provided for," John said, suddenly sounding angry. "As their biological father, he *has* to provide for them. But nothing for you?"

"Not a single bean," Althea joked. Why she was trying to make light of this, she had no idea. She felt as if she could break apart. "I'm not surprised," she told him as she put the papers on the table and reached for her wine. She needed the fortification. "It's what I expected." But stupidly, like so much else, it still hurt.

"May I?" John asked as he reached for the papers, and she nodded. "How old were you when you signed this?"

"Twenty-one."

"Did you have legal representation?"

She shrugged and tossed back more wine. "Just Jasper's solicitor, Edward Fotheringhay's father, as it happened. And it was very much a case of like father, like son."

"Hmm." John was riffling through the papers. "There could be grounds to contest it."

"There could?" The thought exhausted her as much as it gave her hope. A battle with Jasper would be a dreadful thing indeed.

"Would you mind if I asked a solicitor friend of mine? She works in family law in Broughton-in-Furness. I know it's not some flashy London firm…"

"No, it's fine. I don't mind. But…I'm not sure I'm emotionally in a place where I want a big fight."

"You might not need to have one. It's just good to know what the possibilities are." He stood up to put the papers on his desk in the nook. "But enough of that. I didn't ask you over to talk about your prenup."

"Really?" She raised her eyebrows, smiling. "Could have fooled me."

"Sorry. Business is over. Now it's Christmas." He smiled back at her, his eyes crinkling, and Althea's heart did a silly little flip.

"Technically, Christmas isn't for two more days."

"The Christmas season is well on its way, though. More wine?"

Had she already finished her glass? "I shouldn't. I'm driving."

"Ben drives, doesn't he?"

"Yes…"

"Then you're sorted." He filled her glass and Althea watched the ruby-red liquid glint in the lamplight. She was already halfway to feeling rather tiddly.

"Do you know," she said as she took another sip, "the first time I saw you, I thought I could like you."

"Oh?"

"But then I was horrid and so were you and I felt like I'd read you wrong. I've read a lot of people wrong, over the years."

"You didn't read me wrong." His voice had roughened, a throb of sincerity making Althea feel that little flip again.

"So I can like you?" All right, she was more than halfway to tiddly. Three-quarters, at least. Why was she saying these things? Yet it felt good to say them, to say what she liked, to be herself. It had been a long time coming.

"Yes," John answered, his voice holding that roughened edge. "You can like me."

"Good." She looked away then, because she felt as if she had to. She'd meant to be light but the mood had suddenly turned intense. Or was she imagining it? She felt too unsteady in herself to know.

After a few seconds John cleared his throat. "So how are the plans for turning Casterglass Castle into South Cumbria's number-one tourist attraction coming along?"

Althea let out a laugh, grateful for the change in subject. "They're not really coming along at all. Ben's on board, at least, and I think Poppy and Tobias will get there." She paused, thinking of her daughter's sorrow. "Eventually."

"And the actual plans?"

"I haven't really got that far. I suppose the first thing we need to do is figure out how to finance it all. Ben suggested looking for treasures like an episode of *Antiques Roadshow*, and while the castle is full of stuff, I'm not sure how much money we'll get for any of it."

"You might be surprised."

"I hope so."

"So Poppy and Tobias wouldn't mind living here? Going to school here?"

"That's a work in progress." She paused. "I think it would actually be a good thing for Poppy to leave her friends from Surrey behind, but I'm not sure she's on board with that plan yet."

John gave a sympathetic grimace. "Teenagers are hard."

"They are, although Alice seems like a lovely kid."

"She is, but she's had her moments. So have I. Things weren't easy for a while."

"No?" She waited, wanting him to tell her more. Wanting to know. "Do you mean after your wife died?" she asked hesitantly, when he seemed to be struggling to put whatever he was thinking into words.

"Yes…and no." He hesitated. "It wasn't exactly…" He let out a huff of breath. "The truth is, I don't think I've been entirely honest with you about that. About…her."

"What?" Althea looked at him in surprise, and some unease. She wasn't sure she was emotionally stable enough to handle a surprise like that, although she didn't even know what *that* was like. What could he possibly mean, he hadn't been honest?

John scratched his jaw, not quite looking at her. Uh-oh. "The truth is a bit more complicated than I made it sound," he began, only to have Alice run into the kitchen, breathless.

"Dad, where are the batteries? My Wii remote isn't working!" She waved the controller for emphasis, flushed and happy.

John slid Althea a wry, apologetic look before he went to fetch the requisite batteries.

When he returned, Althea had taken their wine glasses to the sink and was smiling at him in a brisk sort of way. "Can I lay the table?" she asked, and she didn't miss the flash of relief in his eyes before he nodded. So, he didn't want to talk about whatever he hadn't been honest about. Which was just as well, because she wasn't sure she was ready to hear it, which was why she'd changed the subject so abruptly. Maybe that was cowardly of her, but she had enough complicated in her life already.

The rest of the evening passed in a blur of good fun and boisterous company, as the children jokingly trash-talked their Mario Kart skills or lack thereof. Althea was grateful to see how involved Poppy looked, the sulky pout she'd been beginning to think was permanent had, at least for the moment, disappeared.

It was clear all the children got along, and Althea was happy to sit back and sip wine and let their burbling conversation flow over her. Once in a while she caught John's eye and he smiled, and she smiled back, feeling warm inside. It was enough. For now, it was more than enough.

She was tottering only slightly as they made their way out to the car a couple of hours later, and she handed Ben her keys.

"Thank goodness you got your licence," she told him as she buckled herself into the passenger seat.

"Maybe we should get a proper all-terrain vehicle if we're going to stay here," Ben said as he started the car, and Poppy emitted a squawk from the back seat.

"What do you mean, if we're going to stay here?"

Ben glanced back at her, unperturbed. "You know, if we don't go back to Surrey."

"Ben…" Althea began, rather feebly. She hadn't quite got round to talking to Poppy and Tobias about her plans, at least not in any great detail.

"Mum?" Poppy demanded. "Are you serious? Did you actually make this decision without even telling me?"

"I haven't actually *made* a decision…" She was not in the right frame of mind for this discussion, three glasses of wine down.

"Come on, Poppy," Ben said in his easy way. "It could be fun. You'd be the girl who lives in a castle. Plus, Alice is in your year."

"*I'd* like to live here," Tobias ventured.

Poppy didn't reply and Althea resisted the urge to jump in with placating promises. "I'm glad you feel that way," she told Tobias.

The castle came into view, its lights glimmering in the distance, the trees along the drive festooned with lights. Althea's heart lifted. It was Christmas, and this was home.

"Alice is nice," Poppy said, her face to the window, her voice so quiet Althea almost didn't hear what she'd said. She stared out the window and smiled, as her heart lifted with hopeful thanks.

Chapter Fifteen

Tomorrow was Christmas. Althea woke up on Christmas Eve morning with a surprisingly buoyant feeling of hope. So much was still uncertain, not to mention a mess, but she couldn't help but feel it—a persistent seed, springing to life. It was certainly a lot better than what she had been feeling recently—despair, doubt, guilt, regret. No, she was going to stick with hope now.

Not that there weren't some bumps along the way. Last night after they'd returned from Appleby Farm, she'd attempted to have another heart-to-heart with her daughter, but Poppy clearly wasn't in the mood. Althea had spent the rest of the evening playing Parcheesi with Tobias in the sitting room, while Ben and Seph had gone out to the pub, Poppy and Olivia had stayed in their rooms, and her parents had watched something ancient on TV. Tobias had thrashed her three times, but he'd been good-natured about it.

"Did you mean what you said, Tobes?" she'd asked as they both focused on the game. It had been easier to talk that way. "About liking the idea of staying here?"

"Yeah."

"What about school? Friends? Won't you miss them?"

He'd shrugged, his head bent over the board. "A bit, yeah."

"But not too much?"

Another shrug. Althea had wondered how much to say. "I'm sorry about all this," she'd said after a few moments. "All this upheaval and uncertainty. I know it can't be much fun."

Tobias had looked up for the first time, his expression endearingly earnest. "You don't need to worry about me, Mum."

Althea's heart had swelled with love. "Well, you don't get a choice in that matter, love," she'd teased. "I'm going to worry about you, no matter what. But I'm glad you like the idea of staying here. I do, too."

Now, in the frosty light of morning, Althea practically bounced down to the kitchen. She wasn't sure what had put her in such a good mood—perhaps simply the *possibility* of life. She hadn't felt as if she'd had options for a long, long time, but right now the future seemed as if it were practically shimmering in front of her. She didn't have to answer to anyone, or at least not to Jasper.

Goodness, but it was positively *liberating* to realise that. That snarky, sneering in her voice was slowly but surely getting quieter. Soon it would hopefully be silent. And meanwhile she could start discovering what she wanted to do, who she wanted to be. Maybe like Olivia had said, it wasn't too late at forty-one.

An image of John's warm gaze flitted through Althea's mind, making her blush even though she was alone in the kitchen. He definitely made her feel fizzy, and she wasn't sure what to do with that information. It was surely too soon to contemplate romance, and in any case she had no idea if John felt the same way. Her self-confidence had been *seriously* knocked in that department.

"Happy Christmas Eve!" Olivia sang out as she came into the kitchen. "Is that coffee you're making?"

"It is, indeed."

"Is there enough for me?"

"Absolutely."

Althea smiled at her sister as she poured out two steaming mugs. Here was something else she was grateful for—a stronger relationship with her sister. Next she'd tackle Seph.

"Is now a good time to talk about why you don't want to go back to York?" she asked, and Olivia grimaced as she took a sip of her coffee.

"On Christmas Eve? Please, no. I will tell you, I promise, but…"

"After Christmas. Along with everyone else."

"Who else is telling you something after Christmas?"

Althea shrugged, smiling good-naturedly. "Our dear father doesn't want to discuss any plans for Casterglass till after the big day. I understand, but I feel as if I'm champing at the bit, raring to go."

Olivia lowered herself into a chair at the table, her slender hands cradled around her mug. "Are you serious about taking on Casterglass, Althea?"

Althea hesitated for the barest of seconds. "Yes, I am. I know it's early days, but I've got a lot of ideas." She'd bought a Moleskine notebook in Kendal, and last night she'd scribbled down some thoughts about how to start. It had been next to nothing, yet it had made her feel proactive. Anti-ostrich.

"And you think I could take on the gardens?"

Althea's heart leapt. "I absolutely think you could. It would be brilliant, Liv. And what a project! There's so much here to work with."

Olivia gave a little grimace. "There are certainly a lot of nettles."

"It's a big job, no question. But just because it's big, doesn't mean it can't be done."

"I like you this way." Olivia gave her a sudden grin. "It reminds me of how you'd boss me about when you were in Sixth Form. Boss both of us about, actually. You were like our den mother, telling us to wash our PE kit and do our homework."

"I'd forgotten that," Althea said with a self-conscious smile. She *had* been bossy, back when she'd been confident, before she'd had it knocked out of her at school, and then with Jasper. Her smile faltered for a second, and Olivia covered her hand with her own.

"No regrets, remember? Life is a learning curve."

"A long one," Althea agreed, turning her smile up a few watts as she held on to that hope. "Well, like I said, you'd be brilliant with the garden. Are you at least tempted to try?"

"I am," Olivia confessed, and Althea's smile upped its wattage again, this time of its own accord. She would love to share this adventure with her sister. "It's an amazing space. I was envisioning something slightly wild…not a neatly tended flower beds-and-hedgerows type of thing, but a little bit as if it's only been partly reclaimed. Does that sound mad?"

"It sounds amazing," Althea assured her. "And easier than manicuring everything!"

They both laughed, and that persistent seed of hope started to sprout.

ALTHEA SPENT THE morning wrapping presents and listening to Christmas carols, before she went in search of Poppy, determined to try again. After finding her bedroom empty, she wandered around the castle, poking her head into dusty, junk-filled rooms she hadn't been inside of in decades before she finally found her daughter in a small dressing room adjoining a bedroom at the front of the castle. Poppy was curled up in the window seat, her knees to her chest, her face turned to the window and its view of purple, frost-covered fells, the sea a stormy glint in the distance.

"I felt as if I was playing a game of hide-and-seek," Althea remarked as she braced one shoulder against the doorframe. "Did you not want to be found?" Poppy shrugged without replying, her gaze still trained on the view. "This bedroom historically belonged to the Baroness of Casterglass," Althea told her. "This dressing room was her private room. No one was allowed to disturb her in here."

"Which one?" Poppy asked after a moment, her chin still on her knees.

"Which baroness? I think the stories Granny told me were about the eighth one. Late 1700s, I think. She was a very romantic figure. There's a portrait of her on the stairs—all powdered hair and a distant, soulful look. She wrote lots of poetry. We have it somewhere, sheaves of it, never published, but I don't think it was half bad." Not for the first time Althea marvelled at her own history, and how much of it there was. No, they definitely could not give up this place, and yet she knew she had to get her daughter on board.

"Poppy, will you talk me through what happened with your friends?" she asked gently as she came to sit next to her on the window seat. "How did it end up like that?"

Poppy shrugged, little more than a twitch of her shoulders. She was still staring at the sky. "Like you said, they weren't really my friends."

"But you thought they were…"

"I was always on the outskirts of it all," Poppy said with

another shrug. "Not as cringy as you were, but close."

Althea smiled at that. "Yeah, I was rather cringy, it's true."

"Sorry, I didn't mean it like that." Poppy gave her a quick, hooded glance. "It's just...it was so much work, trying to be cool. Having the right clothes. The right attitude." She gave Althea a look that held a surprising hint of humour. "Those Prada boots were seriously going to boost my street cred."

"We can still get them—"

"I don't want them anymore." She sighed, settling her chin more firmly onto her knees. "I don't know what I want anymore." Althea waited, saying nothing, sensing more. "I don't really want to go back home," Poppy said slowly. "Alice and I looked at the comp here, and it does the same A levels as I was taking before."

"That's good..."

"But I don't really want to live here," Poppy burst out. "I mean, we're in the middle of *nowhere*. And I have, like, one friend." She hunched her shoulders. "It will probably all suck."

Althea hesitated, knowing she needed to choose her words carefully. This moment felt like a precious opportunity, but also very, very fragile. "It might suck," she finally agreed. "There is that risk to just about everything."

Poppy gave her one of her old looks, but the aggro seemed half-hearted at best. "It's more likely when you're living way out in the sticks."

"Perhaps, but if you weren't really happy back in Surrey…" She paused, giving her daughter time to deny it, but Poppy didn't. "Then maybe there's a greater chance you'd be happy here, because it's so different." Still no reply, but silence was much better than an outright no. "We could at least try it," she suggested. "There's no guarantee it will actually work, saving this old heap, but it feels like something worth doing. Worth taking a risk for." She paused, trying to gauge her daughter's mood. Poppy's face was pensive rather than sulky, but a shadow of sorrow remained in her eyes. "I was thinking, with your mad decorating skills, you could help restore some of the bedrooms." She'd had that idea just now off the cuff, but why not? If Olivia could get involved, why not Poppy? Why not everyone?

Poppy lifted her chin from her knees. "Really?"

"We'll have to get some specialists in, I imagine, to deal with some of the antique stuff, but I'd certainly appreciate your discerning eye. I was thinking we'd have a few shops and craft rooms—maybe you'd like to be involved in that, as well?"

"How?"

Althea spread her hands. "I don't know. I'm just feeling my way through it, but what I do know is I want everyone to be involved. Everyone to feel they have ownership of this place. I'd welcome your ideas, Poppy, I really would."

A fragile smile bloomed across Poppy's face before sliding

off again. She looked out the window, and although she didn't look sulky, she still looked sad. Hearts didn't heal overnight, Althea knew. This was all going to take time.

"Maybe," Poppy said, and she left it at that.

THE REST OF the day was spent getting ready for Christmas, with all the jollity that entailed. Ben and Tobias raced to bring presents down to put under the tree—Althea was surprised and pleased to see her parents had presents for everyone, a thoughtfulness she hadn't expected but was starting to wonder if perhaps she should have.

Then they played an epic game of Monopoly, a Christmas Eve tradition from decades ago, and Olivia took command of the kitchen to make their traditional Christmas Eve meal of shepherd's pie and salad.

"We can't have you cooking all the time," she told Althea. "If we're all really going to go into this together, we need it to be fair."

"I'll make a schedule," Althea promised with a laugh. "Everyone can have a chance to cook, I promise."

As they all sat round the table in the kitchen that evening, a candle in front of each place setting, the shepherd's pie golden and bubbling in the middle, Althea felt a deep contentment steal through her. She'd tried to replicate this back in Surrey; she'd made the shepherd's pie, set out the candles, but it hadn't been the same. Jasper had always been, at best, a reluctant participant, and Althea herself had been fraught with nerves, skittish and anxious with everyone. *This* was how she'd wanted it to be, loving and peaceful, but it never really had been.

As much as that realisation held the power to make it sad, she chose instead to focus on the future. The hope. They were happy now, and that was all that mattered.

After supper they went to the hall to assemble around the Christmas tree and sing 'Silent Night', accompanied by her mother's less-than-adequate guitar playing and croaky voice. It had been a tradition since Althea could remember, and she loved it now, warbling at all. She met Ben's eye and he grinned at her, and then Tobias did, as well. Even Poppy managed a flicker of a smile. Goodness, but her heart was full. She really did have so much to be thankful for. Althea glanced at Seph, hoping to keep the smile streak going, but her sister scowled and looked away. Never mind. There was still work to be done. That was okay.

Then, as her mother's voice was reaching a screechy crescendo—*Jesus, Lord at thy birth*—a big fat raindrop splashed onto the slate floor in front of them all. Althea blinked at it, trying to make sense of the concept that it was raining indoors, when another splashed down, and then another, and another, and another.

Within the space of about thirty seconds it had become a steady drizzle. Althea glanced up. "The roof is leaking," she said, which by that point was obvious. And it was trickling all the way down through three floors, which meant it had to be really bad.

"We need to find the leak," Ben said briskly, suddenly turning all Bob the Builder. "And fix it."

Maybe not so much Bob the Builder as Captain Obvious. "Yes," Althea said, "but how?"

"With some, um, plastic sheeting?" He looked hopeful but bewildered. Althea realised how ill-equipped they all were, to deal with an emergency. And yet this couldn't have been the first time something like this had happened. She recalled having a bucket in her bedroom for over a year, for such a time as this. She turned to her father. "Dad?"

"Plastic sheeting sounds like a capital idea."

"Er…"

Briefly Althea closed her eyes. She wanted to be in control, capable, confident. All the things she used to be yet had forgotten how, over the last twenty years. "Okay," she thought aloud. "We need some plastic sheeting, at least until we can call in the professionals. Where can we get some plastic sheeting?"

"John has some," Seph offered, in her semi-sullen way.

"John?" Althea repeated dumbly.

"John Braithwaite. I saw it in his barn, when I was working."

"Right." For some reason she had a reluctance to call John, to have him come in and save the day, but as the water continued to drizzle down, Althea knew they were running out of time, and were already out of options. "Okay. Can you ring him, Seph?" She didn't actually have his mobile number, although for some reason she felt as if she should have.

"Okay."

Althea took a deep breath and smiled around at everyone, trying to be reassuring. This felt like the first hurdle, and by heaven, she was going to clear it.

Chapter Sixteen

THE SIGHT OF John Braithwaite clambering capably out of his battered Land Rover made Althea feel both grateful and ashamed. She'd wanted to handle this on her own and she could have, if not for the lack of some plastic sheeting. For want of a nail…

"Thank you for coming," she told John, realising belatedly that she sounded as if she were at a funeral. He gave her a smile as he shook off the rain droplets from his hair, a roll of plastic sheeting bundled under one arm.

"Where's this leak, then?"

"It's in one of the storerooms on the top floor. It could be worse, I suppose. Ben and my father are up there now, moving things out." Olivia had shepherded everyone else into the kitchen for hot chocolate. Althea held one hand out for the sheeting. "I can take it from here."

Something like hurt flashed in John's eyes. "You don't want me to help?"

"It's not that," Althea said quickly, although it was, at least a little bit. She wanted to be able to handle this on her own, and yet she also liked having John here. "It's Christmas Eve," she reminded him. "Don't you want to be with your family?"

"Alice is watching some soppy holiday romcom," John told her with a wry smile. "I'd rather be hammering sheeting to a roof than watch it, if I'm perfectly honest. Or sticking pins in my eyes."

"Oof." Althea smiled back. "All right, then. I'm sure we could use the help."

"Good. You're doing me a favour, really." His look was so warm, his eyes dancing, that Althea felt a flush steal over her whole body.

"We'd better get a move on, then," she said, her voice just a little bit unsteady. "Before the whole castle is awash."

She turned to head up the stairs. John following closely behind, so she could hear the whisper of his clothes as he walked.

"I've never been up here," he remarked as he glanced around, the walls crammed with portraits and paintings—muddy oils and faded watercolours. "It's quite something."

"Yes, I suppose it is. I'd give you the full tour, but we're in a bit of a hurry." She turned her head to give him a smile meant to take any possible sting from her words, but doing so caused her to trip on the step and John reached out with one hand to steady her.

"Whoa there."

"Sorry." She sounded breathless, conscious of how close

their bodies were. She breathed in the scent of him—good, clean soap. Simple, and exactly what she would have expected. Then she made the mistake of glancing up at his face, and her stomach did a somersault. He was so close she could see the gold flecks in his eyes, the stubble on his chin. Her breath came out in an unsteady rush.

"Sorry," she said again, her voice little more than a whisper, and this time she didn't know what she was apologising for. She took a step backwards, righting herself, and John dropped his hand from her arm.

"No harm done," he said easily enough, but then he cleared his throat, and Althea had the tantalising suspicion that he was as affected as she was.

Except, of course, she shouldn't be affected. Shouldn't want to be. Being attracted to someone was a complication she really didn't need right now, especially when she was still technically married. She definitely needed to keep a lid on those troublesome feelings, and she hoped John would, as well.

Another set of stairs, and they were on the top floor of the old part of the castle, a series of narrow stone chambers with windows like slits that looked exactly like what they were—about eight hundred years old.

"Wow," John said quietly, looking around.

"Daddy? Ben?" Althea called. "John's here with the sheeting." Her father poked his head out of the storeroom. He was soaking wet and grey-faced with exhaustion. "Oh,

Daddy…" She looked at him with concern while her father managed a brave smile.

"We've moved most of the things out. The water is coming in a treat, though, I tell you." He gave John a genial smile. "Hello, John. Thank you so much for your help."

"It's no trouble."

"Especially on Christmas Eve—" Her father's voice wavered and for a second he looked as if he might stagger.

"Daddy," Althea said in some alarm. "You look tired." She gave Ben a pointed look. "Ben, why don't you take Grandad downstairs? Olivia is making hot chocolate."

"But—" Ben began, clearly wanting to be part of the rescuing party, but then he caught sight of his grandfather's grey face. "All right." He took her father's arm as he led him unprotesting out of the storeroom.

"Sorry," Althea said after they'd gone. "I was just worried he was getting a bit tired."

"Good call. I'm sure we can manage just the two of us, anyway." He tilted his head to look at the hole in the roof— some slates had clearly been ripped off by the window, and the underlay had fallen, soaking and ruined, onto the floor. "Now it would be a good deal easier to nail the sheeting over the ceiling, but the problem with that is water will collect over it and cause a bulge. Eventually the weight of the water will cause it to collapse."

"Okay…so what's the other option?"

"Nailing it on the roof side, which means someone

scrambling through that hole."

"Through…? But then how do they get back in?"

"If they nail most of it, they can come back down and we'll fix the last bit underneath. I wouldn't advise wandering around on the roof, looking for the nearest exit."

"Okay."

"The trouble is," he said, nodding towards the gaping hole, "I'm not small enough to go through there."

Althea gulped. Nodded. Well, she'd wanted to prove herself, hadn't she? And here was ample opportunity. "All right. I can do it."

"Are you sure?"

"Yes."

"All right. I'll give you a leg up. Once you're through, don't think about having a little explore—"

"Trust me, I won't."

"I'll pass the sheeting up and you can nail most of it down. Then I'll bring you back down and finish it off on this side. Sound good?"

It sounded terrifying and impossible, but whatever. Althea straightened her shoulders as if she were in the army. She had an urge to salute. "Yes. Sounds good."

"All right, then." John braced his legs and then laced his hands across his thigh. It took Althea a minute to realise he wanted her to put her foot there.

Gingerly at first and then with more conviction, she put her foot on John's hands and then let out a startled 'oof' as he hoisted her upwards. Her head went sailing through the hole and she was instantly drenched, sluicing rainwater out of her eyes as she gazed around at a landscape she didn't often get to look at—the steep inclines and crenelated towers of Casterglass Castle's enormous roof.

"Okay," she called down. "I'm ready."

He handed her up the hammer, and then a couple of nails, and finally the sheeting. Althea's fingers cramped with cold as she tried to spread the plastic over as much of the hole as she could. This was definitely not as simple as John had made it sound. The wind made the sheeting flap, and she had to lean backwards as much as she could in order to get the plastic across. All in all, she decided, it was a complete and utter faff.

Then she suddenly became aware of John bracing her by her hips. It made sense of course, and yet she couldn't keep a warm, tingling awareness from spreading through her as she became even more conscious of the firm grip he had on her. Really, this was ridiculous, considering the situation. And yet she felt it all the same.

Concentrate, Althea, she told herself sternly. *And just nail this stupid sheeting. Don't think about the fact that John Braithwaite is gripping you in a way no man has done in many a year. Don't think!*

"Ouch." She skimmed the hammer across the her thumb fortunately not too hard. John's hands tightened on her hips.

"Are you all right?"

"Yes." Heaven help her, though, if she farted in his face. Which was unfortunately a bit likely, considering how nervous she was. *Don't think.*

Somehow she managed to nail three sides of the sheeting down, leaving a small gap for her to duck back down underneath the roof and out of the rain. She handed down the hammer and then, as she started to lower herself, John's hands moved from her hips to her waist. Althea knew he was simply trying to steady her as her feet hit the floor, but in the process her body slid down the length of his, coming into contact with every single part—chest, hips, legs—so that as her feet finally landed, her breasts were pressed against his chest, her hips locked with his—*oh.*

John's face flushed as Althea stared at him in surprise, her hair plastered to her head, her mind spinning, her blood surging—

And then, somehow—she didn't know who moved first—he was kissing her. Or she was kissing him. Either way, they were kissing, their arms wrapped around each other, their bodies pressed so tantalisingly close together, so Althea could feel *everything.*

She found herself backed up against the wall, although she didn't know which one of them had moved first, the stone pressing into her back. John was still kissing her, or she was kissing him—Althea didn't know if it really mattered, except that there was a lot of kissing going on. Her knee was pressed between his legs, her hands in his hair, and she couldn't remember the last time she'd felt this way—so desired, so desiring, so *alive*. Every nerve sparked.

"Mum?" Ben's voice coming down the hall had her jerking so hard away from John that her head hit the wall and she saw stars.

"Althea—" He looked concerned about her head, his hair still mussed, his eyes dazed, his breathing ragged, and Althea knew she simply did not have the emotional capacity to process what had just happened, never mind the headache that was rapidly coming on.

"Don't," she said sharply, and he blinked, rebuked, maybe even hurt.

Althea scooted away from him as she pulled at her clothes. Somehow her jumper had become rucked up—when had that happened? Everything was still buzzing, but inside her stomach she felt a great hollowness opening up, like a cavern inside her. How could she have done that? How could she have kissed another man when she was still married? All right, the divorce papers were downstairs, and Jasper was currently bonking his latest affair in a line of several dozen, but *still*. This wasn't who she was.

Except she'd told herself this morning she was still finding out who she was.

"Hey, is it fixed?" Ben came into the storeroom, his glance moving between Althea and John, before glancing up at the ceiling. Althea tried to assume an innocent air, which she feared had the opposite effect of making her look guilty.

She *felt* guilty. Her stomach churned, and not in a good way. She folded her arms protectively across her body, determined not to look at John even once.

"Yep, all fixed," he said, sounding sunny and completely normal. "It should hold until you can get a roofer in, after Christmas."

And how much would that kiss—er, cost? Althea pressed her fingers to her lips and then immediately dropped them. She could not think properly about anything.

"There's still some hot chocolate if you want to come down," Ben said, with another glance between the pair of them. Did he suspect? Oh dear heaven, do not let her son suspect that she'd been snogging their neighbour in the castle storeroom.

"That's a very kind offer, but I should be getting back," John replied, just as easily as before.

"I'll see you out," Althea told him, although she dreaded having a private conversation about that kiss. What would he say? What would she?

John cleaned up his tools and Althea didn't think she was imagining the tension in the room. She glanced at Ben, who gave her a quizzical look back that she ignored.

"All right, then," John said, and Althea did not look at him as she headed downstairs. Ben went off to the kitchen as they came into the main hall, and Althea started towards the castle's main door.

"Actually, my car is around back," John said in a low

voice. She couldn't tell anything from his tone. "Do you mind if we go through the kitchen?"

"Oh, er, no, of course not." Except she feared what they'd been doing would somehow be written all over their faces.

"Althea." John reached for her arm, his grip gentle but sure. "What happened up there…"

"Don't." The word came out in a shuddery rush. "I can't."

John was silent for a second, and Althea risked a glance at his face. His expression was thoughtful, his eyes narrowed. "Can't what?" he asked finally.

"I just can't." She stared at him helplessly, her gaze trained on his chin rather than his eyes. "I'm sorry. It's Christmas. Can we…can we talk about this later?" Preferably in about three years?

"Yes, of course. I wasn't…I didn't mean to put any pressure on you, or…" He seemed almost at as much of a loss as she was.

"It's fine," Althea said quickly. "It's fine." It wasn't, but whatever. "Anyway, I should…"

"Yes, I should." He started back towards the kitchen, and Althea followed. As they came into the brightly lit room, she felt as if 'harlot' was stamped on her forehead. Or maybe 'just been kissed'. She was torn between the two.

Everyone smiled and greeted John cheerfully enough, and then her father, naturally, insisted he stay for 'a cup of good cheer' before heading off into the wild and windy night. John, after a moment's hesitation, agreed. Althea had to bite her tongue to keep from saying something imprudent, like *John needs to leave right now.*

She helped herself to a mug of hot chocolate and slid into a seat at the opposite end of the table as him, sipping it silently and feeling as if she were about fourteen, all blushes and sneaky looks. Olivia gave her a questioning glance; nothing slipped by her sister. Maybe this would, although Althea wasn't holding out much hope.

The conversation flowed over her—questions about Christmas, and something about Appleby Farm's honey, and Althea found she couldn't focus on any of it. Her mind was going in fits and starts, like the engine of a bad car. She couldn't hear herself think above the sound of its coughing.

Then, finally, thankfully, John was rising from the table, with a flurry of farewells from everyone else. Althea thought she mumbled something. Olivia was giving her another look.

Althea couldn't keep from letting out a sigh of relief—at least, she thought it was relief—when John was finally through the door.

"Well." She slapped her hands down on the table. "That was a bit of excitement, but it's getting quite late so we should probably all think about going to bed."

Poppy gave her a strange look. "Mum, it's only nine o'clock."

"Is it?" She felt as if she'd lived a lifetime in one evening.

"Well, it is Christmas Eve."

"And?"

"The sooner you go to bed, the sooner Father Christmas will come."

"Mum, I'm not *four*." Poppy sounded as amused as she was disgusted. "What is with you?"

"Yes, what is with you?" Olivia asked, her tone all too shrewd.

"Nothing," Althea replied a bit desperately. She pulled her cardigan more closely around her as she avoided absolutely everyone's gazes. "Nothing at all. Now come on, everybody. It's *Christmas*."

Chapter Seventeen

ALTHEA WOKE UP to drumming rain and darkness, which was about right for a Cumbrian Christmas. She lay in bed, blinking in the gloom, as memories tumbled through her mind in a kaleidoscope of emotions and sensations. *Kissed.* She'd been kissed. Within an inch of her life!

A smile spread across her face like syrup and her toes curled underneath her heavy duvet as she recalled every glorious second of that life-altering kiss. Then reality slammed into her. She was married, the mother of three children, with a castle to save. She had no business kissing John Braithwaite, making life complicated.

"Happy Christmas!" Poppy sang out, giving a perfunctory knock on the door before she waltzed in with Ben and Tobias in tow. Poppy was holding a mug of tea, and Tobias a plate of toast. Ben was just grinning.

"What is this!" Althea exclaimed, smiling.

"We thought you deserved breakfast in bed," Poppy announced as she handed her the mug. "A chance to relax."

"Oh…" Althea blinked back tears, still smiling. All it

took was her children to be sweet for her to dissolve into a puddle. "Thank you, all of you. That's so kind."

"Plus, we finished our stockings," Tobias chimed in as he gave her the toast. "Thanks for the Minecraft annual, Mum."

"You're welcome." Just as she'd done ever since they'd been tiny, she'd filled their stockings and put them at the end of the bed. Normally by now, she realised, she'd have been placating Jasper, who would have been irritated by being woken up, or the kids being too loud, since he was usually hungover on Christmas Day. She would have been scurrying around to make a meal, make everything perfect, longing to capture those cosy family moments that seemed forever out of reach. This, Althea realised as she took a sip of tea, was *so* much better. Why had it taken her so long to understand that?

Never mind. No regrets. She had tea and toast and three children on her bed. And she'd been kissed last night. No, better not to think of that. But still, life felt pretty perfect as she smiled at her brood and sipped her tea, which was far too sugary, but still. Perfect.

She'd barely finished her toast when Tobias started getting antsy, and even Ben was bouncing around, excited to go downstairs for presents. Laughing, Althea shooed them out while she grabbed her dressing gown and put a brush to her hair, before coming into the kitchen to find Olivia pulling a tray of cinnamon buns out of the oven, and her parents sitting on the sofa, sipping coffee. It was such a cosy, happy scene, that Althea paused on the threshold to savour it. *This is what I want*, she thought with sudden, fervent certainty. *This is what I want all the time.*

"Althea!" Her father beamed at her. "Happy Christmas!"

"Yes, happy Christmas, darling," her mother added with a vague smile in her direction.

"Happy Christmas," Althea returned, emotion making her chest go tight. "Those cinnamon buns smell absolutely scrummy, Liv. Can I have one?"

"Of course."

She took one, burning her fingers and not caring in the least, as she bit into the buttery, sugary goodness and burned her tongue as well. "Where's Seph?" she asked as she licked her fingers.

"Still sleeping," her father replied. "She likes her lie-ins, our Seph does."

"But it's Christmas," Althea protested with a laugh, only to have her sister practically snarl from the doorway, "Well, don't worry, I'm here."

"Oh." Althea bit her lip as Seph slouched into the kitchen. Her dreadlocked hair was even more of the bird's nest than usual and she sent a scowl her way before flinging herself into a chair. What *was* her sister's problem, Althea wondered. Did she have it in for her personally? She really needed to make getting to the bottom of that a priority.

"Happy Christmas, Persephone," their father said cheerfully, and Seph gave him a smile.

"Happy Christmas."

Okay, it really was just her, then. Althea did her best not to feel stung. It was Christmas, after all.

After everyone had fortified themselves with coffee and cinnamon buns, they trooped into the hall where the Christmas tree stood in all of its tinselled glory. Ben and Tobias dragged chairs and even a sofa in from the grand drawing room that nobody ever used, making Althea wonder aloud, "Why do we have the Christmas tree in the hall? It would surely make more sense to have it in the sitting room."

"Oh, but it's so lovely in here," Olivia exclaimed.

"Let me guess," Seph flashed, "you want to change that, too."

Wait—what? Althea squinted at her sister as she tried, yet again, to figure out what was going on. "I don't want to change anything," she said, although that wasn't exactly true, when she thought of all her ideas scribbled in her notebook. "I was just wondering why we put the tree out here." It had been a throwaway comment, meant as something of a joke, but Seph was scowling at her. The easy joy Althea had been feeling started to drain away.

"Stop looking like a wet Wednesday," Ben told Seph with a good-natured laugh. "It's Christmas. You can open my present first."

Seph managed a smile and mumbled her thanks as Ben handed her a present and everyone settled into their chairs.

Althea watched, curious, as Seph unwrapped Ben's present, and her face broke into an entirely genuine smile.

"It's brilliant, thank you, Ben!" she exclaimed as she brandished what looked to Althea like a small axe. "It's perfect."

"No problem."

"What is it?" Althea asked, because she had no idea why her sister would need what looked like a weapon.

Seph gave her yet another dark look. "It's an adze," she said, in a well-duh voice while Althea tried to look a little less blank.

"An adze?"

"For wood carving," Olivia filled in, as if this would somehow make sense.

Althea was starting to resent her own ignorance, along with seemingly everyone else's knowledge. "I didn't know you were interested in wood carving," she said brightly, only to realise immediately that this was precisely the wrong thing to say. Seph scowled and said nothing while the silence stretched on to several awkward seconds.

"Open my present, Mum," Poppy finally said, lunging forward to retrieve a small, wrapped box from under the tree.

"Thank you, darling." Althea was doing her best not to feel stung by her sister's animosity. She unwrapped Poppy's present to discover a pair of earrings similar to the ones she'd bought her in Kendal, only a bit more understated. "Poppy, you sneak!" She laughed. "How did you get these without me knowing?"

"I went back when we were at the café—"

"You said you wanted to look at shoes!"

Poppy shrugged modestly, and Althea pulled her into a quick, tight hug. "Thank you. They're beautiful."

As they continued to unwrap presents, Althea tried not to let Seph's obvious snark bother her. She would get to the bottom of it, but not while everyone was around the Christmas tree. And not while she wanted to enjoy her children having the kind of Christmas they'd never been able to manage when Jasper had been around—easy and light-hearted, good-natured teasing and genuine gratitude mixed together.

By mid-morning they were all finished, and Althea went into the kitchen to help Olivia with the Christmas dinner while everyone else cleared up the drifts of wrapping paper and put the presents away.

"Do you know why Seph seems to hate me?" she asked bluntly as she peeled potatoes and Olivia stuffed the turkey.

"She doesn't hate you."

"She certainly acts like it. I feel like I'm constantly saying the wrong thing. And it's not like I don't try."

Olivia sighed, one hand up the back end of the bird. "It's hard for her, I think."

"You sound like you know more than I do."

"Not really. Not much, anyway. Seph always keeps to herself. But I got the sense that maybe she felt a bit…abandoned, when we all left."

"I can understand that." Althea focused on the *scritch scritch* of her paring knife as the long, dirt-speckled peels came off in curls into the sink. "But that's not just my fault. She seems to reserve her rudeness for me alone."

"She's always been a bit sullen to me too, if that helps. It's better when we're alone together."

"When are you alone together?"

"She's come to York a few times for the weekend."

"Has she?" Guilt curdled in the pit of Althea's stomach. Seph had never come to Surrey, not once in twenty years. *Was* that her fault? "Maybe I should make more of an effort."

"It can't hurt," Olivia agreed. "Especially now that you're planning to stay at Casterglass. It behoves you both to get along."

"True."

"But now I have a question for you." The turkey stuffed, Olivia pointed a finger at her. "What's going on with you and John Braithwaite?"

"What?" Althea blustered, badly. Olivia clearly wasn't fooled. "Nothing—"

"Right, and so why were you scarlet when you came into the kitchen last night? And refusing to look at him even though you kept sneaking glances when you thought he wasn't looking?"

"Olivia…" Althea began half-heartedly, because actually

part of her wanted to tell her sister what had happened.

"Well?"

"Well…we kissed. He kissed me," Althea clarified, although she wasn't sure if that was true, since she couldn't remember exactly how it had happened. Perhaps she'd lunged at him and he'd had no choice but to kiss her back.

"Did he?" Olivia raised her eyebrows, looking impressed. "Well, isn't that interesting."

"It just sort of happened," Althea said. "I wasn't expecting it at all."

"Of course you weren't."

Her sister sounded amused, and Althea let out a huff of exasperation. "Olivia." Then guilt slammed into her. "I'm married," she whispered. "I shouldn't be kissing other men." To her surprise, her sister suddenly looked stricken. Althea's own guilt dropped away in the face of her sister's expression. "Liv? What's wrong?"

"I need to get this turkey in the oven," Olivia said, shaking her head. "And then I need a large sherry."

It was only eleven o'clock in the morning, but it was Christmas. Althea finished the potatoes while Olivia did the turkey, and then poured them both large glasses of sherry.

"Okay," she said, and they sat at one of the kitchen tables, sipping Bristol Cream. "The reason I don't really want to go back to York? A man." She paused, biting her lip as she tried to keep her face from crumpling. "A married man."

"Married…" The word came out in a breath. Althea

tried to keep her expression concerned and compassionate, rather than showing the lightning streak of judgement she instinctively felt.

"Yes, I know." Olivia's mouth twisted. "Go ahead. Judge. I judge myself."

Apparently she hadn't been as successful at hiding as she'd hoped. "What happened?"

"I met him at the garden centre. He came in quite a lot, started asking for gardening advice, we'd have a chat. It was all very friendly, a bit flirty. I liked it. I didn't actually think it would go anywhere, you know? It was just a bit of fun."

"Did you know he was married, then?" Althea asked, striving to keep her voice neutral.

"No." Olivia glanced away. "Not *exactly*." Althea didn't reply, and she continued, "I suspected. But I didn't let myself think about it. I didn't even acknowledge that I suspected, until later. Much later." She sighed. "It was just a bit of light flirting, it didn't *matter*." She dropped her head into her hands and with a rush of sympathy Althea squeezed her shoulder.

"It must have been very hard."

"I just buried my head in the sand, you know?"

Althea thought of her own ostrich-like actions over the last two decades. "Yes, I know. But…what happened? Did it go further than flirting in the garden centre?"

"Yes. He asked me out. I agreed. We had dinner…we kissed. I told myself to be happy, even though I wondered why he could be so cagey about things. Details like where he lived, what he did on weekends…I don't know. There was just a feeling that something was off, and I did my best to ignore it."

"Oh, Liv."

"We went out a couple more times." Olivia gazed at her, her eyes full of tears. "The truth is…I wanted what you had, Althea, or a version of it. I'm thirty-five, and I want to be married. Have children. A baby…this guy seemed like my best chance."

"Trust me, Liv, you don't want what I had."

"But you know what I mean."

Althea sighed. "Yes, I do. So…what happened?"

Olivia let out a shuddery breath. "His wife came into the garden centre when I was working. Confronted me about seeing her husband." Briefly she closed her eyes. "I was mortified, utterly mortified. She called me all sorts of names and told me to leave them both alone. I felt like…like a criminal. And everyone heard. Everyone gave me such looks. This old woman who comes to the centre every week and has always been so lovely glared at me and told me I should be ashamed of myself."

"Oh, Olivia."

"And I get it," Olivia said with a sniff. "I do. I am ashamed of myself. But I feel like no one looks at me the same way now, and the truth is, I don't look at myself the same way. I feel…dirty."

"It wasn't exactly your fault though, was it?" Althea said gently. "If he never told you…"

"There were enough signs. Missed calls, texts he quickly swiped so I wouldn't see. Weekends when he wasn't available. And once he came in with a little girl. Yes," she said to Althea's silent question, "he had children. He was surprised to see me there—I'd told him I wasn't working that weekend, but then I'd swapped shifts. I must have looked stunned because he quickly explained, so she couldn't hear, that this was his goddaughter. Then she turned around and called him Daddy."

Althea couldn't help but wince. "That was near the end. But even then I just ignored it. I told myself—well, okay, he has a child. That's fine. It doesn't mean he's married. But you know what? I didn't even ask him about her. I just pretended I didn't hear her call him Daddy, and carried on." She sniffed and wiped her eyes. "His wife came in a week later. In some ways it was a relief. She saved me from myself…but I still don't want to go back."

"How long ago was all this?"

"It ended a couple of weeks ago, at the start of December. I know it will get better, time heals all wounds, et cetera, but coming to Casterglass was such a relief."

"Well, I want you to stay," Althea told her staunchly, and Olivia gave her a wobbly smile.

"You don't hate me?"

"Liv. Of course I don't hate you. We all make mistakes.

And I do understand about burying your head in the sand—trust me. Hopefully you've learned from it all, and you will heal. So will I." She reached over and hugged her sister. "It's all going to be okay, I promise." Casterglass would be their Christmas miracle, just like in the soppy holiday film life wasn't supposed to be like. She would make sure of it.

With that thought firmly planted in her mind, Althea decided to broach the subject over Christmas dinner, a meal of epic proportions that Olivia had organised, in the castle dining room with its table seating twenty and its walls of back-to-back portraits.

"I have an announcement," she said grandly, and everyone gave her looks of mild curiosity.

"Oh?" her mother asked as she placed the orange paper crown from her Christmas cracker on top of her updo. "How intriguing."

"I want to stay here at Casterglass and turn it into a tourist attraction. Of a sort," Althea clarified, only to be greeted with a variety of nonplussed expressions.

"Mum, we knew that already," Ben said kindly.

Instinctively she glanced at Poppy, who smiled and shrugged. Her daughter seemed to be at least somewhat on board. "Well, yes, I know I've said something about it," she said, deciding it didn't matter that her so-called announcement was more of a damp squib, "but I mean it seriously now. I really want to do this. And I want everyone to be involved. Olivia can do the garden, and Poppy wants to help with some of the interior decorating—"

"Could I design a maze?" Tobias asked eagerly.

"Why not?" Althea answered, although she wasn't quite sure how that would work. Hedgerow mazes took centuries to grow up, didn't they?

"Seph could have a woodworking studio," Ben suggested. "That would be brilliant." Althea glanced at her sister, who shrugged and looked away.

"Yes, that would be amazing," she agreed. "I'd love to have several studios run by local artisans, Seph included." She tried to catch her sister's eye with her kindly smile and failed.

"I thought Sam, when he comes back, could manage the glamping and maybe an assault course. Some country houses have 'Go Ape' things, you know—treetop adventures, that sort of thing."

"I could curate a collection of classical objects," her mother suggested. "I think people would find that very interesting."

"Er, yes," Althea said. "Absolutely. And I thought a tea room, perhaps, and a gift shop…"

"Can I do the gift shop?" Poppy asked. "Because you really don't want it to be lame."

"No, you don't," Althea agreed. She glanced at her father. "What do you think, Daddy?"

"I think it sounds absolutely wonderful, darling. But there is the question of money…"

"Yes, I've thought of that, too. When I looked online there are loans available to help ancestral estates monetise. And I also thought…" She hesitated, unsure if her parents would be on board with this idea, "it's just, there's a *lot* of stuff here, isn't there? Heaps and heaps of antiques and paintings and things. If we sold even just a few pieces that looked valuable…"

Her father's forehead crinkled in thought. "Well, it's an idea, but I have to be honest with you, I don't think we're sitting on an undiscovered Holbein or something like that. And I wouldn't want to sell too much…"

"I know," Althea said quickly. "Of course not." She glanced around everyone, a hopeful smile curving her mouth. "So…do you think this could actually work? The Penryn family business?"

The resounding yeses and cheers had her breaking out into a full-fledged grin.

Chapter Eighteen

Boxing Day was usually all about lying in front of the telly eating chocolates and leftover turkey, or in Althea's case, tidying up while everyone else did that, but this year she woke up to dawn's pink sky and a heart full of determined optimism. She was more than ready to get properly started on the Casterglass Makeover, never mind the tidying that needed to be done inside.

Quickly she dressed, made herself a flask of coffee, and headed outside into the fresh morning, the last shreds of pinkish cloud dissipating over the fells, the air as clear and cold as ice water. The frost-tipped grass crunched under her boots as she took a sip of coffee and glanced speculatively around.

Yesterday they'd spent the entire afternoon and most of the evening daydreaming and brainstorming ideas to make Casterglass a viable proposition. At one point they'd even had Sam on Skype—admittedly a very dodgy connection— talking about glamping yurts and rope courses while he'd blinked at them sleepily—it was four o'clock in the morning in New Zealand. They'd sketched plans for the artisan shops, including Seph's woodworking. She'd mentioned, in a slightly less sullen way, about a woman she knew in the village who threw pottery. After perhaps a few too many glasses of sherry, her father had tottered upstairs and come down with a couple of would-be treasures—a rusted helmet and a painting that could have been by someone slightly famous.

"We'll have to get an assessor in, do the thing properly," he said. "But I'm hopeful a few of these things might fetch a bit at market."

Althea wasn't sure about the helmet—it looked like something you'd give to a child for dress-up—but she appreciated her father's enthusiasm. If they all pulled together, this had at least a chance of happening.

Of course, they needed to tackle the paperwork before they started pulling down walls or putting up roofs, and to make sure the money was there. But as the week between Christmas and New Year's was not one for doing business, Althea had decided to use this in-between time to make a plan. Then, come the second of January, she'd be knocking on the door of the bank, paperwork in hand. Hopefully.

She was also conscious that, as excited as she was about Casterglass's future, she had a few loose ends to tie up back in Surrey. All her stuff was there, as well as the children's. At the very least Tobias and Poppy would want their schoolbooks and personal effects, but Althea had a deep, deep reluctance to go back and face Jasper, or even the house and all its memories. Still, she knew it needed to be done. She was planning to make the trip this week, so he'd still be in Switzerland.

So that was also part of her plan to get her life on track and the castle up and running. And come the new year, she'd be looking only to the future.

Althea ducked into one of the old sheds that made up one side of the courtyard to the rear of the castle. The musty but not unpleasant smell of damp straw and dirt filled her nostrils as she looked around the shadowy space. Poppy had been brimming with enthusiasm last night about making the stables into a tea room and shop, with these old barns as the artisan workshops. Olivia had thought of having a small plant and flower shop as well, with blooms taken from the garden and greenhouse.

"We could sell orchids, Daddy," she'd said, full of enthusiasm. "It could become our speciality."

Now, as she walked through the half falling-down barns with their bits of broken machinery and tools, Althea could almost see it all. She continued to make her way through the ruin of buildings, making notes on the pad of paper she'd brought, the empty flask tucked into the deep pocket of her jacket. They'd all have to be reroofed—that much was clear—and electricity and plumbing put in. How much would all of that cost? Althea had no idea. Plus, her father had cautiously mentioned last night, everything would have to be insured. Another expense Althea wasn't sure about, and then of course there was the two hundred thousand pounds for the roof. A rusted helmet and a muddy painting weren't going to stretch that far, and when she'd had a brief gander on the internet, business loans for this kind of thing were in the tens of thousands, not the hundreds. Where *was* the money going to come from?

Althea pushed that unpleasant thought to the back of her mind. Today was for dreaming. She spent another hour going through the ragtag collection of buildings that made up the estate—in addition to the barns there was a gatekeeper's cottage that had been empty for twenty years and was now half hidden by briars. They'd rented it out, Althea recalled, when she'd been a child, but then the tenant had left and they hadn't been able to get anyone else in. Like so much else, it had fallen into disrepair.

There were also four brick cottages a ten-minute walk from the castle that had been tied to the estate's farms a hundred or so years ago, and now, like so much else, were empty. Althea peered into the downstairs of one to see a few sticks of furniture and olive-green flocked wallpaper circa 1980. Why hadn't her father kept these rented out? Was there really not enough demand? If they did them up nicely now, perhaps they could rent them out as self-catering holiday accommodation.

She pictured offering a luxurious gift basket of locally produced goodies on arrival, a jar of Appleby Farm's honey…

Which made her think of John. Ever since her discussion with Olivia, she'd been trying not to think of John. Hearing her sister's heart-breaking story had made Althea realise that kiss had been a mistake. No matter what Jasper may have got up to, she respected her marriage vows, and she wasn't divorced yet. It was far too soon to think about dating anyone else. At some point she'd have to screw up her courage and tell John as much, a conversation she really wasn't looking forward to, but maybe he'd understand. Maybe he'd even agree.

Now why did that possibility make her feel just a tiny bit disappointed? All right, more than a tiny bit. Halfway to gutted, but she was choosing to ignore the feeling.

The sun was high in the sky, and Althea decided to head back to the castle. Perhaps she'd do a fry-up for everyone, talk through some of what she'd seen. With the dew glimmering on every blade of grass, the whole world seemed to shimmer with possibility. As long as she didn't think about the money…

When Althea came into the castle kitchen ten minutes later, she saw Seph standing by the stove, stirring a pot of oatmeal. Her dreadlocks were piled on top of her head, and her expression was distant and dreamy until she caught sight of Althea, and immediately looked guarded and sullen.

Althea decided now was as good a time as any to ask her sister just what her problem was. Nicely, of course.

"Hey, Seph," she said as she took off her boots and coat. Her sister grunted in response. Althea took a deep breath. "Look, I wanted to talk to you." Nothing. "I feel like…I feel like you're angry with me," she confessed in a rush. "And I'm not sure why. But if I've done anything to…to upset you, then of course I'm sorry. And since we'll both be living here for the foreseeable future, I'd like for us to get along. So…is there anything I can do to make things better between us?"

The question hung in the air as Seph continued to stir the pot of porridge. She hadn't looked at Althea once.

"Seph?"

"No," her sister said shortly, and started spooning the porridge into a bowl.

Althea bit her lip to keep from snapping something un-helpful. "Really?" she finally said, striving to keep any possible edge from her voice. "There's absolutely nothing?"

"Not really." Without looking at her, Seph took her bowl and plonked herself down at the table, spooning the porridge into her mouth with methodical grimness.

"Not really? Then it sounds like there's something." Althea adopted a jokey tone she sometimes used with her children, and her sister looked up at her, exasperated.

"Why do you care?"

"Because—because you're my sister."

"So?"

Althea drew back, nettled, a little hurt. "What do you mean, so? You're my sister, Seph. I'm trying here. I've always tried—"

"Oh, right." Seph let out a huff of hard laughter. "You've always tried," she repeated sarcastically. "Riiiight."

Ouch. Slowly Althea lowered herself into the chair opposite. "Okay, I feel like I'm missing something here. I know I haven't been the most attentive sister, it's true. I suppose that's in part because of our age difference. We've been in massively different stages of life, but I'm here now and I want things to be better between us. Can you…can you just tell me why you seem so angry with me?"

"I'm not angry."

"What are you, then?"

Seph shrugged. "Indifferent."

Ouch again, and even worse this time. Althea blinked, appalled to realise she was near tears. She hadn't expected Seph to be so blunt, so cruel. She had, she realised, been harbouring some secret fantasy that she and her sister would fall into each other's arms, any misunderstanding cleared up in an instant. Why she'd persisted in believing such a ridiculous notion, she had no idea, except perhaps that today had been about daydreams, about possibility and hope.

"Indifferent," she repeated, her voice hollow. "All right. Can you tell me why you're indifferent?"

"Why shouldn't I be? You've been indifferent to me my entire life." Abruptly Seph rose from the table and dumped her bowl in the sink. Her back was to Althea as she washed the bowl, her body seemed to bristle with tension.

"I haven't been indifferent," Althea protested. "It's just…" What? "You're a lot younger than me, Seph, and I feel like I never got a chance to know you."

"I wonder why that was."

"I did try," Althea said, the edge she'd been desperate to avoid creeping into her voice. "I invited you to come down to Surrey."

"When I was twelve. And it was all 'I don't know if you can manage the train, and we are quite busy with school…' I got the picture, Althea. Don't worry."

Althea bit her lip. Had she said it like that? She probably had. Mostly because she'd been worried about how Jasper would react. "I sent you birthday cards and Christmas presents," she said, and Seph turned around, eyebrows raised.

"Oh yes, thanks for the gift card once a year. Much appreciated."

"I didn't know what you'd like—"

"You've never known, because you have never, *ever* tried to get to know me." Seph's voice shook with emotion, shocking her. "If you've ever made any kind of overture, it's only been to assuage your own guilty conscience, not because you were actually interested. That much was always abundantly obvious. 'All right, Seph?'" She mimicked Althea's high, faux-jolly tone. "No, I bloody well wasn't, sometimes. You probably don't even remember, but I had a hard time of it when I was sixteen. Six years ago now. I wrote you, asking if I could come stay. You said no."

"What…" The word escaped in an appalled breath. Had she? How could Althea not even remember that? "What did you say?"

"I said that school here was rubbish and I needed to get away. You wrote now wasn't a good time."

Briefly Althea closed her eyes. Now she remembered. Jasper had been in one of his icy rages, and she'd thought her sister had just meant for the weekend. "I'm sorry," she said quietly. "I didn't realise how bad it was for you. I thought you just wanted to visit."

"Yeah, well, you didn't ask, did you?"

Althea held on to her temper. "I had things going on in my life, Seph—"

"Yeah, I know. Your husband was—is—an arse. I get that. But you were a grown-up, Althea, and I was a kid. And you know what Mum and Dad can be like. I love them to bits, but they're not exactly on the ball about stuff, are they? And you had Sam and Olivia. I didn't have anyone."

"Right." Guilt and frustration warred within her. "Why me, though? I mean, you don't seem angry with Olivia—"

"She tried more. She'd invite me for weekends and mean it. She'd come here, a lot more than you ever did. I would have lived with her in Sixth Form but she was in a little studio flat and didn't have space."

"Oh." The word was little more than a whisper. "And Sam?"

"Sam is gone three-quarters of the time," Seph replied

with a shrug. "I barely know him. Maybe it's unfair of me to put so much on you, but you're the oldest. My sister. It made a difference."

Althea could understand that. Goodness, but she felt about two inches tall right now. She couldn't blame Seph for how she felt, and she wished she'd tried more when she'd been younger, but at the same time she wished her sister could give her a bit of a break. Life had been hard for her, too.

And yet you're the big sister. The bossy one. You should have made more of an effort.

She rose and took a tentative step towards her sister. "I'm sorry, Seph. Truly. You're right. I should have done more. I can see that now, but...can we have a second chance? I want to—"

"A second chance? What, so you can swan back here and save the day?"

"I'm not—"

"You so are. You never even thought about asking me how I felt about you doing up Casterglass."

Althea stared at her incredulously. "I asked everyone—"

"I mean, before it was a done deal."

"It's hardly a done deal," Althea protested. "We haven't got the funding, for a start."

"All I mean is," Seph said coldly, "this is my *home*. I'm the one who actually lives and works here, and you didn't ask me about anything, ever."

"You never even *talk* to me—"

"Because you never listen."

Althea's mouth dropped open and she snapped it shut. "So everything's my fault?" she demanded through gritted teeth. "I'm the one who should have made all the effort, every time? Because you're twenty-two now, Seph. You're an adult, and at any time you could have said: 'You know what, Althea? I'd like to talk about this.' But you never bloody did."

"There wasn't any point."

"Of course not." Althea rolled her eyes, and Seph gave her a glare that could have singed the hair on her head before stomping out of the room.

That had gone well. Not. Althea let out a huff of frustration and hurt. She shouldn't have lost her temper, she knew that, but Seph hadn't made it any easier. She still didn't fully understand why her sister practically hated her. All right, she could have made more effort over the years. She'd always known that. But she hadn't been entirely AWOL, and even if her invitations to visit had seemed half-hearted, she'd still made them.

Although perhaps a half-hearted invitation was worse than none at all. With a sigh Althea sank once more into a chair. How on earth was this going to work, if she and Seph were at daggers drawn all the time? She had a terrible feeling she'd just made things worse, not better, and she had no idea where to go from here. The ideas she'd scribbled in her notebook all morning suddenly seemed as substantial as fairy tales. If any of this was going to work, they had to get along.

And, she acknowledged, she wanted to get along with her sisters simply for their sakes. They were *sisters*. Family. She wanted a better relationship than this. But, she knew, sometimes that wasn't in her hands.

With a groan Althea wondered how, after feeling so hopeful this morning, she could now feel so low. And how on earth could she make things better with her sister?

Chapter Nineteen

THE HOUSE IN Cobham looked exactly as Althea remembered it, and yet somehow less. Made of golden brick, with six dormer windows glinting in the wintry sunlight, it looked both elegant and depressing. Soulless, somehow. As she pulled into the driveway, she let out a long, low breath she hadn't realised she'd been holding before exchanging an uncertain look with Poppy.

"How are you feeling?"

"Okay, I guess." Her daughter shrugged, her gaze on the empty house. "It's only been two weeks, but it feels weird to be here."

"Yes, it does." Althea glanced back at the house, wondering why she felt such a dread about going inside. It felt like going back in time, and she wanted to focus on the future. *Their* future.

It was the twenty-eighth of December, and she and Poppy had driven from Casterglass to Cobham to get their stuff and then head back home. Althea was planning to spend only one night at the house, and Poppy had been, somewhat surprisingly, in agreement.

"You don't want to see any of your friends?" Althea had ventured cautiously, because she knew this was a big wrench for her daughter, and Poppy had shaken her head.

"Like you said, they weren't really my friends. I don't want to see them."

Tobias and Ben had declined to come at all, which had given Althea pause. Did they really have so little connection to the only home they'd ever known? It brought her both relief and sadness. She'd been so intent on creating a welcoming home for her children over the years, and yet they all seemed quite happy to leave it behind. She supposed that taught her what home really was—people, not a place, and certainly not this place. Home was now Casterglass, and everyone there, including Seph. She hadn't managed to make any headway with her sister since yesterday's unfortunate argument, but Althea was determined to remain hopeful.

"Right." Taking a deep breath, she opened the door and got out of the car. Poppy followed. A few seconds later she'd unlocked the front door and stepped into the vaulted marble-floored foyer she'd always felt more suited to a hotel than a home, shoving aside the drift of post that had piled up in the last few weeks. The air smelled stale, of old air freshener and emptiness. The carpet underneath the Christmas tree in the sitting room was decorated with a layer of needles that had fallen, and the Christmas tree, having gone two weeks without water, was looking decidedly woebegone, its boughs drooping under the weight of the ornaments.

"Weird," Poppy said softly as she looked around. "It already feels like I don't live here anymore."

Althea knew exactly what she meant. Even after twenty years, so little connected her to this place. "Is that a good thing or a bad thing?"

"A good thing," Poppy answered. "I think." She gave Althea an encouraging smile. "Casterglass is much cooler."

"Agreed." Again Althea understood what her daughter was feeling. This was hard, painful, but it was still moving forward. "Shall we start going through things?" Ben and Tobias had made lists of what they wanted; there had been surprisingly little, just some clothes, books, and a few odds and ends.

Poppy nodded. "Yeah, I guess."

"There are some plastic bins in the garage," Althea told her. "I'll bring them up."

A wave of sorrow swept through her as Poppy went upstairs and she walked through the house to the adjoining garage to find the bins. As homey as she'd tried to make it, this house had never truly felt as if it belonged to her. Jasper had bought without her even looking at it, insisting she should be thrilled, and he'd hired the interior decorator and approved of all the choices, not entrusting her even with that. The result was that Althea had often felt as if she lived in a sterile and overpriced hotel, a show house, not a home, which she supposed was exactly what Jasper had wanted.

And yet… She paused in the family room that adjoined the kitchen, a stack of bins cradled in her arms. They'd played epic games of Monopoly and Uno here; when the kids had been really little, they'd played Hot Lava, a game where no one was allowed to touch the floor as they clambered around the furniture, screeching and giggling. Jasper hadn't been present for those exuberant times but there had also been birthday celebrations and family dinners and fun and *love*. She couldn't regret it all. She didn't want to.

And even though she was now in the position of having to look back at her life through a different lens, she realised there had been good mixed in with the bad, like streaks of gold in granite. She had a sudden memory of Jasper giving Ben helicopter rides on the floor of the family room, Ben balanced on Jasper's feet as he giggled hysterically…

All right, it had been a long time ago, but it had *happened*. Her children had memories of Jasper as a good father… She even had a few memories of him as a good husband. She remembered how he'd swept her up in his arms and carried her across the threshold when they'd moved into this house. Always one for an exuberant gesture, Jasper had been his most charming self then, and she'd loved him. Twenty years of intervening unhappiness couldn't take that memory away. With a sigh she turned and went upstairs to start packing.

In the end, Althea didn't take very much. She thought about packing all her designer clothes and selling them on eBay, but she didn't want the reminders of a life she no longer wanted to live and so she stuck with packing her comfortable clothes along with a few of her favourite nicer outfits. She left her jewellery—most of them were presents from Jasper, half-hearted apologies for his affairs—and she didn't want those reminders, either. She took a family portrait from a few years ago, all of them smiling in it, her toiletries and clothes, and a few books. That was it.

Finished, she went in search of Poppy, to find her sitting on her bed, a framed photo in her hands, a pile of clothes heaped at her feet.

"Pops? I have the bins." Althea put a couple on the floor as she glanced at her daughter in concern. "Is everything all right?"

"Yeah." Poppy sniffed. "I was just looking at this." She gestured to the photo. "Do you remember?"

Althea stepped closer so she could see the picture—one of Poppy and Jasper when she'd been about ten, a father-daughter dance at school. Jasper was on one knee, his arm around Poppy. She was beaming.

"I do remember that," Althea said quietly. Jasper had texted her that afternoon to say he wouldn't be able to go because of some work thing, and Althea had, in a rare moment of bolshiness, insisted he had to go, for Poppy's sake. She knew Poppy would have been heartbroken if her daddy had bailed at the last minute. And so he had, and he'd even been cheerful about it, saving his ill grace for Althea alone, and this memory was the result.

"It wasn't all bad, was it, Mum?" Poppy asked, her voice wobbling a little.

Althea sat down on the bed and put her arm around her. "No, darling, it wasn't. You have loads of happy memories of your dad, and that's the way it should be. He can be a lot of fun, sometimes, can't he?" Poppy sniffed again and nodded, and Althea continued cautiously, "I don't want to keep you from having a relationship with him, sweetheart. Moving to Casterglass doesn't mean you can't visit or spend time with him. He is, and always will be, your dad."

"He's changed, though." Poppy put the framed photo aside. "He doesn't have time for us anymore. He hasn't for a long time."

It was true Jasper had become more distant with all of them in recent years, but Althea wanted to believe he still loved his children. "I know he's busy," she said, "but that doesn't mean he doesn't love you."

Poppy gave her a narrowed look. "Well, that kind of love doesn't do anyone much good, does it? I mean, telling someone you love them isn't the same as showing it. Showing up." She sighed and rose from the bed to start packing. "It's okay. I'm used to it."

Althea felt as if her heart were splintering into pieces. "Oh, Poppy…"

"If he wants to make an effort, that's one thing. But right now I don't have time for him." She continued chucking her clothes into the bin. "I'll be done in a few minutes, and then can we go out somewhere? I don't feel like hanging around here anymore."

"Sure." Althea managed a smile even though she felt as if she could cry for the pain she knew Poppy felt, and needed to feel. Some things in life you just had to wade through. "Of course."

It only took them another hour to get everything they needed, including Ben and Tobias's things. It really wasn't much at all. While Poppy had been finishing her packing, Althea had written a note to Jasper and left it on his bedside table, where she hoped he would see it at some point. After twenty years of marriage, it had seemed depressingly brief:

Dear Jasper, I've taken everything I need. Feel free to dispose of the rest as you like. I'm staying at Casterglass with the children for the foreseeable future; if you want get in touch with them, you have their numbers and email addresses. I hope, for all your sakes, you can continue to have a relationship with them. Althea

She put the pen down and gazed around the bedroom with a dispirited air, doing her best not to give in to the regret that threatened to roll over her in waves. *Half your life over. Wasted.* No, not wasted. She had beautiful children, and she was a lot stronger. She'd learned some tough lessons. And she really was looking towards the future now.

"Ready, Poppy?" she called.

HAVING LOADED EVERYTHING into the car, they went to a local Italian restaurant for dinner. Althea couldn't remember the last time she'd done anything alone with Poppy. She might have suggested things, but her daughter would have disdained 'Mum and me' time. Now Poppy smiled at her as she ordered a fruity mocktail and a big plate of pasta, and Althea was grateful that, despite so much hardship or perhaps because of it, they'd arrived at this moment.

"I was thinking about the shop," Poppy said as she drew on her straw, her eyes alight. "What do you think about having a line of things—napkins, tea towels, scarves and stuff—with a signature pattern? The Casterglass pattern? We could have someone local design it or maybe incorporate something of the heraldic shield…? And it would only be for sale at the castle. Really, you know, elite."

"I think that's a brilliant idea," Althea said, impressed and full of love. She adored seeing her daughter looking so animated. "Why don't you design it?"

Poppy's eyes widened. "Me?"

"Why not? It was your idea, and I bet you could do it. You were always good at art, and you love those design shows on TV. We could hire someone to reproduce it, but you could come up with the original pattern."

"Wow…" Poppy sucked down some of her mocktail. "That would be so cool."

They kept chatting as their meals came, and Althea revelled in the simple pleasure of getting to know her daughter all over again. In the midst of dealing with her teenaged attitude, she'd forgotten how funny and surprisingly astute Poppy could be. She was fun to be with, and that filled Althea with grateful joy. Then, halfway through their bowls of spaghetti, Poppy's expression clouded.

"What is it?" Althea asked, and then followed her daughter's gaze to a nearby table of girls who had recently arrived—blonde, thin, laughing raucously. They looked vaguely familiar and they reminded Althea of crows, bright-eyed and picking at their food. "Do you know them?" she asked quietly and Poppy nodded.

"Yeah, that's the group I used to belong to. Well, *thought* I belonged to."

"What exactly happened, Poppy? Was it just that party—"

"I guess the party was like your friends' holiday," Poppy said, and to Althea's surprise, humour flashed in her eyes. "I guess I am as much of a saddo as you were, even if I wanted to deny it."

"There's worse things than being a saddo," Althea replied lightly, although her heart ached for her daughter and the hurt she'd so obviously been feeling. "So what happened with this party?"

"I wasn't invited." Poppy sighed. "Even before we went to Casterglass. And Elise was. She is—was—my closest friend, but then she made this big thing about how she was going to the party and I wasn't and it was like I wasn't cool enough for her anymore." Her gaze slid over to the table. "She's over there now, with her new, cooler friends. And I know it isn't even that big a deal—it was just a party—but it's more than that." She paused. "I don't want to be like that. And I don't want to try to be like that anymore."

Althea reached over to put her hand on top of her daughter's. "I'm proud of you, Pops."

"I'm going to go tell them," she said suddenly, and Althea sat back in surprise.

"Wait—tell them what?"

"What I think." With a bit of her old attitude, Poppy flicked her hair over her shoulders as she stood up and sashayed over to the table. Althea watched—appalled, amazed, and then ridiculously proud as Poppy spoke to them. She couldn't hear what she said, but predictably all four girls at the table gave her sneering looks. Inwardly Althea cringed. If those blonde crows hurt her daughter now...

But to her surprise Poppy just laughed. She turned around and walked back to their table, her smile wide and determined.

"What did you say?" Althea asked.

Poppy reached for her mocktail. "I told them if you had to put someone down to feel important, you were clearly the one with the problem. And then I wished them a nice life." She shrugged. "I'm done with them." For a second her bravado dropped to reveal a hint of vulnerability. "I may only have one friend up at Casterglass, but at least she's decent."

"She certainly is. And one friend is better than none." Althea thought of the text she'd received from Jenna that morning, agreeing to meet up for coffee in Ulverston next week. She'd been heartened by the reply, since Jenna hadn't seemed all that keen when she'd talked to her in person. Life was definitely looking up. "Besides," she assured Poppy, "you'll make loads more friends once you start school."

"I hope so." Poppy looked uncertain for a moment. "Starting a new school in the middle of Lower Sixth isn't exactly ideal, you know?"

"I know," Althea agreed quietly.

Poppy's chin tilted upwards. "But it's better than going back."

IN THE END, they decided to start driving back to Casterglass that very evening. Poppy had confessed she didn't want to spend the night in the house, and Althea rather agreed with her. It meant fuelling herself with travel mugs of coffee and spending the night at a shabby Travelodge on the M6, but it was worth it to roll up to the castle at eleven o'clock the next morning, to everyone's surprise and delight.

Already things had happened in their absence—Seph, Ben and Tobias had all started clearing out the old barns, and her father had arranged for another estimate for the roof.

As everyone helped bring in the bins of stuff, her father was jubilant, telling them that he'd contacted 'an old friend' about the dented helmet and he thought it might be from the Viking era.

"Viking!" Althea had exclaimed, impressed. "Really?"

"If so, it might be worth quite a bit. There's only one genuine Viking helmet in a museum in all of the UK."

"That's amazing, Daddy." Althea kissed his cheek. "Well done."

Her father beamed.

Later, when everything had been unpacked and Althea had been filled in on the surprising number of developments that had occurred in her twenty-four hours of absence, she finally found a quiet moment to deal with the text that had pinged on her phone that morning.

We need to talk. –JB

She didn't know how he'd got her mobile number; perhaps one of her children had given it to him. Neither did she know what a talk would entail, only that it made an uneasy dread pool in her stomach. She didn't want to lose John's friendship, and she was afraid that kiss—exciting as it had been—might pose a serious risk to it. Still, he was right. They needed to talk.

Curled up on the window seat in the sitting room while everyone played a board game downstairs, Althea watched the sun sink slowly behind the purple-fringed fells. The world was so peaceful, the darkness falling like a velvet blanket, the only sound the hooting of a barn owl, and the occasional burst of laughter from downstairs.

She was *happy*, she realised. Despite all the remaining uncertainty—the details of her divorce, her entirely precarious financial position, Casterglass itself—she was happy. She was glad she'd come here, that she was staying. It hadn't been quite the montage of movie moments she'd joked about when she'd first arrived, but close enough. *Close enough.*

She glanced down at her phone. Yes, she was happy, but she wasn't ready to embark on a relationship with John Braithwaite, and yet at the same time she didn't want to close it down completely. What to do? What to say?

She hesitated for a few more moments and then she texted back: *Yes, we do. When is a good time? —A*

A few minutes later a reply pinged in. *Tomorrow morning, 10ish? I'll bring the coffee and we can go for a walk.*

A walk? But not a date, surely? Her stomach churned with a mixture of uncertainty, excitement, and sheer nerves.

Sounds good, she texted back, and then she put her phone aside as she leaned against the window and watched the last of the sun's rays sink beneath the fells.

Chapter Twenty

I T WAS ONE of those brilliant, blue-sky days that so rarely came to Cumbria, with absolutely everything sparkling, the air as fresh and clear as a drink of water. Althea stepped outside with a feeling of nervousness bordering on dread. The weather was most definitely not matching her mood, because she was not looking forward to this conversation.

Last night she'd given herself a stern talking-to; she was forty-one, not fourteen, and she could talk about kissing without coming over all giggly and embarrassed. Of *course* she could. She'd birthed three children, after all, in blood and anguish, and she'd been relatively unfazed when it came to discussing the facts of life with her three children.

And yet, when it came to John, she felt as if she were about fourteen, silly and blushing. She had something of a crush on him, she realised, and it was most ill-timed, considering everything else that was going on in her life.

Well, she could deal with a crush. She would have to. She took a deep breath and straightened her shoulders as John's mud-splattered Rover appeared around the curve in the drive. He couldn't keep her stomach from doing a little flip, however, as John emerged from the car, his shock of chestnut-brown hair glinting in the wintry sunlight, his lanky form encased in his usual get-up of wax jacket, faded jeans and battered boots.

He hoisted a flask. "I brought coffee."

"Wonderful."

Her smile flitted across her face and disappeared as her heart rate kicked up a notch. *Easy, Althea*, she told herself. *Easy.* "Where would you like to walk?"

"I thought you could give me a tour of the estate. I've been round the edges, since your land borders mine, but I haven't seen much of the interior."

"Um, okay." Her voice sounded so high and nervous. As discreetly as she could Althea wiped her palms along the sides of her jeans before pulling on her fleece-lined gloves. "That sounds like a plan."

John gave her a smile that was both knowing and sympathetic, and made Althea want to cringe. He clearly could tell how nervous she was. "Okay, so where should we start?"

"Umm…" Why did her head feel as if it was full of cotton wool? Althea nodded towards the meadow that ran along one side of the castle, the sea beyond. "How about we walk along the ha-ha, and then back through the woods? We'll end up by the barns and gardens."

"All right."

The tufty grass squelched beneath their boots as they

started along the meadow towards the sunken ditch and retaining wall that made a border with the next field. Seagulls wheeled high overhead and in the distance a sheep bleated, the sound plaintive. A fresh, salt-tinged breeze from the sea blew over them as Althea dug her hands into the pockets of her coat and lowered her head against the window.

"Did you have a nice Christmas?" she asked, sounding so very polite.

"Yes, nice enough. Alice was happy with her presents and we cobbled together a roast dinner. She's more of a cook than I am."

"Is it…hard?" Althea ventured cautiously. "On holidays? I mean, without your wife… I know it's been a few years…"

John was silent for a long moment and Althea wondered if she should have asked. He'd told her before he hadn't explained that situation as well as he should have, and that it was all a bit more complicated, and she still had no idea what that meant.

"Yes, it has been a long time," he said finally. "I think Alice and I are both used to it being just the two of us, to be honest."

Althea nodded slowly. "How did she die?"

"Ovarian cancer. It was…quick. About three months from start to finish."

She couldn't keep an appalled expression from her face. "That must have been so—"

"Yes. Well." John rubbed his jaw uncomfortably. "Like I said, it was a bit more complicated than it might appear to you."

"Do you want to tell me how?" Did she want to hear?

He shrugged and sighed. "Not really. Just that…we didn't get along all that well, truth be told." He hesitated, as if he was going to say more, but then he just shrugged again and said, "But like I said, it was a long time ago." He'd texted her saying they needed to talk, but not about that, obviously. Althea decided to drop it. "So where were you thinking of setting up the glamping?" John asked, and she wondered if they were going to talk about anything serious at all.

"At the top of this field, perhaps, where you can get a view of the sea. We were thinking about doing those pods, with wood burners… It would get pretty cold, especially with the wind."

"True."

"Sam had the idea of doing these tree houses in the woods. Apparently they're the next big thing." She nodded towards the acre or so of cedar and larches that bordered the north end of the estate. "Deluxe accommodation, apparently, to sleep among the trees."

"Sounds quite interesting. When is he coming back?"

"End of February, apparently. Although whether he'll stay…" She shrugged. "He's always been a bit of a wanderer."

John slid her a thoughtful look. "What was it actually like, growing up in a castle? Because I can't imagine it, even though I lived right next door."

"It's strange, isn't it? I don't even remember you from when I was young," Althea confessed. "Although we must have met."

"I saw you from afar, mostly," John told her. "Everyone did. It was 'there go the Penryns' kind of thing. A bit of craic about what the castle was like, from people who did odd jobs on the estate."

"And what was the craic?" Althea asked, curious yet not entirely sure if she really wanted to know.

John let out a little laugh. "That you were all a bit mad, actually. I remember hearing from a mate of my father's who did some plumbing that you all ran through the castle like a herd of banshees. He said, I recall, that it was 'bloomin' crackers'."

Althea gave a little huff of acknowledgement. "That's true, I suppose."

"So what was it really like? Because for a long time I thought you were all toffee-nosed snobs, but now I'm starting to wonder."

"Only wonder?" Althea pretended to look insulted, although she wasn't sure if she really was pretending. "Do I seem like a snob to you?"

"No, you don't," he said quietly. "So tell me the truth. How was it?"

Althea was silent for a long moment as she tried to organise her thoughts. "It was mad," she finally said. "And for
a long time I resented the—the lack of normality. When I
got to about nine I hated being homeschooled, and I just
wanted to live in a regular house with a regular family. A
bedroom that was warm, a sitting room with a TV." She
glanced at him to see how he was taking this, afraid he'd see
her honesty as a shameless bid for sympathy when yes, she
knew how privileged she was. She really did.

"I can understand that," John said quietly.

Heartened by his compassion, Althea continued. "My
parents are wonderful. They really are. They love us all, they
always have, but when we were growing up they'd forget
things. Birthdays, dentist appointments, just the normal day-
to-day stuff that other parents seemed to get. Like snacks."

"Snacks?"

"When Olivia and I went into the village we'd see kids
with crisps and biscuits and things and we were so envious.
We never had anything like that growing up. We never had
any food. I mean, we didn't starve, of course, but my parents
weren't great about shopping. Sometimes we'd just scavenge
for what we could. And I dreamed of going to school and
having a lunchbox with a ham sandwich and a bag of crisps
in it. Which sounds ridiculous, I know."

"But you did go to school," John said after a moment.
"For Year Six, didn't you?"

"Yes…and I was instantly out of my depth. I must have

seemed so odd to everyone there. And I packed my own lunch." She gave him a quick smile. "Look, I know how this sounds. I've always known how this sounds. Poor little rich girl, sniff, sniff. But you did ask."

"I know."

"Anyway, it wasn't all bad. Coming back here has helped me remember the good times—and there were loads of good times. We really did have so much fun. I think it's just…you can fixate on things, can't you? And for so long I fixated on wanting to be normal. It was all I thought about. All that mattered. And I let it guide so many of my choices."

John glanced at her with a frown. "How so?"

"Well…my marriage, for one. At the start Jasper could be very charming and he threw a lot of money around and to me that looked like love. And when love came with all that wonderful normality—a nice house, children who would go to a normal school—I went chasing after it."

"That's understandable."

She let out a sigh. "I suppose. Anyway. That's my bit of self-therapy for the day. How about some coffee?"

They found a few tumbled stones that were mostly dry and sat down, the sea a sliver of slate blue on the horizon, the fields rolling onwards in an undulating canvas of green. John retrieved two plastic mugs from one of his voluminous pockets and poured them both coffee.

They clinked mugs and then drank as the wind from the sea buffeted them and sunlight sparkled on every stark tree and blade of grass.

"Look, I've found something out," John said after a moment, and Althea tensed instinctively.

"Found something…?"

"My solicitor friend, the one I told you about? She looked at your prenup agreement and she doesn't think it would stand if challenged."

"What?" This was so unexpected Althea nearly spluttered her coffee. She'd assumed the prenup would be rock solid, because this was Jasper, after all, and he surely would have made certain it was. She'd already become used to the idea that she wouldn't see a penny from him, although she hoped he'd provide for the children.

"You were only twenty-one, and you didn't have your own legal representation. And the terms of the agreement are remarkably unfair. Put it all together, I think it would be a very unfeeling judge who would accept it as it stood."

"Wow." Althea shook her head slowly. "I never even thought it could be challenged. But what does that mean, exactly? I don't want a big court battle. I don't think I could handle that right now."

"And you might not have to have one. If my friend sends an opening salvo to Lord Pompous Fotheringhay, that might be all that's needed."

"Or it might make Jasper even more furious." Her stomach curdled with dread at the prospect.

"There's not much more he can do, is there?" John asked

reasonably. "But of course it's up to you."

"I don't know." She took a sip of coffee, her gaze on the sea while John sipped from his own mug and waited. She didn't want to be an ostrich anymore, she reminded herself. She didn't want to accept what little she was given because she didn't dare ask for more. And yet here she was, contemplating doing just that.

"I suppose an enquiry couldn't hurt," she said, giving John an uncertain smile. "Just to see."

"All right."

"She must be billing for her time," she realised with some alarm. "I don't have any money to pay at the moment…"

"Don't worry about that. She'd been doing it as a favour to me."

"A favour?" Althea raised her eyebrows, curious now. What, was this lawyer some old girlfriend? And was she actually jealous?

"Yes, a favour." Clearly this was something else he didn't want to talk about.

"All right. Thank you."

They finished their coffee in silence, and Althea wondered if they were actually going to talk about that kiss. Perhaps they would just pretend it hadn't happened, something that sort of suited her, but also felt disappointing. Maybe she would have to be brave enough to mention it first.

"Should we walk through the woods?" she suggested, and

John nodded.

Underneath the spreading boughs of the larches and cedar, the forest was quiet and dark, a thick carpet of needles underneath their feet. They walked in silence for a few minutes, as Althea's heart started to thud.

"Look," she finally blurted, "about that kiss."

John slanted her a bemused look. "I was wondering which one of us was going to mention it first."

"Why didn't you?"

He shrugged. "I was working up to it. But I can't get a read on how you felt about it, and that was giving me pause."

"Well." She cleared her throat, her gaze on the ground in front of her. "I...I think it was a mistake." As soon as she said the words, she sort of wished she hadn't. She didn't think it was a mistake, not exactly, just badly timed. She glanced at John and saw his expression had closed right up, his gaze on the ground, as well.

"Ah. I see."

"It's just...I'm still married."

"I know."

"And I know Jasper has been having affairs left, right, and centre, and we're about to be divorced, but...I said vows. I meant them. And we have children together..." Her words were garbled, her tone desperate. She didn't even really understand what she was trying to say, except that it was too soon. Way too soon. "Besides, with the castle and sorting out my children, and just everything…I'm not remotely in a place for a relationship. Not," she continued quickly, flushing, "that you were proposing a relationship, or anything at all. Of course. I know that." Why on earth had she used the word *proposing*? "I just meant…it's not the right time."

"I understand." The words were toneless, his face giving nothing away. Althea felt her heart sink right down to her muddy boots.

"Okay," she said after a moment. "That's…good." Even if it didn't feel good. It actually, she realised, felt very *not* good. Which was confusing.

They walked in silence for a few more minutes, the forest dark and quiet all around them, the only sound their footsteps, muffled by the carpet of needles. Althea struggled to think of something to say; she felt as if she'd lobbed a grenade into the middle of their conversation, their whole friendship, and she didn't know how to recover.

They came out of the forest onto an overgrown track that led back to the castle's barns, and still they didn't speak. Then, finally, John said something.

"I like you," he told her bluntly. Althea nearly faltered in her step as she stared at him in surprise. "I really like you."

"Oh…"

"I'm not asking you to like me back. I know I'm a grumpy old codger when it comes down to it, but I wanted you to know. I understand it's not the right time. I really do.

And I understand that things might change, and nothing might come of it, of us, but I want you to know where I stand."

He stopped right there in the road to look at her directly, his gaze steady and sure as Althea stopped too and faced him. "I'm not the sort of bloke who goes around kissing women willy-nilly. Maybe you've gathered that already. The truth is, I've only had one relationship since Laura died, and it was short-lived. For Alice's sake, as well as my own, I haven't looked too hard for another one. But then you came along and…" He spread his hands. "I thought you were so unsuitable. At the start I thought you were a snob. But I've come to know you, not all that well yet, admittedly, but what I've seen, I've liked, and I've wanted to know more. A lot more."

Althea's stomach fizzed at the look of heat in his eyes and she struggled not to look away, simply as some sort of self-protection. She'd never had such an honest conversation. It *sizzled* with truth. It was both painful and thrilling, like her nerve endings were being exposed to light and air, like everything in her was pulsing.

"I…" She licked her lips, trying to frame a response, but John held up one hand to forestall her.

"You don't need to reply. I'm not expecting you to say anything. I just didn't want you to leave this conversation thinking it had just been the heat of the moment, because in fact there was precious little heat in that storeroom with the rain coming in." He gave her a wonderfully crooked smile.

"So there we are. Or at least that's where I am. The next move is yours."

Althea nodded, half-tempted to kiss him right then and there and yet knowing she couldn't. Not until things were sorted with Jasper. Not until she had her head on straight. Not until she was a free woman…and even then, only if she was brave enough.

"Okay," she whispered. "Thank you."

John nodded, and then he kept walking. Althea fell into step beside him, and after a few moments he asked about her plans for the barns as they came into view, and within a few minutes they were talking about reroofing and workshops and she almost wondered if that lovely conversation had happened at all.

Chapter Twenty-One

"JENNA!"

Althea half-stood as she waved to her friend from across the crowded coffee shop in the garden centre outside Ulverston. It was a few days after New Year's, and for Althea the start of a new life. After charades in the sitting room and fireworks in the garden to celebrate the new year, she had busied herself with preparations and plans for Casterglass. She'd filled out forms for bank loans and grants from various charitable organisations; she'd mucked out barns and helped to catalogue the castle's many possessions for the antique assessor who was coming next week, and she'd registered Tobias and Poppy for school at the comprehensive here in Ulverston. They started tomorrow.

Althea felt both exhausted and elated by it all, even as so much remained uncertain. Seph still wasn't talking to her. Olivia had gone back to York, and was still deciding whether she'd move to Casterglass permanently. There had been no word from Jasper, and she'd only seen John once, when she'd brought Poppy over to Alice's for a sleepover. They'd had a few glasses of wine in front of the fire and chatted about nothing terribly important, but it had been relaxed and lovely and made Althea wonder if maybe she was ready for something more. The evening had ended with nothing more than a smile and a wave goodbye, which felt right, and yet…also didn't.

"Hey, you," Jenna said with a slightly brittle smile as she unwound her scarf and then collapsed into the seat opposite Althea. "How are you?"

"Good, good," Althea replied. "Busy. Thanks for meeting up." Jenna nodded somewhat abstractedly, not meeting her eye, and Althea wondered if she was pushing this association a little too much. They'd had so much fun in Year Six, but there could be no denying Jenna didn't seem quite as into renewing their friendship as she was. "Shall I get the coffees?" she suggested and Jenna flashed her a quick smile of thanks.

"That would be fab."

Althea queued for coffees, wondering if she should ask Jenna outright if something was off. After their cosy chat at the Christmas drinks evening, Jenna had seemed more and more unenthused about meeting up. Yet she'd agreed to this coffee.

No hiding your head in the sand, Althea reminded herself. She was determined to confront things head-on, even this.

"So tell me what's going on in your life," she stated breezily as she handed Jenna her vanilla latte and sat down with her own mocha, complete with whipped cream and chocolate sprinkles. She didn't have to watch her weight anymore, or at least not as much, and she wasn't touching another Pilates class with a barge pole for the rest of her life. "How was your Christmas?"

"It was so-so. Matt had the kids for Christmas Day, so…" She shrugged and took a sip of her latte, wiping the foam from her upper lip.

"That must be hard. Do you have a fifty-fifty custody agreement?"

"Pretty much. He's a good dad, but he's with someone else and I'm not and it always feels a bit…" She shrugged and took another sip of coffee.

"I'm so sorry, Jenna. That must be really tough."

Jenna brushed her sympathy aside, seeming almost impatient. "What about your ex? Will you guys split custody equally?"

"I very much doubt it." Although what if Jasper insisted? No, he wouldn't. Couldn't. And in any case, Ben was an adult and Poppy and Tobias would get to decide for themselves. "He's more of a Christmas and birthdays kind of father, although he used to be a bit more involved when they were smaller." A small, sad sigh escaped her as her mind snagged on a memory—Jasper rocking Ben to sleep when he'd been six weeks old and it had all been wonderful and new. She couldn't remember him rocking Poppy or Tobias to sleep.

"So, how are things up at the castle?" Jenna asked brightly. "I heard a rumour you were thinking of staying." She spoke so incredulously that Althea felt her hackles rise.

"Actually, I am."

"What?" Jenna looked completely incredulous. "Why? I mean…"

Quickly and succinctly Althea explained about her plans for the castle. Jenna still looked disbelieving. "Is it so hard to imagine?" she asked, slightly stung by her obvious scepticism.

"No…it's just…I didn't think you'd be staying."

"Well, I am." Althea tried to smile. "So we can see a bit more of each other, maybe." Although she was seriously starting to wonder whether that was something Jenna wanted.

Jenna looked down at her half-drunk coffee and then up again. "Althea…" she began, and then stopped.

Now she was feeling decidedly uneasy. "What is it?" she asked, hoping her voice sounded normal.

Jenna let out a heavy sigh. "I feel like such a fake. I haven't…that is, I haven't really been that nice to you. About you."

Althea's questioning smile froze on her face. "Oh?" she asked, because she had no idea what else to say.

"I didn't…" Jenna blew out a breath. "When I saw you in Booths, it was such a shock. And you looked so…I don't know, glamorous."

Althea let out a hollow laugh. Yes, she'd worked hard to

look the part Jasper wanted her to play, but she'd never really felt it. At least she'd fooled someone, she supposed. "What does that have to do with anything?" she asked, although she had a feeling she already knew. She remembered John's look of surprise when she said she was friends with Jenna—and Jenna's look of guilt now.

"I was envious," Jenna admitted. "Of your life. Your clothes. Even your kids. They looked so…confident."

Althea thought of Poppy's attitude and heartbreak, Tobias's shyness and online world, and could only shake her head.

"And you know, you always had so much when we were growing up… I mean, you live in a *castle*."

"Yes, but you know what that castle is like. Falling down as we speak."

"It's not falling down that much," Jenna said, a trace of bitterness in her voice.

Althea felt a hot flare of anger and a deeper one of hurt. "Jenna," she said, "what are you trying to tell me?"

Jenna hung her head, her gaze firmly on the table between them. "I…I've been talking about you," she said in a low voice. "Gossiping, really."

Althea wasn't surprised, based on all Jenna had said so far, and yet she was. She felt a cold, prickly flush break out all over her body and as she reached for her mocha, her hands weren't quite steady. Why did this hurt so much? She didn't even know Jenna anymore, not really, and she'd known Jenna wasn't that into their friendship. This shouldn't feel like the body blow it did, and yet...

It did, because this was her new life, her new start, and already it felt like old hat. Friends who weren't friends. Mean girls who gossiped. People who judged her. Hadn't she had enough of that?

"I'm sorry," Jenna whispered. "I did it because I was envious. I wanted what you had."

Althea let out a hollow laugh. "What, an adulterous husband and a messy divorce? And absolutely no money?"

Jenna's gaze widened. "No money...?"

"I think I've given you enough craic already," Althea retorted, and now she sounded bitter. She realised she was angry, really angry, and it felt better than being hurt. "I don't get you, Jenna. I was honest with you. I told you about my husband, my life, how disappointed I felt...and you go and talk about me behind my back? I mean, I know we're not really friends anymore, but..." She shook her head. "What did you even say?"

"It doesn't matter—"

"I think it does." Althea's voice came out hard as she recalled John's disbelieving look. No wonder he'd been so incredulous! He must have heard some of the gossip. "So tell me, what?"

Jenna hunched her shoulders. "Really?"

"Really."

"I just said you'd, you know, swanned back here and you

were acting the la-di-da lady of the manor. And how you thought you'd have all Casterglass eating out of your hand." Jenna looked up, clearly miserable. "I know I must sound like a complete and utter bi—"

"Yes, you do." Althea took a steadying breath, willing the hurt back. "I thought you knew me better than that."

"Althea, I hadn't seen you in thirty years!"

"Exactly. So why would you think… What had I done to make you think…"

"I told you, I was envious." Jenna leaned forward. "When I saw you in Booths, chucking whatever you liked in your trolley, dressed to the nines…you seemed like you had it all sorted. And I admit, when you told me about your ex, I was thrown. But you still had a castle to come back to, and your family…" She took a deep breath. "My parents divorced when I was four. I barely know my dad."

"That's very sad, and I'm sorry for you, but it doesn't justify—"

"I know, but Althea, you've always been cool. I remember seeing you in year seven and you were so haughty, with your nose in the air—"

"What?" Althea stared at her in disbelief. "You mean when you were hanging out with all your friends by the train station and I was completely alone?"

"Butter wouldn't melt in your mouth—"

"Or yours. You ignored me that day—"

"*You* ignored *me*."

"What…" The word came out in a rush of breath. Althea felt as if her life was a kaleidoscope and someone had just given it a twirl. She'd been so lacking in self-confidence, so unsure of her place in the world, that she'd made assumptions. So had Jenna.

"I really am sorry, Althea. I'm telling you now because—"

"Because you knew I'd found out?"

"Well, yes." Jenna gave her a shamefaced smile. "And also because I regret what I said. It was at the pub one night and I'd had one too many. I was being stupid."

Althea nodded slowly. She understood, even if she didn't like it. She wondered how many people she'd misread over the years, how many opportunities she might have missed.

"So you forgive me?"

Althea took a breath, and then nodded. "Yes." It would take a little longer to trust her, but Althea didn't want to hold grudges. This was her new life, after all, and everyone deserved a fresh beginning, a second chance. "Let me get us another coffee. We have a lot of catching up to do, I think."

A smile broke across Jenna's face. "Let me get them," she said, and with an answering smile, Althea let her.

JENNA'S REVELATIONS WERE still running through Althea's mind when she walked Poppy and Tobias to the bus stop by the turning to Appleby Farm the next morning. She'd been surprised they'd been willing to let her come along; they weren't in primary school, after all, and yet starting a new school felt like a big deal. Last night Althea had gone a bit teary when Tobias had tried on his new blazer.

"We'll be fine, Mum," Poppy had assured her with an eye-roll and a shrug, but she hadn't protested when Althea had suggested she come along this morning.

It was another fresh morning, wintry and clear, and despite the hurt of Jenna's admissions Althea felt hopeful. She'd dealt with the situation, and she believed she and Jenna could still be friends even if it took a bit more time and trust. She was still moving forward.

"Is the antique assessor coming today?" Poppy asked as they walked down Casterglass's drive towards the main road. She seemed more interest in renovation developments than her school day, something that made Althea smile.

"Yes, but just for an initial look. We have so much stuff… It will take them ages, and there will have to be several specialists involved."

"What if they found something that was worth, like, a mint?" Tobias asked excitedly.

"Well, the Viking helmet didn't pan out that way, but it would be amazing." Apparently the helmet had been too dented and damaged to be of much value. Althea had a feeling they would be hearing that familiar refrain for most of her family's antiques. Still, any money they could raise would be a bonus.

As they came to the bus stop, Poppy slowed down.

"Mum, not to be rude or anything, but could you walk behind us a little bit? I mean, I am sixteen."

"All right." Althea dropped back as Poppy and Tobias headed towards Alice, who was already waiting by the little shelter. It wasn't until Althea had walked closer that she saw John had walked to the stop, as well.

"I thought I was the only helicopter parent in this situation," Althea said with a smile and he gave a rueful nod of acknowledgement.

"First day back and all that. But I'm trying not to kill Alice's vibe, whatever that means."

Alice threw him a dark look before she and Poppy began to chat excitedly. Tobias looked a little adrift, and Althea's heart ached for him. She hoped he'd be able to find good, like-minded friends here in Cumbria. She knew he was a little shy, a bit quirky, but surely there were kids like that at this school?

"He'll be fine," John said quietly, following her gaze. "But I know it's hard."

"I think I'm more nervous than they are." Althea let out a slightly wobbly laugh as the bus pulled up and Poppy and Tobias did their best to ignore her as they climbed on board. She understood; waving your teenaged children off did not exactly help their street cred.

"Do you fancy a coffee?" John said once the bus had trundled off, leaving Althea feeling a little flat. "And then I could drive you back to Casterglass."

"Oh…"

"No pressure." He held his hands palm up, smiling easily, and Althea smiled back.

"None felt. I'd love a coffee."

It was strange, she mused, how relaxed she felt with him, considering how heightened her awareness had become. Several times a day his words had replayed in her mind—*I like you. I really like you*—and a thrill had run right from her head to her toes. And yet it still felt wonderfully easy and companionable to walk alongside him up to the farmhouse, smoke curling from the chimney and the dogs barking excitedly as they approached the door.

"Tobias was asking for a dog," Althea remarked as she followed John into the kitchen. "We never had one in Surrey. Jasper didn't like the mess or bother."

"Do you think you might get one now?"

"I'm thinking about it."

"Tess here is having puppies in the spring," he said, as he patted one of the springer spaniels. "You're welcome to one, if you like. I usually keep one for myself and sell the rest, but I'll give you a freebie."

"Oh, wow, that's so kind."

"It's no trouble." His gaze lingered on hers as he reached for the kettle, and Althea felt her face warm. Yes, this was all so very companionable, and yet it also…wasn't. She looked away first.

"It feels strange," she said after a moment, willing her

blush to fade, "to think about making things permanent here. I was talking to Poppy and Tobias about giving their rooms a bit of a personal touch—everything is old and shabby, and I'd like them to feel as if they have their own rooms."

"But…" John prompted, clearly sensing something more.

"But I don't feel like I should change anything, even as I am contemplating changing everything." She let out a little laugh. "It all feels so strange, now that Christmas and New Years have passed. I'm *staying* here. I can't quite put my head around it. I can't quite make myself believe in it."

"I suppose that's understandable," John stated after a pause.

Althea thought he sounded a bit reserved, and she wondered at it. "I'm excited, of course," she said hurriedly, in case he thought she was complaining, but John just sipped his coffee and smiled.

They chatted about relatively innocuous things then—the antique assessor's visit and the imminent lambing season—and Althea thought they'd mostly regained their ease of conversation, but she still sensed John was holding something back, although she wasn't sure what.

"Everything's all right, isn't it?" she made herself ask once they were in his Rover, heading back to Casterglass.

He glanced at her with a frown. "Why wouldn't it be?"

"I don't know. Just my Spidey sense, as Tobias would

say." Althea tried to smile. "I…I like being your friend." She flushed as she said it, both hating and needing to be so vulnerable. Something flashed in John's eyes and he nodded.

"I like being yours."

But Althea still had a lingering sense of uncertainty as he pulled into the castle drive, both of them staring in surprise at the sleek forest-green Jaguar already parked there.

"Antique assessors must make a mint," John remarked dryly, and as the familiar figure emerged from the car, his cashmere overcoat flapping behind him, Althea felt her stomach drop down her toes.

"That's not the antique assessor," she said in a thready voice that sounded nothing like her own. "That's my husband."

Chapter Twenty-Two

ALTHEA DIDN'T CATCH John's response as she climbed out of the Rover on wobbly legs. She hadn't seen Jasper in just over a month, but it felt like years. And yet he looked the same—the same blond hair swept away from his high forehead, the same electric-blue eyes and hard, chiselled jaw. He was movie-star handsome, but in a way that now seemed cold and distant.

"There you are." His gaze swept over Althea and then moved to John, his eyes narrowing slightly. "And who is this?"

"This is my neighbour, John Braithwaite." Her voice still sounded scratchy. John gave a terse nod, his gaze just as assessing as Jasper's.

"Your neighbour," Jasper repeated, and his tone made Althea flush with both anger and shame. She knew her indiscretion was next to nothing compared to Jasper's, and yet she still couldn't keep from feeling a needle prick of guilt.

"Jasper, why are you here?"

"To see you, of course." A pause and then he added

swiftly, "And the children, of course."

"They're at school, and Ben's gone back to Durham." He'd left yesterday afternoon, promising to come back for the weekend as soon as he could.

"It's you I want to speak to, Althea. We have things to say to each other." He met her gaze directly, his eyes so very blue. "Please." He sounded surprisingly sincere.

From behind her John cleared his throat. "I should go."

"Yes. I'm sorry—" Althea stopped abruptly, because she didn't know what she was sorry for. John gave a shrugging sort of nod and climbed back into his Rover. Althea watched him reverse and then head down the drive with a helpless incredulity; her world felt like it was spinning out of control. She'd never expected Jasper to come all the way to Cumbria. Why was he here?

She turned back to face him; he was in his casual clothes, a cashmere polo jumper and perfectly pressed chinos. He looked handsome, yes, but he left her feeling utterly empty. "When did you get back from Switzerland?" she asked coolly.

"Yes, about that." Jasper looked, amazingly, a little sheepish. Well, that was a first. "Can we talk inside? I always manage to forget how bloody freezing Cumbria is." He offered her a rueful smile, a twinkle in his eyes, and in the past Althea would have tripped over herself in gratitude for him throwing her even that much of a bone. For him not being a complete and utter arse for once.

"All right," she said, her tone still cool even as she felt her composure slipping. When it came to a face-to-face confrontation, she feared Jasper would be the victor. But what did he actually *want*?

She walked around to the back, Jasper following, and into the kitchen, stilling when she saw Seph at the sink.

"Seph, you remember Jasper?" she asked, and her sister, who still wasn't talking to her, gave her husband a dark look.

"Yeah, I do," she said with emphasis, and Jasper looked slightly disconcerted by the savagery in her tone. "You want privacy, I suppose," she said.

"Please, if you don't mind…"

Seph stalked out of the kitchen without another word. Jasper raised his eyebrows.

"What's her problem?"

"You're not exactly a firm favourite around here," Althea told him. "But surely that can't be a surprise?"

"I suppose not." He gave a grimace.

Althea leaned against the Aga railing, grateful for its warmth on her back. She folded her arms and gave Jasper a level stare as he shrugged off his overcoat before running a hand through his hair. He seemed uncomfortable, and she was rather enjoying that. "Why did you come all this way, Jasper?"

"I wanted to see you."

"Why? I thought the divorce papers were obvious enough. Message received loud and clear, thank you."

Another grimace, seemingly sincere. "Look, Althea, I was angry then…"

"What?" She stared at him in disbelief. "Are you saying you didn't mean it?"

"At the time, yes, I suppose I did. It felt like we'd grown too far apart, in too many ways."

Althea couldn't keep from snorting out loud. "That's one way of putting it."

"But I've had a think," Jasper persevered, "and I don't want to throw away twenty years of marriage. We were good together, Althea. We used to be, anyway. I think we could get that back, if we tried."

This was so unexpected she struggled to respond for several seconds. "We were never good together, Jasper," she finally said, and he looked shocked.

"How can you say that? We had a good life, three beautiful children…"

"You started having affairs less than a year after we were married," she told him matter-of-factly, grateful that her voice didn't wobble. "When, exactly, were we good together?"

Jasper sighed heavily as he sank into a chair at the table. "I know I wasn't perfect, Althea," he said, and she bit her lip to keep from laughing—or maybe crying. She felt weirdly close to doing both.

"I wasn't expecting you to be perfect," she managed after a moment. "Just faithful to your wedding vows." At a minimum.

Jasper sighed again, looking regretful. "I admit I've made mistakes. A lot of mistakes. But I want another chance." He glanced up at her then, his blue eyes wide and so very appealing. She'd forgotten just how susceptible she could be to her husband's charm, to that seeming wry honesty. Perhaps that was at least part of why she'd stayed for so long.

"Another chance?" she repeated, struggling to form the words. "Are you serious?"

"Very serious." His blue, blue gaze remained trained on hers. "I still love you. I know I haven't always shown it, and I can admit, I've been a bastard sometimes. I know I have." He shook his head slowly. "I never meant to hurt you, but I was thoughtless. Very thoughtless."

"Thoughtless is leaving your wet towel on the floor," Althea told him. "Which is something else you did. But regular infidelity is more than *thoughtless.*"

"All right, I'm sorry, wrong choice of words. I've been…cruel." Althea could tell it cost him something to say that. "But this separation has shaken me up, Althea. It's not what I want. I want our family to be whole again. I want us to raise our children together." Heat flared in his eyes as he added, his voice dropping meaningfully, "I want you."

Althea turned away, stunned and reeling. She had no idea what the expression on her face was; she couldn't even figure out what she felt. Shock, yes, and also stupidly flattered. Appalled as well, but also hopeful. It was all far, far too confusing.

"I really didn't expect this," she said after a moment, her back to him as she grasped the Aga railing with both hands, needing to anchor herself.

"I know." Jasper's voice was quiet, contrite, and unlike anything Althea remembered. "And it shames me, that you didn't."

Shamed him? Had Jasper ever admitted feeling shame for anything? Slowly she turned around. "This is so unlike you, Jasper." He hung his head, spreading his hands wide, the epitome of helpless apology. "So...what are you exactly saying?" Althea asked.

"I want us to get back together. For our sakes, for our children's sakes." He took a step towards her. "Let's be a family again, Althea."

"And what about your affairs?" She spoke through numb lips. He was saying everything she once had dreamed of him saying, but it didn't feel anything like the way she'd thought it would. *Hoped* it would.

"They're in the past. I know I have a lot to atone for, a lot of trust to regain." He spoke steadily, his gaze unwavering. "And I just want you to give me the opportunity to do that. To give me a chance, Althea. That's all I'm asking for."

Slowly, on unsteady legs, Althea walked over to a chair and half-collapsed into it. "Jasper...I can't believe you're saying this. I've made plans, though. I want to live here at Casterglass. The children do, as well." For a second surprise flashed across his face, and Althea steeled herself for his scathing rejection of that idea. Then what would she do? She had no idea how to move on from here.

"If that's important to you," Jasper said after a moment, "then we can make it work."

"What?" Althea goggled at him. It was as if he'd a complete personality transplant, although perhaps that was being unfair. He could be kind, and thoughtful, and compassionate. *When it suited him.* Althea pushed that niggling thought away. "Do you seriously mean that?" she asked. For a few tantalising seconds she let herself envision it—a successful marriage, Jasper mucking in with everyone, bonding with his children, being the husband and father she'd longed for him to be. The last twenty years of her life *wouldn't* have been a failure.

"Yes, I do," he told her. "I'd have to travel for work, of course, and it might make sense for me to take a flat in London. But if you feel happier up here, then I want to support that."

Something about the urbane smoothness of his tone, the swift and complete willingness to adapt to her plans, made Althea pause. "So, we'd basically live separate lives?" she asked after a moment.

"Not completely separate, no, but I can hardly make the daily commute from Cumbria to London." He spoke in a jocular tone, but she saw a flash of irritation in his eyes, and it felt familiar. He wanted to get back together, but he wanted his own life, too. As always. The words *cake* and *eat it* came to mind.

She put her chin in her hand, her narrowed gaze on him. "So talk me through it."

"Talk you...?" Jasper looked uncharacteristically discomfited. "Well, I supposed I'd stay in London Monday to Friday and come to Casterglass for the weekends and holidays. Maybe not every weekend, but as much as I could manage. That seems sensible." He smiled, and Althea didn't smile back.

"That hardly seems ideal, if you really want to give our marriage a second chance," she said after a moment. "Does it?"

He looked baffled, and then uneasy. "I'm not sure what you want me to say. If you want to stay here, and I have to work—"

"I don't know what I want you to say, either," she admitted honestly. "I still don't really understand why you're here."

"I told you, I want to give our marriage a second chance—"

"Yes, you did say that." She paused. "Where's Marie?"

"Marie?" He said the name of his latest mistress as if he'd never heard it before, and Althea actually wondered if he'd forgotten.

"Yes, Marie. You know, the friend I went to Pilates with whom you took to Switzerland for a lovefest instead of spending Christmas with your family?"

Jasper had the grace, at least, to look apologetic. "I really am sorry about that. That was…a poor decision."

"That's certainly one way to describe it."

"I'm not sure what you want from me, Althea." Jasper paused. "I know I haven't been faithful to you. We both know it. I've said it, and that I'm sorry."

As if a single apology could be enough. "Are you really saying you're going to be different now? No more affairs?" His second's pause gave her a sick feeling. Why was she even considering this? *"Jasper."*

"Look, I admit, fidelity has not been my strong point. If it makes you feel any better, I didn't go into our marriage thinking I was going to cheat on you."

Did that make her feel better? Not really. "And yet you did, again and again and again."

"Do we really need to talk about this?" Jasper asked. He was starting to look irritated rather than apologetic, and with a sick wave of understanding Althea realised he'd expected this to be easy. And why shouldn't he have? It always had been before. She'd never had a backbone before.

"Yes, we do need to talk about it," she told him sharply, "because just a few weeks ago you were willing to walk out on our family for a woman I called my friend. Am I supposed to just overlook that?"

"Look, it wasn't so much about Marie," Jasper said, his tone turning what she suspected was meant to be conciliatory. "It was about me. I was having something of a midlife crisis…"

"Then you've been having one for nineteen years," Althea said in a hard voice. "Since you first began to cheat on me."

"I apologised for that," Jasper said through gritted teeth, and she let out a humourless laugh.

"Oh, right, one half-hearted sorry and the matter's closed? You're ready to move on? Sorry I can't get in line that quickly."

"What do you want from me, then?"

Althea was silent for a moment. "Nothing," she said slowly, an epiphany. "I don't want anything from you. Our marriage is over." As she said the words she realised how true they were.

"But I want to get back together…"

"And I don't." It had to be a revelation, for Jasper not to get what he wanted. "Too much has happened, Jasper. Too many affairs. Too many petty cruelties. I believe you think you can do better, but it's not enough. I don't trust you. I don't think I ever will."

His jaw was clenched tightly. "Althea, I'm trying…"

"And I don't want you to try." Although for a little while there she'd almost been willing to be convinced. She'd wanted the fairy-tale ending, the proof that her marriage hadn't been a mistake, that she hadn't been a failure. Ostrich Althea yet again. "For twenty years I was a good wife to you," she told him. "Loyal, loving, diligent, determined to overlook all your indiscretions to make our marriage work. Maybe that's *not* being a good wife, now that I come to think about it. I let you get away with everything."

Jasper didn't reply, and she forged on determinedly. "But coming up here has made me see it all in a new, more truthful light. And I don't want to go back to being the woman I was. I certainly don't want to go back to that sham of a marriage. You sent the divorce papers, Jasper, and I signed them. I looked it up and the divorce can be finalised in less than four months if we agree on everything." She paused as a sudden suspicion assailed her. "This isn't about the prenup, is it? John's—my—lawyer phoned Edward. You didn't just come up here because you're scared of losing money…" The thought was horrifying yet all too possible.

"Of course not," Jasper said with scathing dignity. "This isn't just about money, Althea."

"Yet it has something to do with it." Had Jasper realised he stood a chance of losing a good deal of his money, as well as someone who ironed his shirts, made him meals, provided a welcoming home to return to after a hard day in the city? He'd probably convinced himself he was up here for the good of their marriage, but Althea suspected otherwise. He wanted his easy life to go on just the way it always had. "You haven't even asked about the children," she told him.

"Because I was trying to save our marriage!" He was starting to sound angry.

"Some things can't be saved."

He stood up. "And that's all you have to say?"

She nodded as a sudden, surprising rush of sorrow went through her. This really was the end. "Yes."

Jasper stared at her in cold disbelief as he shook his head slowly. "I don't know what you think you'll gain from this, Althea. Do you really want to spend the rest of your life in this falling-down heap?"

"I do."

"Whatever that country solicitor says, you won't get much from the settlement."

"I'll take that chance." She paused. "I hope you'll provide for the children, at least, Jasper. They're legally entitled to that."

He looked insulted. "Of course I will."

"But not me?" She let out a humourless laugh. She didn't really care, and yet somehow his disregard still stung a little. How had he almost convinced her he could change? That their marriage could work?

"You signed the prenup," Jasper told her flatly. "And you didn't bring a penny to the marriage. Why should I give you anything?"

Althea folded her arms. "Oh, I don't know," she drawled. "Because I was your wife? Because we said vows to each other, before God? Because I raised your three children and made a home for you for twenty years? Any of the above?"

He had the surprising grace to look slightly abashed. "I wanted to make another go of it."

"And that justifies that horrible prenup?" She shook her head wearily, realising she'd never get through to him. He had tried, and that made him a saint in his own eyes. She felt both relieved and exhausted, and now she just wanted him gone. "Jasper, the best thing is for us to communicate through our lawyers. I don't want this to be any more difficult or dramatic than it needs to be. And I don't actually want your money for myself. I want it for our children, which you seem to, as well, so hopefully we can come to a reasonable arrangement. I'm not looking to fleece you—trust me."

He hesitated. "Althea, has it really come to this?"

"Yes, it has." She met his gaze steadily, and with a flicker of sympathy. Jasper had always had everything served to him on a silver plate. Not getting what he wanted instantly had to be an uncomfortable novelty. "Goodbye, Jasper," she said, and she almost sounded gentle. "Unless you want to return so you can see the children come back from school?"

"I need to get back." Of course he did. Althea nodded wearily. "I'll text them," he said defensively, and she didn't bother to reply.

"You're making a mistake," he told her, and again she said nothing. Then, with a huff of exasperation, as if she were being entirely unreasonable, he grabbed his coat and strode out of the kitchen. A few seconds later she heard his car start up, and her breath escaped her in a long, weary exhalation. She sank back into her chair and rested her head on the table as emotions clambered for space inside her. Sorrow, for what never could have been. Relief, that he was gone. Elation, that she'd just stood up to him. And a deep grief, for what she and the children had lost. A husband, a father. The hope of one. Gone for good.

Would he try to salvage his relationship to his children? Althea hoped so, but at this moment she questioned it, and maybe, eventually, that would be okay. Maybe it was better for them to have no father than one like Jasper, who couldn't see past his own wants, a possibility that made her feel unbearably sad but also weirdly hopeful.

A door had forever closed; a window had been cracked open. She was finally free. She'd thought she'd been free before, but until she'd seen Jasper face to face she realised she'd been holding on to some faint, frail hope that life could go back to the way it had been, even though she'd already convinced herself she didn't want it to. The human heart was complicated—that was for certain. She'd been willing to let him convince her, but she was glad she'd had the strength to stop the futility. To tell both him and herself that their marriage really was over.

"Wow, he's an arse."

Althea lifted her hand to see Seph standing in the doorway, her arms folded, her expression as sullen as usual except... There was an unexpected spark of humour in her sister's eyes. This was the first time she'd talked to her for days.

"Yes," Althea agreed, "he is. And he doesn't even realise it."

"You sent him packing?"

"I did."

"Good thing."

Then, to Althea's surprise and gratitude, Seph smiled. She hadn't seen her sister smile directly at her before, and it felt like sunlight flooding through her heart, lighting up all the dark spaces.

"Yes," Althea agreed, her tone heartfelt. "It is a very good thing."

Chapter Twenty-Three

T HREE WEEKS BLURRED by in a flurry of activity— scrubbing and cleaning and filling out forms, visiting the bank and touring the property, writing up schemes and dreams and also helping Tobias with his English homework. Althea had never felt so exhausted, so overwhelmed, so alive. In the midst of the chaos, she was happy. She was settled in herself in a way she didn't think she'd ever been before.

Whether it was dismantling the dozen mannequins in the ballroom with her mother, and laughing all the while, or having Seph, admittedly rather sullenly, show her some of her wood carvings, or chivvying Olivia on the phone to come to Casterglass permanently, Althea felt as if she were settling into life at Casterglass and it felt *right*.

Poppy and Tobias had both settled into school, and Ben was enjoying his second term at Durham. Jasper had, both to her surprise and relief, reached out to all three of his children. They'd come to her in turn, asking her if it was okay if they stayed in touch with their father, and Althea told them, meaning it utterly, that of course it was. She didn't know how much of a relationship they'd have with Jasper, but she certainly wasn't going to stand in the way of it.

And yet…as the days and then the weeks ticked past, she realised she hadn't seen John since he'd left her and Jasper to it back in early January. At first she hadn't noticed, because there had been so much else to consume her, but as the days slipped by Althea started to feel his absence. Admittedly, it wasn't as if they'd spent every second together, far from it, but they'd had a ramble or a coffee or just a little chat every once in a while, and she'd counted on those times—on the comfort as well as the spark. Why was he keeping his distance now?

Had he lost interest? Had seeing Jasper in the flesh made him realise he didn't want to wait for whenever she was ready? And why should he? They barely knew each other. She wasn't exactly a sure thing. In fact, she was pretty much the opposite, with a crumbling castle, three kids, and a soon-to-be ex. Complicated barely began to cover it.

As the days continued to pass, Althea tried to decide what to do. Anti-Ostrich Althea would stride over to Appleby Farm and confront him. But she wasn't sure she was feeling that brave, because what if she didn't want to hear whatever she'd compel him to say? What if he told her he was happy to be neighbourly, but that was it? She pictured him telling her, her smile faltering as she tried to rally. It would be so, so awful.

Besides, she told herself, it had only been a few weeks.

Lambing season was about to start; John was busy, too. She could just leave it, and see how thing went. That didn't have to be hiding her head in the sand.

And besides, she was busy; every day felt full, and there was Tobias and Poppy to think of, as well, as they navigated a new school, new friends, new lives. Admittedly it all seemed to be going swimmingly and so as January melted into February, Althea had less of a reason to stay away from John except for the fact that he seemed to be staying away from her, which was really no reason at all.

Then, the first week of February, she received a letter from Edward Fotheringhay and Associates proposing a split of her and Jasper's marital estate—thirty per cent to Jasper's seventy, which shocked her with its unexpected generosity. With the sale of the house in Surrey, it would, she read with a dropped jaw, amount to *seven hundred thousand pounds.* She'd had no idea Jasper was so rich. *She* was so rich.

And she was amazed that Jasper had agreed to it at all; she realised he must have known the prenup wouldn't stand, and she'd be legally entitled to a full fifty per cent. Either that or he'd actually had an attack of conscience. Either way, Althea was happy to accept. She didn't want a court battle and three-quarters of a million pounds would do her just fine. She could finance the re-roofing, and put a tidy sum away for her children. That was all that mattered.

Receiving the letter seemed as good a reason as any to talk to John, since it had been his idea to contest the prenup in the first place. And so, on a sunny afternoon in February with the ground scattered with the delicate white buds of snowdrops and the children at school, Althea pulled on a pair of welly boots and a waterproof jacket just in case and headed across the muddy fields towards Appleby Farm, just as she had less than two months ago, but what felt like a lifetime.

The wind from the sea was as brisk as ever, buffeting her and stinging her face with cold. She dug her hands deep into her pockets and breathed in deep, grateful for just about everything in her life, even an icy wind.

A few sheep glared at her balefully as she walked across, but this time Althea didn't falter. She felt as if with each step she was growing in confidence and determination. She was, in some sense, becoming more herself—shoulders back, head held high, smiling.

Perhaps that being fanciful or just a bit weird, but she felt it. She lived it. She was still smiling as she crossed the final field, clambered over a stile, and walked down the track towards the farm house. She caught sight of John in the doorway of one of the barns, dressed in mud-splattered plus-fours, looking every inch the irascible sheep farmer. Her smile widened. He frowned, which made her falter for a moment, but then she kept walking. Determined. Head held high, and *not* in the sand.

"Hi there," she called out when she was close enough so he could hear.

John gave a nod in response. "You look like you've had some good news."

"I have, actually." Why was he *still* frowning?

"I thought you might have," he replied, and the way he said it, sounding so grim, made Althea stop right where she stood, hands planted on her hips.

"Are we talking about the same thing?"

John folded his arms. "You tell me."

This was really not going the way she'd hoped. Her stomach was starting to cramp. Had John completely changed his mind about their friendship? *I like you. I really like you.* Not right now, apparently.

"Are you busy?" Althea asked, trying her best not to sound uncertain. "I thought perhaps we could have a coffee."

John looked as if he wanted to refuse, but then with a shrug and a sigh, both of which stung, he headed towards the house. "I suppose."

Wow. Ringing endorsement it was not. Trying not to feel miffed, Althea followed him to the house. He stripped off his plus-fours and hurled them into the corner of the kitchen, the movement seeming unnecessarily fierce.

"So," he said flatly. "Tell me your good news."

His back was to her as he filled the kettle, and Althea didn't know whether to laugh or groan. "Well, since you're sounding so thrilled, I guess I will."

"I'm sorry if I can't put my game face on." He sighed as he turned around. "I am happy for you, Althea. Really. More than I seem, I'm sure."

"That's not saying much, actually."

He raked a hand through his hair. "What do you want me to say?"

She shook her head slowly. "What's going on? I feel as if we're having two different conversations." She paused, then plunged. "I haven't seen you since…since Jasper came up here. Have you…have you changed your mind?"

He blinked at her for several seconds. "Have *I* changed my mind?"

"Yes, you know, about…waiting." She flushed. "Because I'm, I don't know, too much work, I suppose. I still want to be your friend," she continued hurriedly, "and I'm not ready for anything else yet, but…" *One day I'm pretty sure I would be.* "What is it?" she asked, for John was looking at her as if he was completely flummoxed.

"What…you…" He shook his head slowly as the kettle switched off.

Althea stared at him in bewilderment. "John…?"

"Just a minute." He turned back to make their coffees, shaking his head and muttering to himself the whole while, although Althea couldn't make out any words. What on earth was going on?

Finally they were both seated at the table, mugs of coffee in front of them. John took a deep breath and let it out slowly.

"Althea, I thought you and Jasper had got back together."

"What?" She stared at him in surprise; in all her ruminations about why John might have been keeping his distance, this possibility had never even occurred to her. "Why would you think that?"

"Because he came all the way to Cumbria to find you. Because you told me you'd said vows and you meant them. Because you said you couldn't quite believe you would be staying here. And because Alice mentioned that Poppy was back in touch with her dad." He shrugged helplessly. "Because it's what I feared would happen."

"But…" The word came out in a slow exhalation. "Why didn't you *ask*?"

"I wanted to give you space, especially if you and Jasper were trying to make a go of it… Heaven knows I didn't want to come between the two of you."

"You really thought I'd go back to him? After the serial cheating, the lying, the putting me down?"

John glanced down at his mug, his hands wrapped around it. "Marriage is a big deal," he said quietly. "I know that. And who was I to say that Jasper couldn't change?"

"He tried to convince me he had," Althea admitted. "He came to Casterglass to ask me to give him another chance."

"He did? So I wasn't far wrong."

"He didn't mean it. He acted contrite but it was just that. An act." She swallowed. "When I started to suspect, the mask dropped pretty quickly. He didn't stay for more than twenty minutes."

"Ah."

"The reason he came up at all was because he was worried about the prenup agreement. Your lawyer friend scared him, I think, so I have you to thank for that."

He smiled wryly, still looking unconvinced and a bit shaken. "For having him come up at all?"

"No, for having Edward Fotheringhay offer me thirty per cent of all our marital assets."

John raised his eyebrows. "Only thirty—"

"Trust me, it's enough," Althea assured him. "I don't want a court case, and I have enough for the children and a new roof. I can't complain."

"Still…"

"Besides, it means the divorce will be finalised in just a few months. Less than three now, in fact." She smiled at him. "And I'm ready for that."

John smiled back, but then it wavered and he looked down. Althea started to feel uneasy again. "I don't know what to say," he said after a moment.

"You could say 'that's great', maybe?" she suggested. "I mean, nothing's changed, that is, between us…" She trailed off, for John was shaking his head. Oh, no. She'd feared this, hadn't she? He didn't want to wait around. Who could blame him?

"I haven't been honest with you, Althea."

Uh-oh. She tried not to gulp. "In what way?"

John looked at her seriously. "About my wife."

"Ah." She nodded. "The complicated bit."

"Yes. The truth is…Laura left Alice and me—well, me, mainly—just two years after we married. Alice was only a baby."

"Oh…" She stared at him in confusion. "Why didn't you tell me?"

"Because I was embarrassed," John stated bluntly. "What kind of man has a wife who leaves him like that?"

"Surely it's a reflection on her, not you—"

"Well, everybody loved Laura. She was a lot of fun. And for her to leave her own *child*… They wondered just how wrong our marriage must have gone. You know how people like to gossip here. They mean well, but it still can hurt."

"Yes." She certainly knew that. "But surely you knew I wouldn't have thought that way, John?"

"I suppose I didn't want to find out."

"Why did she leave?"

He sighed heavily. "She had a romantic view of farming life, I suppose. She grew up in Manchester… We met at university. When we first got married, we went travelling for a while… You might have seen the postcards in the bathroom? I sent them to my dad." He gave a reminiscent smile. "He always got a kick out of them. But even when we were travelling, I always intended to come back here and make a go of the farm, especially after my father died, and Laura understood that. I think she thought it would be all picnics by the sea and bouncy little lambs. The long hours, the lack of holidays, the sheer drudgery…she wasn't so keen on any of that. Looking back, I think she must have been suffering from some sort of postpartum depression, although I didn't realise it at the time. She left a literal 'Dear John' letter and walked out one morning while I was seeing to the lambs and Alice was sleeping in her cot."

"Oh, John." Althea couldn't imagine something so sudden and dreadful. "That's awful."

"It wasn't great. I was shocked at first, and then angry, and then despairing. And then I just *was*."

Her heart ached for him and all he'd gone through. Neither of them, she realised, had had an easy time of marriage. Was that why he was being so hesitant and wary now? Maybe, like her, he wasn't quite ready.

"So when you said she died of cancer…" she said slowly, waiting for him to fill in the blanks.

"That's true, she did. When Alice was ten she showed up at our door, after nearly eight years of virtually no contact— just a few calls and cards. She'd been diagnosed with terminal cancer and she had nowhere else to go. Of course I took her in. I even hoped there might be some kind of healing through it, some kind of reconciliation, like in some soppy film, I suppose, but there wasn't, not really." He rotated his mug between his hands, his face cast into lines of remembrance and regret. "In some ways things were even more difficult than before, because she was ill and she hated that, and sometimes she hated me for…for not being ill, I suppose, which I could understand. She was only thirty-five. It was bloody unfair."

"Yes." Althea had to speak past the lump forming in her throat as she imagined the sorrowful scene. Sometimes things were just hard, without redemption.

"And then she died," John said simply. "And in some ways, it provided more closure than her just walking out had, but it also just felt…like a loss. A pointless one. Which it was."

Silently Althea reached over and put her hand over his. He gave her a small smile and then wiped his eyes. "Sorry," he mumbled, and she squeezed his hand.

"You don't need to be sorry."

"We're a pair, aren't we?"

They certainly were, both of them with difficult pasts, trying to come to terms with what it meant for the present, never mind the future. "So you stayed away because you thought I might make a go of it with Jasper like you tried with Laura when she was ill?" she guessed, and he gave a half-shrug.

"Something like that. I'm not even sure what I was thinking. Just that I couldn't interfere between a husband and wife."

"You didn't."

He nodded, and they sat in silence for a few moments, holding hands. It was nice, Althea thought, rather than romantic, although perhaps there was a little of that, too. But mostly it was just nice.

"So," John said after a moment, gazing down at their twined fingers. "Is this…I don't know…a new beginning?" He glanced up at her with a smile that was both hopeful and shy. "Because I meant everything I said before. I like you."

"You really like me?" she filled in, smiling, and he gave a little laugh.

"Yes."

"Good, because I really like you. But for now…"

"Just friends." She nodded. "Good," he said, and that was enough.

They finished their coffee and then John walked her back to Casterglass as the sunlight started to fade from the violet sky. Although it was only February, crocuses were poking their bright heads up through the grass, a lovely harbinger of spring. They didn't speak, but Althea felt they didn't need to. Everything was understood.

As they were walking up the drive, Poppy and Tobias appeared behind them, walking from the bus stop, talking and laughing together. Althea was heartened by the sight; since moving to Casterglass, they had been getting along so much better.

John slid her a smile, as if he knew what she was thinking. As if he knew how full and happy her heart was.

"Do you want to stay for dinner?" she asked impulsively. "Poppy could text Alice to have her come along. Just…you know…"

"Yes," he told her with a smile. "I know. And yes, that would be…great."

As Tobias and Poppy joined them, Althea mentioned the plan and Poppy whipped out her phone to text Alice. Together the four of them walked around the castle to the warmly lit kitchen where her father was waiting for them.

"I saw you coming up the drive," he told them, "and I thought I'd put on the kettle. Your mother has almost finished her chapter on Ovid's legacy." His brow crinkled. "At least, I think that's what she was writing…"

"I'll make the tea," Althea told him with a smile, and as she reached for the teapot, she felt a rush of love sweep over her, a rush of warmth and contentment and thanks. There was nowhere else she'd rather be, and no one else she'd rather be with. Her gaze met John's across the kitchen and she had a shivery feeling that he was thinking exactly the same thing. It was early days, definitely, but it was a beginning, just as he'd said. Just as she'd hoped. And right now, that was more than enough.

She glanced at her father, chatting with John, and Poppy and Tobias bickering good-naturedly, and then she looked out the window and saw Seph coming in from the barn, looking, perhaps, slightly less sullen than usual. From upstairs she heard her mother's sing-song trill.

"Hel-*lo*! Is that the kettle I hear?"

Laughing, Althea called up that indeed it was. Then, as

she was pouring out the tea, her phone pinged with a text, and she glanced down to see it was from Olivia.

Get a room ready! I'm coming home.

The End

Find out what happens next for Althea and John as well as Olivia in the next book in Keeping Up with the Penryns: *A Casterglass Garden.*
Coming in February 2022, pre-order now!

Join Tule Publishing's newsletter for more great reads and weekly deals!

If you enjoyed *A Casterglass Christmas,*
you'll love the next book in the….

Keeping Up with the Penryns series

Book 1: *A Casterglass Christmas*

Book 2: *A Casterglass Garden*
Coming February 2022

Available now at your favorite online retailer!

More books by Kate Hewitt

The Return to Willoughby Close series

Book 1: *Cupcakes for Christmas*

Book 2: *Welcome Me to Willoughby Close*

Book 3: *Christmas at Willoughby Close*

Book 4: *Remember Me at Willoughby Close*

The Willoughby Close series

Book 1: *A Cotswold Christmas*

Book 2: *Meet Me at Willoughby Close*

Book 3: *Find Me at Willoughby Close*

Book 4: *Kiss Me at Willoughby Close*

Book 5: *Marry Me at Willoughby Close*

The Holley Sisters of Thornthwaite series

Book 1: *A Vicarage Christmas*

Book 2: *A Vicarage Reunion*

Book 3: *A Vicarage Wedding*

Book 4: *A Vicarage Homecoming*

Available now at your favorite online retailer!

About the Author

After spending three years as a diehard New Yorker, Kate
Hewitt now lives in the Lake District in England with her
husband, their five children, and a Golden Retriever. She
enjoys such novel things as long country walks and chatting
with people in the street, and her children love the freedom
of village life—although she often has to ring four or five
people to figure out where they've gone off to.

She writes women's fiction as well as contemporary romance
under the name Kate Hewitt, and whatever the genre she
enjoys delivering a compelling and intensely emotional story.

Thank you for reading

A Casterglass Christmas

If you enjoyed this book, you can find more from all our great authors at TulePublishing.com, or from your favorite online retailer.

TULE
PUBLISHING

Made in the USA
Monee, IL
12 November 2021